"I don't think Isa
such tenderness

Polly's heartbeat returned to its original state. At least Mitch hadn't noticed her foolishness over him. And instead, he'd brought her focus back to where it should have been in the first place—his children. "I imagine it's been hard, having so many nannies, and with her mother now gone, love is all the little dear needs. And I'm happy to provide it."

But Mitch didn't return the expression. Instead, his eyes looked haunted, his brow furrowed. "I don't think she even had that before." He rubbed his forehead, then shook his head slowly. "How could I have missed it, all this time?"

"Missed what?" Polly reached forward and touched his arm tenderly.

Oh, if he were only a little boy like Rory or Thomas, she could take him in her arms and hold him. But Mitch wasn't a boy, and the longing in her heart felt different from how she felt toward his sons. But it didn't change her wish to somehow make whatever was going on in his mind better.

Danica Favorite loves the adventure of living a creative life. She loves to explore the depths of human nature and follow people on the journey to happily-ever-after. Though the journey is often bumpy, those bumps refine imperfect characters as they live the life God created them for. Oops, that just spoiled the ending of Danica's stories. Then again, getting there is all the fun. Find her at danicafavorite.com.

Books by Danica Favorite

Love Inspired Historical

Rocky Mountain Dreams
The Lawman's Redemption
Shotgun Marriage
The Nanny's Little Matchmakers

DANICA FAVORITE

The Nanny's Little Matchmakers

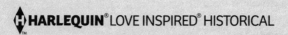

HARLEQUIN® LOVE INSPIRED® HISTORICAL

Recycling programs
for this product may
not exist in your area.

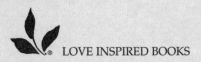

LOVE INSPIRED BOOKS

ISBN-13: 978-0-373-28376-7

The Nanny's Little Matchmakers

Copyright © 2016 by Danica Favorite

www.Harlequin.com

Printed in U.S.A.

As iron sharpens iron, so one person sharpens another.
—*Proverbs* 27:17

To Shana, thanks for helping my books shine, and for making me a better writer.

Chapter One

Leadville, Colorado, 1882

The door to the Mercantile jangled and Mitch Taylor looked up from the books. Before he could greet the customers, his sister-in-law, Iris, had already stepped into action. A good thing, since the customers appeared to be a pretty young lady and her father. The lady seemed to be a proper miss, in a pale blue gown edged with lace, ribbons and all the fripperies that went with the latest style. Her strawberry blond hair arranged in a similar fashion to those he'd seen back in Denver, the young woman could have graced any parlor with ease. She laughed at something Iris said, a soft musical tone escaping her pink lips and a pretty smile lighting her face.

Mitch turned away. Not only was the young lady young—too young—but he had no business admiring ladies of any sort at this point in his life. He'd never imagined that he'd end up crawling back here. *Here* not being precisely the correct term, as the Leadville store hadn't opened yet when he'd made the decision to remain in Denver and run his own store while his brother worked to expand the family mercantile empire. Besides, he hadn't crawled. He'd run.

Hattie was dead.

The words rolled in his mind as he considered them. Hattie was dead. Some days those words still didn't seem real.

But the ensuing scandal was real enough. He could only hope that it would be a while longer before talk reached Leadville and he would have enough time to—

A crash and a screech from the back of the store made him set his pen down. Mitch took a deep breath, then casually turned in the direction of the noise.

As seemed to constantly be the case, before he could even get to the other side of the counter, one of his children, this time it was Clara, ran toward him. Mrs. Abernathy, their nanny, followed behind.

"You get back here!"

Clara darted behind him and clung to the back of his shirt. "I won't!"

Even the glowering look on Mrs. Abernathy's face would not be enough to convince Clara. Experience had taught him that while all of his children were stubborn, when this particular daughter refused to do something, walking to China would be easier than getting her to change her mind.

"What seems to be the problem?" Mitch asked, offering Mrs. Abernathy a smile.

"Everything is the problem." Mrs. Abernathy's face had turned an unmistakable shade of red. He'd seen it on a number of nannies, all shortly before they'd quit.

Mitch pinched the bridge of his nose and took a deep breath. Could he find a way to convince her to stay?

The young lady he'd been admiring came into view, covered in flour.

No. Even before Mrs. Abernathy opened her mouth to utter the fateful words, Mitch knew nothing would keep her. He supposed he should make the effort, but with this being the second nanny in the space of a month, he'd need all of his energy to convince another woman to come work for him.

"I see," he said instead.

"Those children are out of control." Mrs. Abernathy gave him a sharp look as the flour-coated woman approached.

"I know," he said quietly. He could feel Clara relax behind him. She, too, knew that their nanny was a few words from giving notice. For Clara, as well as the other children, this would be another victory.

The flour-coated woman smiled at him. "You must be the father of the little darling who welcomed me to the store."

Iris rushed over. "Polly, I am so sorry. You see—"

Polly held up a hand. "It's not your fault, Mrs. Taylor. But I think there's a young lady who owes me an apology."

She looked at Mitch firmly, but not unkindly. Not like the many people who'd been terrorized by his children. He'd liked to have said that such occurrences were rare, but in truth, they'd left Denver not just to escape the scandal of his wife's death. He also needed respite from talk of the antics of the Taylor Terrors, as his children had been dubbed by society.

Most people, when they saw his children coming, ran the other way. Perhaps people running away was a small exaggeration, but not by much.

Polly squatted down in front of him. "Come on out now, young lady. I realize that you're new in town, but in Leadville, we don't go throwing flour at strangers.

That might be what you did where you used to live, but here, that's not our custom."

She spoke gently, sweetly. Without the rage of so many of the others who'd insisted that Mitch do something about his out-of-control children. Even her eyes. A bright blue that matched her dress, they looked almost...nice.

Clara didn't budge.

Polly rose and looked him in the eye, then stuck out a hand, which he shook. "Polly MacDonald. I can see why your daughter might be a bit shy, but she does owe me an apology."

Then her blue eyes twinkled as she pointed to a figure peering around a barrel. "Although we could say that our little mishap with the flour was my own fault, since I was so inconsiderate as to be paying too much attention to the dried fruit and not realizing I was stepping into a battle between these two."

Rory. Mitch sighed again. Of course it was Rory and Clara. The two of them hadn't stopped bickering since Rory had the misfortune of being born seven minutes after his sister. A fact she wielded like a weapon in establishing superiority to her younger brother.

"You see! They are positively out of control," Mrs. Abernathy said with the kind of self-righteousness Mitch had resigned himself to hearing from everyone who met his children. "I'm sorry, Mr. Taylor, I really am. But your children are too wild for the likes of me. I never thought I'd say that about any child, but there is clearly something wrong with them. They belong in an institution."

Had he not heard it dozens of times before, he might have been insulted. Instead, he smiled politely and nodded. "Thank you for your service, Mrs. Abernathy."

"I beg your pardon!"

Mitch turned toward Polly, the woman his children had just doused in flour. The kindness had melted from her face, replaced with a level of fury he'd expected from the flour incident.

"There is nothing wrong with those children. I cannot fathom why you would make such a horrible suggestion as to put them in an institution. I hope Mr. Taylor docks whatever wages you have coming to you. Whatever is wrong with these children, it's not a deficiency in them, but in the kind of care they are receiving. You should be ashamed of yourself."

Then Polly squatted down again. "Please come talk to me, little one," she said in a much gentler tone. "I won't hurt you, I promise."

"Well, I never!" Mrs. Abernathy stomped away. Mitch wasn't sure if he was glad to see her go or not. He'd have liked to have thought there was truth in Polly's words, that had he had a better nanny, his children wouldn't behave so terribly.

But he had been through an awful lot of nannies.

Clara came forward. "I'm sorry," she said quietly. "I didn't mean to hit you. I was trying to get Rory back."

"Rory," Mitch said, indicating his son should join them. "I believe you also owe Miss MacDonald an apology."

Which is when it occurred to him. Clara had actually apologized. Never in all of his life had he heard his children apologize. At least not without threats of bodily harm, missing supper and the like.

Mitch looked over at the young lady. "It is Miss, isn't it?"

She gave him the kind of dazzling smile that would have struck him in the heart were it not firmly encased in stone. It had been a long time since he'd allowed himself to be swayed by a pretty face.

"Indeed it is."

"I'm Mitch Taylor. I apologize for not introducing myself sooner. I was caught up in the situation."

He placed his hand on Clara's shoulder. "This is my daughter Clara, who is ten, and that's her twin, Rory." Then he looked around. "Where are the others?"

Dutifully, his other children stepped out from behind the shelves. "This is Louisa, my eldest, who is twelve, and there's Thomas, who is seven." Mitch looked around. "Where is Isabella?"

The children all looked at each other like they'd assumed the other had been in charge of the child.

"I'm sorry," he told Polly. "Would you excuse me for a moment?"

She smiled at him. "Let me help. How old of a child am I looking for?"

"Right." Mitch tried to smile back, but he found he lacked the energy. "Isabella is three, and she has dark curls and is wearing a…"

He looked at the other children. He'd gone out early this morning, before any of them were up. "What is she wearing?"

"A pink dress," Louisa volunteered.

Everyone stood there, staring at him. "Well, let's find her!"

Suddenly, there was a flurry of activity in the store as everyone went off in search of Isabella. Mitch paused at the counter for a moment.

"It's all right," Polly said kindly, her hand resting on his arm. "I'm sure we'll find her."

Mitch nodded. Like all of the other difficult emotions he had to suppress in life, this one should be no different. After all, Isabella disappeared all the time. She liked to hide in small spaces, where she'd curl up and take a nap. The rational part of his brain told him that Isabella was most likely somewhere doing just that. But the ache in his heart…the one that had already borne too much for any man to bear…

"Thank you," he said simply. Then he turned to look for his daughter.

Mitch Taylor was not a cold man, Polly had decided upon meeting him. The simple way he spoke, seemingly unattached, gave an air of coldness that would have driven most people off. But there'd been a catch in his voice whenever he spoke of his children that gave him away. He might want people to think him detached, but Polly could tell by the love in his eyes that he cared deeply for his children.

She paused at a pile of blankets tossed casually on the floor. Mrs. Taylor would never tolerate such disarray in the store. Though she only spoke to the other woman briefly on her visits, Polly knew the pride Mrs. Taylor took in keeping everything in order.

Polly knelt down and moved the blankets. She spied a mass of curly black hair.

She gently touched the child. "Isabella?"

The little girl sighed and pulled the blankets back closer to her.

"I've found her!" Polly stood and waved Mitch over.

The relief spreading across the man's face reaffirmed her belief that there was more to Mitch than he let on. He ran to them and immediately scooped up the little girl into his arms.

"Isabella!" He cradled her against him. Then she lifted her head, yawned and looked around.

Which is when Polly noticed that Isabella was completely unlike any of Mitch's other children in appearance. Her mass of curls was much darker than the straight brown hair of her other four siblings. But it was the deep rich brown of Isabella's skin that struck her the most. Especially as it contrasted with Mitch's fair skin, blond hair and blue eyes.

Her friend Emma Jane had adopted a child, and Polly had always admired her for the ferocity with which she and her husband, Jasper, loved little Moses. But to see this strange man, who wore such a veneer of ice, loving a child so clearly not his own, it made Polly's heart tumble in a funny manner she hadn't expected.

"Yes, she's mine," Mitch said curtly, still cradling the little girl as he moved past her.

"Of course she is," Polly said, knowing how Emma Jane and Jasper often had to correct others who made unkind remarks about Moses not being theirs. "I can see you love her very much."

Mitch relaxed slightly, then peered down at his daughter. "You gave us quite a scare, Isabella. You mustn't hide like that."

"I was sweepy," the little girl mumbled, then rested her head back on her father's shoulder.

"Mrs. Abernathy's lessons were too long today," the eldest girl, Louisa, said as she joined them. "She wasn't paying the slightest attention to Isabella and was more worried about Clara's spelling. Rory told her that Clara cheated on her lessons, so Mrs. Abernathy rapped her knuckles. If I hadn't been forced to work on penmanship, I might have been able to look after Isabella myself."

Louisa gave him a haughty glare. "I'm twelve years old. I don't see why I need lessons anymore. I can watch the younger children, and then you won't need to hire any more dreadful nannies like Mrs. Abernathy. I'm practically a grown woman. I can do it."

Polly fought the urge to laugh. At twelve, she'd thought herself quite the grown woman. And, in truth, she'd taken on much of those responsibilities. Her mother had been busy taking in the washing from other miners and their families, her father had been busy working in the mines. That is, when her father hadn't been too drunk to work. It had fallen on Polly's shoulders to keep an eye on both her younger siblings and any of the other young children in the various mining camps they'd bounced between.

But it was not a life she'd wish on any twelve-year-old child. If a girl had a choice, anything was better than the drudgery of running a household that wasn't hers to run.

"We won't be having this argument again," Mitch said, shifting Isabella in his arms. "You need an education so you can have a good life for yourself."

"I do have a good life," Louisa declared hotly, "at least when I don't have a horrible nanny forcing me to do useless things."

"Your education is not useless." Mitch's voice held the same calmness she'd observed when she first met him. "You have no idea the doors it will open up for you."

Louisa looked like she was going to speak, but then closed her mouth as she nodded grudgingly. Her expression was anything but accepting, but at least she appeared to be listening to her father.

Polly would have given anything to have her only responsibility be her lessons at that age. Instead, she changed diaper after diaper, wishing things could be different. It was only the Lassiters' influence that had allowed her to have an education in the first place.

Pastor Lassiter, or Uncle Frank, as he'd lately insisted he be called by the MacDonald family, and his late wife, Catherine, had come to the mining camps as part of their ministry to spread the gospel to the miners. But more than that, they'd helped Polly's family better their circumstances, and Polly had been able to take lessons with their daughter, Annabelle.

Uncle Frank! Polly looked around, realizing for the first time that while she'd come with the pastor, in all of the excitement, she'd forgotten him.

She spied him at the counter, talking with Mr. Taylor and his wife. Polly started toward the Taylors, noting that Mitch followed close behind.

"Ah! Polly!" Uncle Frank stepped aside to let Polly join the conversation.

"I'm sorry, I got caught up in all the excitement." Three little heads peered from around the corner of the counter.

"Yes, I saw." Uncle Frank smiled. "I think we stopped by in the nick of time."

He turned his attention to Mitch. "Frank Lassiter. I'm the pastor at Leadville Community Church. Andrew wanted me to welcome you to town, let you know that we're here for you if you need anything."

Mitch frowned, then gave his brother a funny look. "You know I'm not much of a church-going man. The church—"

"This church is different. Trust me. Pastor Lassiter can help with your situation," Andrew Taylor said.

Uncle Frank made a face. "Please. I've told you to call me Frank. We're all the same in the Lord's eyes, so don't make me any more than I am."

"I'm sure the church can't do anything for my situation. I need a new nanny, that's all."

The hard set to Mitch's jaw made Polly's heart ache. They'd encountered a lot of pride over the years, both when Polly's family helped take care of other miners' children, and now with helping Uncle Frank with his ministry to the miners and the outcasts of Leadville society. Mitch wanted help. But like so many who'd been wounded in the past, accepting help from the church was almost too difficult to bear.

Uncle Frank looked over at Polly. "That is something we can help with. Polly is wonderful with children, and I know she'd be delighted to help with yours until you can find a replacement."

The familiar resentment rose up in Polly. It wasn't that she didn't like children, or that she didn't like being with children. But her entire life, she'd heard the same thing: "Polly won't mind." "Polly would be delighted." Only no one ever bothered to ask if, in fact, Polly had any opinion on the matter at all.

Surely there had to be more to Polly's life than the same drudgery that seemed to be a woman's lot. Until she married, she was under the direction of her family in doing whatever they wanted. And then, when she finally settled on a husband, it would be more of living whatever life he chose for her. When did Polly get to choose for herself? To live beyond dirty diapers, washing that needed done and cleaning up after everyone else.

And it wasn't that Uncle Frank, her mother and everyone else asked things of her that were intolerable. It was just that…no one ever gave her a choice. All she wanted was to find her own way in the world and choose to live a life she wanted, not having to constantly do what everyone asked her to do.

As for finding a husband, well, Polly had fooled around with the notion of romance. Only a lot of people were not who they seemed, and she'd been taken in by the wrong sort of fellow. There were a lot of wrong sorts of fellows in Leadville, and as much as a girl wanted to believe in the happy endings a few of her friends had, finding an honorable man was just as difficult as finding a good vein of silver. It might happen to some folks, but too many people lost everything in their hunt for the elusive treasure.

So what was left for Polly? Continuing to be "delighted" to perform every menial task her family gave her since she was without the benefit of a husband? Settle for marriage to a man who was nice enough but spent his spare time in the many saloons and brothels in town? No, she had to find a way to make her own way in the world.

A respectable way in the world. She'd met enough working girls to know she didn't want a life outside of the respectable bounds of society. Which left her few options outside of marriage or remaining the dutiful daughter.

But perhaps, with this situation, there was a way for everyone to get what they wanted.

Polly smiled and turned to the gentlemen.

"Actually, Uncle Frank, I would like to apply for the position myself. I think it would be good to earn my own money and start to live my own life."

Uncle Frank stared at her for a moment, then shook his head. "Is there something you need? I thought I paid Gertie plenty to provide everything you could want, and your father is earning a nice wage running the mine. I'm sorry if we haven't been generous enough."

The genuine despair at having thought he'd cheated her family in some way tore at Polly's heart. Uncle Frank had been too generous, to a fault, for many years.

"That's not it at all." Polly sighed. "Everyone my age is married. Annabelle, Mary, Emma Jane. Every time I begin to form a new friendship, the woman finds a husband. I'm sure I'll have to marry eventually, but I don't want that right now. I—"

"I know your heart was broken by that fellow, but you'll find another. In time."

All of the other adults murmured in agreement. All except Mitch, who stared at her intently. His seemingly expressionless face gave almost nothing away. But his eyes…they seemed very interested in what Polly had to say.

"This isn't about what Tom did. I've been over him for a long time. This is about me, and finding what's important to me in life. Surely there is more to life than the drudgery of marriage and children. If I can take a job, earn some money, then I can go off in the world and find what else is out there for me."

"If taking care of children is drudgery, then why would you want to take care of my children?" Mitch asked quietly.

Polly's hand flew to her mouth. She often got into trouble for speaking her mind without thinking. It had almost ruined her friendship with Annabelle, but fortunately, the two of them had been able to mend the rift. Since then, Polly worked very hard to temper her tongue.

"Because they aren't my children, and I'm being compensated for my time. I enjoy working with children, but I also want time for myself. I can have that if I'm taking care of your children."

Polly took a deep breath, then drew the courage to share her plans with Uncle Frank. "I've been thinking of obtaining my teaching certification. If Mr. Taylor does not hire me, then I will find a job elsewhere to earn the money needed to take the course."

Then she turned back to Mitch. "Surely we can work something out. You need a nanny, and I need employment. I'm good with children, you heard it yourself."

"All right," Mitch said, looking at her. "I'm willing to discuss the job with you. Once you've heard what it entails, you can decide for yourself if it's drudgery or not."

Polly almost felt the weight of her life lift off her shoulders. But as she noticed the calculated way Mitch still observed her, she knew that her challenges had just begun. In fact, as she heard one of the boys, Thomas, let out a yelp, she had to wonder if she'd just put herself into an even more challenging situation than the one she was desperate to leave.

Chapter Two

He was crazy to even consider it, Mitch told himself firmly as he followed Polly and Frank back to the parsonage, where Frank insisted they would be more comfortable discussing the issue. The children skipped on ahead, gleeful at having gotten rid of yet another nanny. And, he was certain, already plotting ways of getting rid of Polly.

Mitch kept stealing glances at the girl, who suddenly seemed so young. Too young, but probably the same age Hattie had been when they'd married. Perhaps even older.

Hattie's dreams had not included marriage or family either. But Mitch hadn't understood that when she'd accepted his proposal. Nor had he realized it when the baby, Louisa, had come too soon. He'd been forced to accept that reality when he'd been left alone too many nights with the squalling baby as Hattie pursued her career on stage.

At least Polly had the maturity to realize that she wasn't meant to be a wife and mother. She wouldn't leave behind a brokenhearted husband and children who didn't understand why their darling mummy didn't want to be with them. That had been years ago, of course. Mitch's heart had healed, and the children understood that Mummy had to travel a lot for work and they lived for the moments when she could be with them.

Well, that's how it had worked while Hattie was alive. With her gone, Mitch didn't know what hope the children clung to, or how he was supposed to make up for a lack of a mother. Even one as inattentive as Hattie.

They arrived at the parsonage, a cheerful yellow house that looked like it had been tacked on to several times over the years. Frank escorted them to the parlor, then excused himself briefly to get the rest of the family to make introductions.

Polly sat on the sofa, smiling at Mitch's children, who now regarded her with a great deal of suspicion.

A short robust woman entered the room, wiping her hands on her apron. "What is this nonsense I hear about Polly becoming a nanny? And going off to be a teacher?"

"Maddie, stop." Another woman, an older, stouter version of Polly, entered the room and looked at her. "But you should have told us."

"Ma, I…" Polly looked up helplessly, as though she hadn't quite thought through her plan.

Before Polly could finish, Frank reentered the room, several children following him.

"I realize this isn't a standard part of employment negotiations, but since our families will be connected in the coming months, I wanted you to meet everyone. Besides, I'm sure your children could use some friends."

Frank introduced the children, and Mitch's head spun from all the names. From what he gathered, Frank's son-in-law, Joseph, had recently built a house next door. Joseph was raising his orphaned siblings, and while the eldest, Mary, had recently married, the Stone children rivaled Mitch's own in number. Additionally, when Polly and her mother, Gertie, came to stay with Frank to help with the Stone children, they'd brought along Gertie's youngest daughter, Caitlin. Polly's older brothers and father remained in the mining camp, running the Stone mine. And, apparently, the folks at the parsonage also cared for several other children as well.

All told, Mitch counted a dozen children, in the age ranges of his own. A little girl about the same age as Thomas stepped forward and said, "Hi, my name's Nugget. Want to go play bandits with us?"

His own children looked at him expectantly.

No one had ever asked them to play before. Usually, they would approach other children, ask them to play, and the children's mothers would take them by the hand and usher them away with warnings about "those people."

Polly smiled at him. "It's all right. They'll stay in the backyard." Then she looked over at a little girl standing next to Nugget. "Right, Caitlin?"

"Yes, Polly." The little girl sighed and looked like she was about to whisper something to Nugget.

"And no ropes!"

The two girls sighed like Polly had accurately predicted what they had up their sleeves.

"Or water," Maddie said. "Or you'll all be doing the washing, then sent to bed with only bread and milk for supper."

"And do leave the rocks on the ground," Gertie said, looking pointedly at a boy who appeared to be of similar age to Rory.

Gertie smiled at him as the children went outside. "And now that we've probably frightened you with all the warnings we've given the children about their behavior, let me assure you that—"

"Don't bother," Polly said, pointing at her soiled dress. "His children can take it. I have this courtesy of a flour fight over rapped knuckles and tattle tales."

"More laundry," Maddie sighed. "I do so hate laundry."

"Maddie is our housekeeper," Frank said, patting the other woman on the arm. "And she does a fine job. However, I was thinking that Alan Forester's widow is in need of extra money, and she's been taking in washing. I'm sure she'd be happy for the work."

"What use would I be, then?" Maddie glared at him. "I'll be thanking you to not be giving my work to someone else to do. You just tell those rascals to stop getting so dirty, and we'll be fine. I'll get tea for everyone."

Maddie stomped off, and the other adults laughed.

"Please, sit." Gertie gestured to an empty chair. "I apologize for the craziness, but you should know right off that chaos is something Polly does very well with. The children truly aren't bad, but they are lively. If yours are as lively as ours, you'll need all the help you can get."

Her words were meant in solidarity, that he could tell by her smile. And for the first time in a long time, Mitch didn't feel quite so alone.

"Which is why I offered my services," Polly said, looking at him with a ferocity that surprised him. "Your children are quite a handful, but I know how to handle them."

Mitch let out a long sigh. Polly's offer was probably the best he was going to get, considering he'd gone through every nanny agency in Denver. He'd have to send to New York, or perhaps even London, to find someone willing to take on his children. No one wanted to take care of the Taylor Terrors.

But that wasn't the only reason people didn't want to work for him.

He cleared his throat. "Perhaps. But I feel compelled to share some of our family's circumstances with you before you make a decision."

Then he looked around the room. Could he trust them with his secrets? Some of them perhaps. "I hope we can all keep this information confidential."

"Of course," they all said at once, looking aghast that he'd even suggest it.

Mitch debated about what information to share— most of it could be confirmed by reading the papers, and there were certainly even more rumors and innuendos. But the whole truth? No one knew the whole truth. He wasn't even sure he did.

"The reason we came to Leadville is I needed to leave Denver. Our family owns a successful chain of mercantile stores, but the rumors and gossip surrounding my wife's death were hurting business, and my family was receiving threats. I'm staying with my brother until talk dies down."

Mitch's throat ached as he tried to form the words to explain Hattie's death. "You may have read the story in the papers. My wife was Hattie Winston, the famous actress who was found murdered in her bed at the Orrington Grand Hotel."

Silence rang through the room so loud, it was almost like thunder. But then Mitch realized it was his heart. He'd only admitted the truth out loud to his brother, Andrew, and Iris. To tell strangers seemed almost...

irresponsible of him. Not that he'd given any information that hadn't been in the papers.

"Hattie's scandalous affairs have always tainted our family. The good families have long stopped receiving us, and now, with her death, people are outright hostile. Hattie ruined a lot of lives."

His chest tightened at the thought. He'd liked to have said that Hattie had ruined his life, because in many ways, she had. But without Hattie, he wouldn't have his children, and without them, what would he have then?

Mitch looked up at the others. "My children know few details about what happened. I have deliberately kept the information about their mother's indiscretions from them. They loved their mother, and I won't have their memories tainted. It's all they have left of her."

For all of Hattie's faults, when she was with the children, she did appear to love them. And they had adored her. Everyone adored Hattie Winston. A reviewer once wrote about her that "to be in the presence of Hattie Winston was to be in the sun, and to be without was to be in the midst of the cloudiest of days."

Mitch had spent his time in Hattie's sun. Unfortunately, when a person spends too much time in the sun, he gets burned.

Polly gave him a sympathetic smile. "I think I speak for everyone here when I say that none of us have a problem with that, and we don't judge you, the children or even Hattie."

She glanced over at Frank, who nodded. "One of the many components of the ministry here is that we care for the least of God's children, and that includes those tainted with scandal."

Maddie entered the room, bearing a tea tray. "I have refreshments."

Polly turned away from him and looked at Maddie. "Were the children still out back?"

"Screaming like wild animals. I'm surprised you don't hear them."

"Nugget?" Polly's eyes darted to the door.

"Leading them all as always."

Polly turned back to him. "Nugget is Joseph Stone's half sister. She is the product of a liaison between his father and a woman of the night. I'm not telling you this to gossip, or to single her out from the others. In fact, I would suggest you never say anything to indicate Nugget being any different from the rest of her family or that she is not equally loved and valuable, because every single person in this household will hurt you for it. But I want you to understand. Whatever scandal their mother was involved in, it has no bearing on the worthiness and love your children deserve."

Though Polly's speech was meant in defense of someone else's child, her fierce love for Nugget made Mitch want to weep. He never wept when Hattie died, even though he probably should have. But here, knowing that what he'd always hoped for his own children might actually be possible…

Frank came over and put his hand on Mitch's shoulder. "I know you bear a heavy burden, even more than what you've shared with us. But we are here, as servants of the Lord, to help you bear those burdens."

Mitch's eyes filled with tears. He couldn't help it. For twelve years, he'd carried the shame of the truth about Hattie, listened to the judgment of others over Hattie's behavior and here, in this place, these people were telling him that he didn't have to anymore.

Polly MacDonald wasn't just offering to take care of his children. She was offering him a lifeline he hadn't known he needed.

Polly hadn't expected the rush of emotion from Mitch. She could tell he still fought to maintain control, but his eyes were watery, like he wanted to cry, but couldn't. How many times had she seen that in the people they'd ministered to? People who needed help, and didn't believe it possible.

Even though she'd seen this job as a way out, and a chance to carve her own path, now it was something more. They hadn't even talked terms of her employment, but she knew whatever they were, she'd accept.

The trouble with wanting her own life was that, if Polly were to be honest with herself, there were pieces of her current life that she loved. They'd been given a nearby barn to use for their mission purposes and were slowly converting it to a real place where they could minister to the down-and-out people of Leadville society. Polly loved every minute she spent there.

But the coming home…living with everyone else's expectations…that's where her life had become drudgery.

Thinking about Mitch and his children, Polly felt a renewed sense of purpose, more energy than she'd felt even when considering pursuing her teaching certificate.

Mitch looked up at her. "Aren't you needed here?"

Everyone in the room laughed. Polly groaned. "Trust me, they have plenty of help. The others are just over at the mission today."

Gertie nodded. "We have Mary and Annabelle, and

Emma Jane comes over often to help as well. Plus, Rose has been extremely helpful lately."

Polly was grateful that she neglected to mention that all four women were expecting. Somehow she didn't think Mitch would see four expectant mothers as being much help with such a rowdy brood of children. In truth, each woman had a unique bond with a different child. Annabelle could always get Nugget to behave the best, Mary handled the rest of the Stone children with ease and somehow Daniel, the unruliest of them all, had become besotted with Emma Jane's son, Moses, and would do anything Emma Jane asked.

No, Polly wasn't needed to help care for the children these days. She hardly felt needed at all, other than being an extra hand. Even then, sometimes she wondered what place she had in all of this chaos.

The latest announcement, Mary's pregnancy, a scant two months after her wedding to Will Lawson, made Polly wonder where she fit amongst her friends.

One more reason she should carve out a life of her own.

She turned to Mitch and smiled. "Truly. I've been looking for an opportunity like this for a long time. You could accept me for a trial period, and if things don't work out, then you can hire another nanny. But in the meantime, you'll have someone to care for your children."

The front door opened, and Polly heard the laughter of her friends long before she could see them.

"Oh, my feet!" Rose pulled off her hat as she entered the room, rubbing her swollen belly. "Oh! I'm sorry, didn't realize you had guests."

"It's all right," Frank said, patting the couch beside

him. "Come sit. Rest your feet, and meet Mitch Taylor. He's considering hiring Polly to be his nanny."

Annabelle and Mary followed.

"What's this about Polly becoming a nanny?" Though Mary had barely discovered her pregnancy, she rubbed her own belly as she sat in one of the empty chairs.

"She'd like a life of her own, it seems," Frank said, smiling at Polly. She imagined he was trying to be encouraging, but as she looked at her three expectant friends, she felt guilty knowing that she probably should stay here to help them.

Rose made a noise and patted her stomach again. "I had visions of that myself, and look where that got me. I suppose you're taking a more respectable path, but don't be fooled into thinking that the world is any better out there. At least here, you have a family who loves and supports you."

"It's not as though she's running away with an out-law, Rose, dear." Annabelle gave her sister-in-law a pat on the shoulder as she moved to sit in another chair. Then Annabelle turned her attention to Mitch.

"I am assuming you're not an outlaw, and that you're a man of good character? Mary's husband, Will, is a lawman, and I can assure you that if you engage in any funny business, he will bring you to justice."

Poor Mitch looked overwhelmed, and she didn't blame him.

"I'm sure Will would be happy to make some inquiries," Mary said, smiling at Mitch in the same way she smiled at the children when giving them a subtle threat.

Except with so many people staring him down, Mitch could hardly think that any of them were being subtle.

Polly stood. "I'm sure Mr. Taylor is perfectly respectable. His brother runs Taylor's Mercantile, and we all know how well he speaks of his other family members. Uncle Frank would have never brought him into our home had it been otherwise."

Then she turned to Mitch. "Why don't we go out back so we can check on the children and discuss terms of my employment?"

The creases in his forehead softened as he stood. "I think that's a good idea. My children…"

He looked as though he wanted to say something about his children's capabilities but then thought better of it. Polly bit back a giggle. Oh, if only he knew the sort of antics she'd put up with over the years. He was afraid of terrifying her, but after having endured questioning by her family, he should have realized that there wasn't much that scared Polly.

Polly led him out the back door, not waiting for any of the others to catch up or comment. That was the other problem with being tied to her family. As much as she truly loved them, it seemed like none of them gave her the space to think for herself. To make her own choices.

Granted, some of the overprotectiveness was her own fault. Her failed romance was with a man who'd turned out to be an outlaw, and her blind trust in him had nearly cost Annabelle her life. Polly had failed to see the man's interest in Annabelle, and when he'd kidnapped her, hoping to use her as leverage to gain access to a silver mine, Polly had looked the other way. No, not looked the other way. That implied a level of complacency Polly had lacked. Rather, Polly had been blinded by jealousy and thought Annabelle had stolen her beau.

Love, or at least the thought of being in love, had stolen Polly's good sense. A common occurrence in these parts, since she'd seen too many love-struck women have their hearts broken by men interested in gambling, boozing and brothels. When she'd fallen for Tom, she'd been convinced he wasn't like those men. She'd been only partially right. He might not have spent time in any of those places, but he'd been wicked all the same.

So it was no wonder none of her family and friends trusted her judgment. She questioned it herself. But this was not a romantic entanglement. Rather, it was legitimate, respectable employment.

No hearts to be broken here.

After all, Mitch was mourning the untimely death of his wife. The hint of gray at his temples suggested he was not the sort of man to be interested in her anyway. Although…if she'd been in a room with her friends, before their weddings, she might have indulged in a giggle or two over the fact that despite his age, Mitch Taylor was a handsome man indeed.

But he would not be interested in her. And while she was sure he was a perfectly respectable man, she was also certain that he was not free of secrets. Secrets that Polly would just as soon not involve herself with.

Mitch put his hand at her waist to steady her as she walked down the stairs. Though she'd walked down the stairs to the backyard plenty of times on her own before, there was something almost comforting about the warmth of his hand at her waist. Polly looked up at him, and he smiled.

Flecks of ice sparked in his deep blue eyes, and once again, she was struck by the hidden warmth within. It would be easy enough to believe in the fantasy that Mitch's secrets were all about his hidden depth and warmth, but Polly knew better.

"Children!" Polly stepped out of Mitch's reach and

held her arms out. Her youngest sister, Caitlin, came running.

"We were good," she said in a singsong voice. "Can we have some of the cookies Maddie was baking?"

The other children quickly followed, the chorus of voices joining Caitlin's. But Polly noticed that the Taylor children hung back.

Polly stepped toward her charges and gave them a smile. "Did you have fun?"

The eldest, Louisa, glared at her, but the others hesitated. Nugget tugged at the back of her skirt. "They didn't know any of our games."

Polly turned toward Nugget. "Did you teach them?"

"No." Nugget kicked at a rock. "They didn't want to play."

Polly put her arm around Nugget and turned her toward the Taylor children. "Do you remember when you first came here, and you didn't know anyone?"

"People were mean to me, on account of my mama," Nugget said quietly.

One of the twins, Clara, came forward. "People are mean to us, on account of our mama, too."

Polly watched the expressions flash across the rest of the Taylor children's faces. Her heart ached as she remembered the taunts poor little Nugget used to face. And, to a lesser extent, she used to face. Polly's ma was a woman of the most honorable sort, but her pa... Polly sighed. She did her best to honor her pa, but his gambling, drinking and suspected philandering was the biggest reason she could never see herself settling down.

"Well, I'm not going to be mean to you on account of your mama." Polly held out her hand. "And I am fairly certain that none of the children here will do so either. But if they do, they will answer to me."

Clara came and took Polly's hand. "Everyone says Mummy was wicked. And we're wicked just like her."

Those big brown eyes looked up at her, full of hope, yet fearful.

"You're not wicked," Polly said, squeezing the little girl's hand, then looking over at the rest of the Taylor children. "You might need to learn a few manners, but that doesn't mean you're wicked."

Mitch stepped alongside her. "Thank you," he said quietly. "I don't think anyone's told them that before."

She turned her attention to him. "Why haven't you?"

"I didn't know." The sadness in his voice tugged at her heart more strongly than the wounded expressions on his children's faces.

She'd already been convinced that she needed to help this family. But now, more than ever, nothing would stop her from giving them the support they needed.

Chapter Three

Slipping his hand into Polly's free hand felt more natural than anything he'd done in a long time. Actually, everything about being with Polly felt natural. How had Mitch not seen the misery his children had been living in for so long? How had he not known how the nannies themselves disparaged the children?

Polly squeezed his hand, sending an intense current of warmth through him.

"I'm sorry, children, I didn't know." Mitch looked at his children, wishing he could undo the damage that had been done to them.

Clara let go of Polly's other hand and rushed at him, wrapping her arms around his legs. Before he knew it, the rest of the children were gathered round him, hugging him. Isabella probably had no idea why, but she was still of an age where all she needed was a few snuggles and she was perfectly happy. She hadn't yet realized that people treated her differently because of her dark skin.

Louisa, however, stood apart from them. Watching him. Shooting glares at Polly.

"Just because you say the right things doesn't mean

we're going to accept you as our nanny." Then she looked pointedly at the hand Mitch still held. "Or our new mummy."

Polly immediately jerked her hand away. "Well, I suppose it's just as well that I never have any intention of marrying." She gave Louisa a smile that seemed to be more menacing than sweet. "Or having children. As for being your nanny, if you can prove to me that you are as capable as you say of taking care of your siblings, I will gladly leave my post, become trained as a teacher, then make my own way in the world."

Mitch watched as Polly locked gazes with his daughter. "But I promise you that whatever you try to do to drive me away, it won't work. The only way I will leave is if I am completely assured of your ability to take care of yourselves."

Then she turned her gaze to Mitch. "We haven't discussed terms of my employment yet. Perhaps we can leave Louisa in charge while we take a short stroll to settle things. This could be the perfect opportunity for her to prove her worth."

Polly didn't wait for Mitch's response as she tucked her arm into his elbow and extricated him from his children's embraces. She didn't speak until they were well outside of the children's earshot.

"I think they'll be just fine while we walk. Even though I left Louisa in charge, everyone in Uncle Frank's household is within earshot."

She smiled at him, and again, he was struck by the warmth in her expression. Warm, but tough.

"I'm not comfortable with Louisa raising her siblings. It's no life for a young girl."

"I quite agree," Polly said, a twinkle filling her eyes. "Having lived that life myself, I can tell you that eventually, she'll come to resent it, and be willing to do just about anything to escape."

"Such as become a nanny to five unruly children."

Polly grinned. "Indeed. It's a good thing you only had five, because I'm not sure I have the stamina for six."

Mitch had already been certain in his decision to hire Polly, but her quick wit and sense of humor cemented it. The dour women who'd looked after his children in the past always intimidated him, and sometimes he wondered if that intimidation only frightened the children.

He'd never considered that what the children might need was something completely different. Someone completely different.

"You're sure your family won't mind?"

Polly sighed. "Honestly, other than not having someone to do their bidding, I'm not sure they'd notice. I feel more in the way these days, and I never know what my place is. Other than following orders."

Then she stopped, put a hand over her mouth and turned to him. A few moments later, she dropped her hand, then gave him a dejected look. "I'm sorry. I sound like such an ungrateful daughter. Ma has worked hard her whole life. Even when Pa wasn't up to the task of providing for our family, Ma took over. I know Ma says that Pa means well, but the truth is, she's nearly worked herself to death to do right by us, and I am truly grateful for her sacrifices. Maybe it is selfish of me to want my own life, but I've spent most of it helping Ma. Now that Pa has a good job in Joseph's mine, Ma doesn't have to work so hard."

Another long sigh escaped Polly's lips as she looked at the house, then back at him. "Since I'm not needed so much, I have to take the chance to live the life of my choosing, not what's forced upon me."

She gave him a soft smile, and once again, he was struck by how pretty she was. He pushed the thought away and concentrated on her words instead.

"I didn't mean to unburden myself on you like that, but I don't want you to think I'm a bad person or Ma is a bad person. We've done the best we could do with what we have, and I promise I'll be good to your children."

"I know," Mitch said, trying to ignore the tug on his heart. Her words made him want to hire her not just for his children, not just for him, but to give Polly the life she craved.

But he refused to let himself get attached to her on a personal level. Polly had already indicated her desire to eventually leave, so he had to think of her position as temporary. As for any deeper feelings, those were completely unacceptable.

A man only remarried for love or to get a family for himself. He already had more family than he could handle. Love, well, that was a folly he'd not repeat.

Hattie had bled him dry of any sort of romantic notions he might have had. Polly MacDonald was pretty enough, and he'd admit that she stirred feelings in him he'd thought dead, but Mitch knew better than to act on any of them. The only thing worse than falling in love was falling for a woman he knew wouldn't stay. He should have seen the signs with Hattie, but now that he knew Polly's plans for her own life, he knew how completely off-limits he had to keep his heart.

He had to keep things strictly professional, which was why the question forming on his lips had to be asked. Not for his sake, of course, but for the five children who might become attached to Polly.

"How long do you plan on working for me before seeking your teaching certificate?"

Polly shrugged. "I have no timetable. I'll stay as long as I'm needed and we're both satisfied with my work. I don't necessarily need to become a teacher, but it is one of the few respectable forms of employment for a young unmarried lady. Particularly one who has no intention of ever marrying."

Once again, Mitch found his interest piqued by her strong declaration against marriage. "Was your heart broken that badly, then?"

Polly shook her head. "I know everyone thinks it's because Tom broke my heart. But the truth is, I've seen what falling in love and marriage does to a person. Did Ma know what kind of man Pa would turn out to be when she married him? Of course not. She had stars in her eyes, and even now, if you catch her at just the right time, she'll tell you of the roguish way he stole her heart. But what good did that do her? Backbreaking work, more mouths to feed than she could afford and having to put up with his antics?"

A gust of wind scooted between them, and Polly pulled her shawl tighter against her body. "I know that not every man is bad, and I'm sure you want to defend your gender to me. But honestly, I've had enough of a taste for when things go wrong to not want to venture there myself. In my experience, things go wrong more than they go right."

Mitch couldn't help the sigh that escaped. Part of him wanted to argue with her logic and tell her that exactly not all men were bad, and not all marriages were terrible. But his own experience…

"I understand. As much as I tried to protect the children from knowing the truth about my marriage to Hattie…"

Mitch sighed again. He'd never confessed the truth of his marriage to anyone, not his family, not the few friends who stood by him, not the police who questioned him over Hattie's death.

"I'm sorry that it wasn't good," Polly said softly. "But you did your best to make your children feel safe and secure. Which is what Ma did for us. I respect that. And you won't hear a word against her from me."

Then Polly glanced back at the house. "I shouldn't have told you those things about my pa. Ma would be terribly hurt if she knew I held him in such low regard. She's never spoken ill of him, even on the nights he's come home smelling of drink and cheap perfume."

Her loyalty felt like a warm cloak around his heart. His children were safe with this woman. She wouldn't make them feel small or out of place, and she'd do her best to keep them from the talk that followed their family. And, as he watched her nibble on her lower lip, he knew that he was safe with her as well.

"I won't say anything," Mitch said softly. "Thank you for trusting me. I imagine this has been weighing on you for some time."

"You don't know the half of it," Polly said quietly, once again glancing in the direction of the house. "My friends have all married wonderful men. They all think I'll eventually find someone just as wonderful and live the same wonderful lives they lead. But how can I tell them that marriage isn't always so wonderful when they are clearly so happy?"

"You don't," Mitch said, taking her by the arm and leading her down the road. "I never wanted anyone to know what a fool I'd been, so I simply pretended everything was fine."

Then he stopped. "I'm sorry, I don't know where we're going. And I don't know why I'm telling you all of this. I suppose that both of us needed someone to talk to, and both of us understand what's at stake for the other."

Polly smiled, then pointed at a nearby barn. "Why don't I show you Uncle Frank's mission, and the work he's doing? As for talking, I understand completely. Your secrets are safe with me."

They turned a corner, and Mitch realized that not all of his secrets were going to remain safe. Gerald Barnes, deputy and chief investigator into Hattie's death, was coming toward them.

He should have known that Gerald would show up in Leadville sometime. But what he hadn't expected was the two large men standing with him.

Gerald and his men closed in. "Mitchell Taylor, you're under arrest for the murder of Hattie Winston."

Murder? Polly looked at Mitch. There had to be some mistake.

But Mitch didn't look at her. Instead, he stared at the deputy. "You know I didn't do it."

"I got a witness who says otherwise." The deputy put his hand on the gun at his waist. "I suggest you come peacefully."

The two men with the deputy came toward them, looking like they expected a fight. Once again, Polly stole a glance at Mitch, who wore the same icy calm expression he had in the Mercantile when his children were misbehaving.

"Of course." Mitch held out his hands, almost as

though he'd been expecting this. Then he turned and looked at Polly.

"I'm sorry we weren't able to settle terms of your employment fully, but I can assure you that once we sort out this misunderstanding, I'll pay whatever wages you think fair."

He nodded in the direction of the deputy and his men. "They're witnesses to my agreement to pay you, so you needn't worry that I'll not give you your due."

"I wasn't worried," Polly told him. "I'm happy to care for your children, but—"

"You should be worried, miss," the deputy said, his brow furrowed. "The way poor Miss Hattie died, it was a gruesome scene, and I'm sure she must've suffered in the end. You shouldn't trust the likes of Mitch Taylor. He has a pretty tale to tell, but it's all lies."

Secrets. Everyone had them. Could Mitch have killed his wife? Polly's gut told her no. But with as forthcoming as he'd seemed to be in their discussions, why hadn't he mentioned that he was a suspect in his wife's death?

"I believe, in this country, a man is innocent until proven guilty," Polly said quietly, looking at Mitch. What would he say in his defense?

"There's proof enough," the deputy said. "A fine citizen like Mitch Taylor, you'd have never believed it. But I suppose there's only so much a man can take, and one night, he just lost it."

Then he looked at Mitch. "I suppose you thought she had it coming. But no one, no one, deserves to die the way Hattie did."

Still, Mitch remained silent, and Polly's stomach turned inside out. Why wasn't he defending himself? Why did he seem so calm?

"Can we go now?" Mitch stared back at the deputy.

"I'd rather not cause a scene. My children have already been through enough."

Once again, Mitch brought his icy gaze to Polly. "If you wouldn't mind bringing the children back to my brother's, let him know what's happening. He can notify my lawyer. I trust you'll care for the children as we discussed?"

Polly nodded slowly. "Of course. I could ask Uncle Frank or Will—"

"Please don't." Mitch's shoulders rose and fell. "I know you want to help, but right now, the only help I need is making sure my children are safe and well cared for. That's all that matters to me."

Other than his initial protestation of guilt, not one word about his innocence. Not one word about the heinous crime he'd been accused of. In fact, he stood there calmly as though he'd been expecting this to happen all along.

What kind of man was Mitch Taylor? Had she been wrong in her instincts about him?

As she watched the deputy put handcuffs on him and lead him down the street, Polly couldn't imagine that she'd been wrong. But why was he so meekly accepting this injustice?

Or was it as the deputy had suggested, and Mitch had just snapped?

Mitch stopped, then turned to look at her. "Go. I'm counting on you."

The deputy and his men led Mitch away, and while Polly wanted to run after them, she did the only thing she could do—she ran back to the parsonage and back to the Taylor children.

When she arrived at the house, Uncle Frank was waiting for her on the porch.

"Where's Mitch?"

Polly started spilling the details of Mitch's arrest, hoping that somewhere in her words, something would come out that made sense. Before she got very far in her story, Will Lawson, Mary's husband and a deputy in Leadville, arrived at the house. Both men were silent until Polly finished, but from the expressions on their faces, she knew the situation wasn't good.

Finally, Will spoke. "I've heard of the case. Grisly murder. Everyone figured the husband did it. He got tired of being cuckolded and finally did something about it. The biggest surprise in the whole thing is why he didn't do it when their youngest daughter was born. You don't get much more proof of infidelity than that."

Little Isabella's face popped into Polly's head. "He wouldn't have killed her over that. He loves Isabella. He loves all of his children."

Will shrugged. "His children, maybe. But I don't know a man alive who would put up with that kind of behavior from his wife."

"So you're proclaiming him guilty without having all the facts? What kind of lawman are you?"

A grin spread across Will's face. "The kind who knows better than to mess with Polly MacDonald. You're right, though. I don't have all the facts. But since he's now closely tied to the family, I aim to find them."

Polly's shoulders relaxed. Despite her lack of trust in most men, she had to admit that one of the few men she trusted explicitly was Will Lawson. He'd proven his honor time and again, and his thirst for justice was unequaled. If anyone could help Mitch, Will could.

Her conscience nagged her as she remembered Mitch's instruction not to have anyone help him. But she'd seen his pride in accepting help with the children and knew that getting Will on the case was the right thing to do.

Until Will looked at her with such intensity, she thought it would melt her on the spot. No wonder criminals feared him.

"But if he's guilty, Polly, I will see him brought to justice."

She wouldn't consider that possibility. Mitch had to be innocent. She couldn't be wrong about a man and his criminal involvement twice. Mitch seemed too...

Memories of how Tom had fooled her rattled in her brain. He'd seemed incapable of a crime as well, and look where that had gotten her.

"What will happen to the children if he is?" Polly couldn't help the question that escaped her.

Will shrugged. "Either family will take them, or they'll go to an orphanage. But don't worry, we'll make sure you're not stuck with them."

A blur of dark braids flew at her.

"We will not go to an orphanage!" Clara's fists pummeled Polly in the stomach. "I trusted you! You are not sending us away!"

Polly wrapped her arms around the little girl. "No, I'm not sending you away. I promise. Even if it means staying with you for the rest of my life, you will not be sent away."

As Clara sobbed, Polly could only pray that she wouldn't have to make good on the promise. Yes, these children had already burrowed into her heart. But there was still a part of Polly that desperately yearned to be free. Had she just trapped herself?

Chapter Four

"It's time for bed," Polly called as she picked up a discarded sock from the floor. Mitch had been gone for over a week, but his brother, Andrew, said he'd heard from him and that everything was fine.

Fine. How could anything be fine when a man was in jail? Even Will had little to report on the case, a fact which only made the wait even more maddening.

Four scowling faces looked up from the game of marbles they'd been playing. Isabella, sweet Isabella, toddled over to her.

Louisa glared at her. "We aren't finished with our game."

"I believe I warned you when you began the game that you would not have enough time to complete it. If you like, you can leave everything out and finish in the morning."

"That's not fair!" Rory swiped his arm across the elaborate setup, ruining any hope that the children could continue in the morning.

Polly sighed. The longer Mitch was gone, the angrier the children became. Andrew's explanation for their father's absence wasn't sitting well with any of the children because after so many days, "your father will be home soon" sounds an awful lot like a lie.

"It's a shame you ruined such a lovely game." Polly ruffled the boy's head, and he shied away. "Off to bed now, and in the morning, you can help with the others' chores, since you spoiled their fun."

Clara smirked and flounced out of her seat. "I don't mind going to bed. Because in the morning, we'll wake up, and Papa will be home."

"He will?" Thomas looked up with such innocent brown eyes that Polly wanted nothing more than to agree with Clara. "Papa's never left us before. What if Papa never comes back, like Mummy?"

"Papa is nothing like *her*," Louisa said, picking up the marbles. "He'll be back, you'll see."

"Hey! Those are mine!" Rory snatched at Louisa's hand.

"I won them, fair and square."

"I was going to win them back if *she* hadn't told us to go to bed."

"Well, you didn't, and now that you've ruined the game, they're mine," Louisa said triumphantly, holding up a marble with deep blue flecks. "And this one sure is a beauty. I've been admiring it ever since Uncle Andrew gave it to you."

"Not all of those marbles are yours, Louisa." Clara pointed at some of the marbles in her pile. "You're just taking advantage of Rory's foul temper to gain more for yourself."

"You're just a sore loser."

As the four children's squabbling grew louder, Isabella began to wail. As she often did when the others fought. Polly pressed her fingers to her temple and rubbed gently before speaking.

"Give me the marbles."

Immediately, the voices went from accusing each other to what a horrid nanny Polly was. She smiled and held out her hand.

"All of them. We'll sort out what belongs to who in the morning. Now go get ready for bed, and I'll be in to hear your prayers in a moment."

Thomas was the first to comply. He hadn't yet found the will toward the level of defiance the older children had. After depositing his marbles in Polly's outstretched hand, he made his way to the bedroom he shared with the other children.

The Taylor family lived in a small apartment above the Mercantile. Andrew and Iris had recently vacated the rooms to live in a home they'd built nearby, and were hoping to rent them out as soon as Mitch's troubles were resolved. For now, though, the Taylor children crammed into the tiny space, complaining often about how their home in Denver had much more room. The cozy place featured two bedrooms, a large sitting room that had space enough for a dining area and a small kitchen. Off the kitchen was a tiny room the previous nanny had occupied, but with Mitch gone, she'd taken over his room as her own to be closer to the children. To Polly, room enough. At least when the children weren't all squabbling.

"Don't let Louisa keep my special marble," Rory said as he deposited the few marbles he'd been able to collect into her hand.

"We'll discuss it in the morning."

Clara sighed as she handed over her marbles as well.

Louisa, however, remained where she stood, holding the marbles, chin raised high, her eyes daring Polly to act.

"You, too, Louisa."

"I'm the eldest. I shouldn't have to go to bed so early."

"Your attitude says otherwise. I'm sure if I had more cooperation from you, then you would be rewarded by being allowed to stay up later and read in the sitting room. But clearly, from how you're fighting with your siblings, you're just as tired and cranky as they are."

Louisa's face reddened, and she opened her mouth to speak, but Polly had learned that a single look, the same she'd successfully employed dealing with the children in the Lassiter household, was enough to silence her. Even Louisa knew that the look meant her punishment would be worse if she spoke.

"Fine. But as soon as Papa returns, I will speak to him about this, and he'll tell you how unreasonable you're being."

With that, Louisa set the marbles on the table and flounced off.

Polly couldn't help the smile that curled at the edges of her lips. Every day was a battle with the Taylor children, but it seemed like each one became easier. Mostly because the children were starting to learn that while she was firm, ultimately, she was fair, and in the morning, when the marbles were divvied out again, each child would be satisfied with the results. Not completely happy, of course, but satisfied enough that they'd received their due.

In the meantime, though…she looked over at the sofa, where Isabella had curled up and fallen asleep. The girl had a knack for being able to do so whenever she felt tired and could be found sleeping in the oddest of places, as evidenced by their first meeting.

"Come along with you, then." Polly scooped the

sleeping girl up and carried her to Mitch's bed. Their first night together, Polly learned that Isabella was prone to nightmares, and the easiest solution was to keep the small girl in bed with her. Otherwise, her cries woke the entire household, and it made everyone miserable. Polly had spent enough years with a child in her bed that she was able to quickly comfort Isabella and lull her back to sleep without much fuss.

After Polly tucked Isabella in, she went into the children's room, where they were all in their beds, the girls in one bed, the boys in another, quilts tucked up to their chins. Thomas had already fallen asleep, and Rory seemed to be quickly on his way.

"Good night, boys," Polly said softly, brushing their heads gently and pressing quick kisses to their hair.

Then she went to the girls' bed. As she reached for Louisa, she was met with the usual icy glare. "Don't you dare."

"All right, then. Good night, Louisa."

Polly smiled and looked down at Clara. "Good night, my sweet." She smoothed the little girl's hair and bent to kiss her, but Clara stopped her.

"Why do you do that?"

"Do what?"

"Tuck us in, and kiss us and then say a prayer for us?"

Polly hadn't gotten to the prayers yet. Since the children refused to pray with her, she prayed aloud anyway and hoped that somehow her words, combined with God's love, would reach their hearts.

"Because I care for you, and I want you to know that you're loved."

"You're not our mother," Louisa said, then rolled onto her side, putting her back to Polly.

"No, I'm not," Polly said softly. "But it doesn't mean I can't love you. It doesn't mean that God doesn't love you."

Clara reached up and hugged her. "None of our other nannies loved us."

"Well, I'm not like them," Polly said, hugging her back and kissing her on top of the head. "Now off to sleep with you, and we'll talk more in the morning."

Then, as she always did, she tucked the quilts firmly around the children, saying the familiar prayer her mother had always said when she tucked her in.

"May the Lord be with you, and in your dreams, show you the love He has for you, so that in the morning you wake, full of His love and everything you need for a glorious day. Amen."

She thought she heard Louisa snort, but Clara whispered something softly, something that, if Polly had to guess, sounded an awful lot like "amen."

The wounds these children carried were not something Polly could fix, but if they allowed Him into their hearts, the healing they needed could follow.

Polly exited the room, closing the door softly behind her. She tiptoed through the rest of their home, blowing out the lamps, then banking the fire so it would keep them warm the rest of the night. Though the spring weather was warm during the day, evenings and early mornings still held a chill that needed to be kept at bay.

Satisfied that everything was in order, Polly returned to the bedroom where Isabella slept. She quickly changed into nightclothes and snuggled in with the tiny girl. Another benefit of sharing a bed was that it was already warm when she got in.

She'd just begun to enter the hazy almost dreamlike

state when a crash startled her. Polly's heart leapt into her throat as she sat up in bed.

A scraping sound, then another crash.

Muttered words of anger.

At home, Polly would have lain in bed and prayed that Pastor Lassiter, or Will, or someone, would have dealt with it. Or that it was one of the boys, having fun. But here, alone in this place with these children, she knew it was up to her.

Hands shaking, Polly pulled her wrapper around her nightgown, then grabbed the pitcher from the dresser. It wasn't much, but at least if the intruder got close enough, she could use it as a weapon.

"Please, Lord," she prayed, "don't let the intruder be armed."

Her prayer did little to quiet the rushing sound in her ears or calm her unsteady hands.

Polly eased open the door, then peered out. A large mass lay on the ground, muttering in pain.

She held the pitcher above her head. "Who are you, and what are you doing in our home?"

For a moment, she thought about sending it crashing over the intruder's head, which would incapacitate him long enough for her to get help, but her hesitation gave the intruder time to speak.

"Polly, it's me, Mitch."

Her heart continued to thunder in her chest as she lowered the pitcher, then clutched it tight against her.

"You nearly frightened me to death."

"Why didn't you leave a lamp lit?"

"I had no way of knowing you were coming home tonight. One would think you would have kept me apprised of your circumstances so that I had something to tell the children. Had I known you were coming, I would have been better prepared."

"Point taken," Mitch said, his voice sounding like he was smiling as he spoke. "Could you light a lamp? It seems the furniture has been rearranged in my absence and I tripped over a chair. I think my shin might be bleeding."

Polly took a deep breath, trying to steady her still-frantic nerves. "Of course. I'm sorry. I should have done that sooner."

She lit a lamp, then looked down at Mitch, who was rubbing his leg. The damp spot on his pants indicated he'd probably cut it open. "I'll get some bandages."

Polly quickly gathered the supplies she needed, lighting a few more lamps along the way, then returned to the sitting room, where Mitch had made himself comfortable on the sofa.

"You've done a nice job rearranging things. It's much more open, yet cozy in here."

As she knelt in front of him, Polly gave him a smile. "Thank you. I found that it's easier to give the children their lessons if I can see the older ones working at the table, and I can help the younger ones here. It's so hard for Isabella and Thomas to sit still, so having some open space for them to move around in makes it easier."

As she spoke, she'd rolled up his pant leg to find a deep gash. "You've got quite the injury here."

He smiled down at her, warming her in a way she hadn't expected. Like a sudden burst of sunlight through the clouds.

"Like my children, I suppose I don't do anything halfway."

She couldn't help but smile back. "I don't suppose any of us do."

Polly dabbed at the wound, trying to ascertain its depth.

"You're good at this."

"I've had a lot of practice. In the mining camps, there aren't many doctors, if any, so you have to learn a lot on your own. I can tend most injuries, deliver a baby and, if things get truly desperate, I've taken a bullet out of a man."

She could feel his gaze on her. "A refined young lady like you? But how?"

Meeting his gaze without taking pressure off his leg, she shrugged. "What you see is the product of a lot of hard living, a few refinements here and there, and a good dose of God's grace. I mentioned how Pastor Lassiter's involvement in our lives changed everything for us. Before that, we spent our days in mining camps, doing whatever it took to survive. You couldn't wait for someone more qualified to come do a job if you were the only body around to do it. I've been helping deliver babies since I was ten years old. There aren't too many womenfolk in the camps, and you learn pretty quickly to stick together."

Which is how Polly knew that marriage wasn't always a picnic. She hadn't just experienced her mother's pain, but watched as the other women in the camps struggled as well. She neglected to mention to Mitch that she'd learned to treat a gunshot wound after a woman in camp was shot in the arm by her drunken husband. He hadn't meant to shoot her, of course, but he'd been drunk and... Polly shook her head. It didn't matter.

"You're amazing, you know that?" The warm look Mitch gave her made her squirm. Amazing? Her stomach flipped, not in an unpleasant way, but in a way she couldn't explain. Didn't want to explain, because it meant…

Polly shook her head. "Thank you, but in all honesty, I just did what I had to do. You and anyone else would do the same in a similar situation."

Mitch wanted to argue with her, to let Polly know that there was something more to how wonderful she was, but he couldn't find the strength to put it to words. Besides, how could he start thinking of a nanny as being wonderful?

"How are the children?" he said instead, as she finished bandaging his wound.

Her smile filled her face, lighting her eyes. When had anyone smiled giving a report on his children?

"They're doing quite well, all things considered. They miss you terribly, but we're getting along. It would have been easier had you at least sent word."

He'd forgotten about how readily she spoke her mind. This was the second time in a matter of minutes she'd taken him to task as if he were one of the children instead of her employer. As much as he should remind her of propriety, he knew her chastisement of him came from a place of caring for his children.

Yet the gleam in those blue eyes told him she wasn't finished with him yet.

"My lawyer was in contact with my brother. I believe he kept you apprised of the situation."

"Apprised?" Polly's voice rose slightly, but then she lowered it again, looking over her shoulder at the bedrooms. "If by *apprised*, you mean he let us know you were alive, then yes. We were *apprised* of the situation. However, when one engages a nanny and tells her of the scandal of his wife's death, he should also *apprise* the nanny of the fact that he is considered a suspect."

Polly was right, of course. He should have told her. But he hadn't realized his arrest was so imminent. He'd already known that getting anyone to care for his difficult children was challenging enough, but then to have his extenuating circumstances on top of that…it seemed like madness.

"My lawyer has advised me not to speak to anyone about the case. It didn't occur to me that they would arrest me like that."

She frowned at him. "The press perhaps, but the person entrusted with your children should know what to expect. You should have at least informed me of the potential issues and how you'd like me to address them with the children."

Mitch let out a long sigh. Right again. But Polly didn't understand what was at stake here. He'd sheltered the children from the truth about their mother for years.

"I haven't known what to say," he said quietly, looking down at his hands. He'd always tried to be strong for his children, and yet now, when they faced the biggest challenge they'd ever faced, he had no idea what to do.

"They just lost their mother, and now their father has gone off without word and I've had no explanation for them. You have to say something."

Mitch's heart clanged to the bottom of his stomach, threatening to pull him under. How did a man tell his children that their beloved Mummy was dead, and everyone thought their father did it?

He didn't look up at her. Couldn't really, considering that he already felt the weight of her eyes on him, and to have to face them would be too much. Why was Polly affecting him this way? She was practically a child, and yet the wisdom and experience coming from those eyes…

"I don't know what to say," he said, repeating his earlier words, looking forlorn, still not meeting her gaze.

"How about letting them know you didn't do it and that you're working to find the real culprit?"

Her words hung in the air between them, and it should have been easy enough to agree with her.

But then Polly spoke again, so quietly, it was almost indecipherable. "Unless, of course, you killed her."

Had she tossed a red-hot coal and hit him squarely in the chest, it would not have burned as hard as her words. Mitch jumped up from his chair and stood, towering over her, where she knelt.

"Get out!"

Polly calmly picked up the supplies she'd used to bandage his leg, then rose. "And who will watch your children the next time the deputies come for you?"

Even the accusations from the investigators hadn't stung so much. They'd spewed horrible, disgusting details about Hattie's death, and never had he felt so violently toward them.

"How dare you?"

"How dare *you*?" Polly stepped into his space, mere inches from him, bringing her face as close to his as possible, given that she stood nearly a head shorter than he. "You hire a woman to care for your children, get arrested for a grisly murder and don't have the courtesy to tell her the truth about what happened. At least be so good as to declare your innocence."

The sparks flying from her eyes only served to stoke the fire in him. "I told them when they arrested me that I didn't do it. What more do you want?"

"No," Polly said, taking a step back. "You told them

that they knew you didn't do it. It's not the same as telling me what's happening, and to reassure me that you did not, in fact, kill your wife. It's not the same as telling your children that you didn't kill their darling Mummy."

Everything in Mitch's body burned. But as he thought of the only answer he had, he suddenly went cold. "I shouldn't have to."

He walked toward the fireplace, putting his hands out for the dying embers to give him some warmth. Something to chase away the ice that had seized his heart. "I've never been anything but honorable in all of my dealings. In how I treated Hattie and the children. How could anyone think…"

Memories washed over him. All the times he and Hattie fought, with Hattie storming out and him not hearing from her for months. The scandals Hattie always found herself in, and him, stoically standing by, saying nothing, because he didn't want the children to think ill of their mother.

No, he had never said anything. The papers had always said enough, and regardless of whether or not their stories were true, they said it anyway. What was there for him to say?

Mitch turned back toward Polly. "I didn't kill Hattie," he said quietly. "I hope that satisfies you. But that is all I will say on the matter, and should you require any more information, I suggest you find other employment. For I will not speak of it."

His threat, as much as he'd like it to have more power, floated on the air. Losing someone who cared for his children as much as Polly would be a blow. But already the rumors and innuendos swirling about were too much for Mitch to handle. All were complete lies, of course, but he'd seen how good friends had already closed their doors to him, not wanting to be involved with something so scandalous. And with the way the investigators had already twisted his words and actions, his lawyer had told him that the less he said to anyone, the better. One of the "witnesses" was Mitch's former housekeeper, who'd told the investigators about the violent last argument he'd had with Hattie.

The argument had been violent. But it had been Hattie who'd thrown the lamp at him. Hattie who'd screamed obscenities. Hattie who'd slapped him so soundly it had made his cheek bleed from where her nails had scratched him. She'd stormed out, slamming the door behind her, and he hadn't heard from her since.

Absently, he rubbed the spot on his cheek. The scratches had faded, leaving only invisible scars that left him wondering how he'd gotten caught up in the madness in the first place.

Polly remained standing where she'd been, the shadows too dark for him to see her eyes, and he was glad. He'd just begun to get to know her, just gotten to like her, and now he was driving her away.

Mitch cleared his throat. "I'd also like to make it clear that I won't have you gossiping about my family. If anyone asks, a reporter shows up or anything of the like, you will say nothing. I was arrested based on rumor, and I will not have anyone in my employ who is prone to idle talk."

"I would never gossip about anyone," Polly said quietly.

"Perhaps," Mitch said slowly. "But just as you needed to hear that I didn't kill my wife, I need to hear that you won't be talking to anyone about my family."

Polly nodded. "You have my word." Then she hesitated. "But…my family…"

"I would rather you not share with them." Who knew what, even in innocence, might be shared. And, with all the comings and goings in the parsonage, what would be overheard and misconstrued.

She didn't say anything, but instead, walked over to him and placed her hand on his arm. Then, with those eyes that seemed to probe deeper into his soul than he was comfortable with, she spoke softly.

"It must be incredibly lonely keeping yourself so closed off. As much as they make me crazy sometimes, I don't know what I would do without my family to talk to. I understand that it must be difficult to talk to someone you barely know, but I hope you know that you don't have to go through this alone."

Mitch's throat clogged with anything he might have said in response. What did Polly know of his life? Of the difficulties he could not, would not, share?

Then she squeezed his arm, sending a current through him that seized his heart. "Even if you reject my friendship, please at least consider opening up to your brother. He cares for you deeply, and I know he wants to help even more than he has."

He closed his eyes, willing himself to breathe. Andrew was the last person he'd confide in. Yes, he loved his brother, but how could he let his brother know just how bad things were? How could he disappoint him so?

Polly's soft lilac scent filled his nostrils. *She* was the one he wanted to confide in. Wanted to wrap his arms around her, and have her tell him it was going to be all right. But then he would have to admit to feelings that he didn't have the right to have.

Mitch took another deep breath. "I have everything

under control," he said, pulling away. "We should both turn in for the night. Morning will be here before you know it, and I'm sure I don't need to tell you that the children are early risers."

"Of course," Polly said, bowing her head. She seemed to understand without him having to tell her that theirs needed to be a more formal relationship. There would be no confidences shared, no…none of the things that sometimes crossed his mind. He couldn't afford to have his heart so ensnared again.

He started for his bedroom, but Polly stopped him. "If you'll just give me a moment, I've been sleeping in there with Isabella. It seemed easier to be closer to the children."

"It's all right. I'll take the other bedroom. After the nights I've spent in a cell, any bed has to be more comfortable."

Another dip of the head. "As you wish."

No, nothing was as he wished. But as he watched Polly retreat back into the bedroom, he knew it was the only way to keep his heart safe.

Chapter Five

The children were already eating breakfast when Mitch entered the kitchen, hair tousled and rubbing the sleep out of his eyes. Polly had hoped he'd be able to sleep in, but with the room just off the kitchen, and the ruckus that always came with mealtime, she should have known his peace wouldn't last long.

"Papa!" five voices chorused as they all jumped from the table and wrapped their arms around him.

As much as she wanted to hold Mitch's inability to be forthcoming against him, and wanted to stay angry with him, she found that as she watched the loving interaction between father and children, she couldn't bring herself to do so. For the first time since he'd gone away, Louisa was actually smiling.

"I see Polly still has all her hair," Mitch said, looking up at her and smiling. "I hope that means you were all well behaved."

The cross expression returned to Louisa's face as she made a noise. "Well, she wasn't as horrid as Mrs. Abernathy, but we would have done just fine without her."

As the younger girl wound herself up for what Polly imagined was yet another argument for why she should be allowed to take care of her siblings, Mitch seemed to sense the direction Louisa was taking as well.

"I don't want to hear it," he said, shaking his head. "I need an adult taking care of you, and Polly is doing a wonderful job."

"How would you know? You've been gone." Louisa's dark eyes flashed, and she stepped away from her father, crossing her arms over her chest.

Polly turned to help Isabella get back in her chair, but not before she caught the reciprocal flash in Mitch's eyes.

"It couldn't be helped," he said, his voice quiet, yet with an undercurrent of tension that made Polly's heart ache.

She supposed he couldn't be forthcoming with the children; after all, having their father be accused of killing their mother was a tragedy no child should have to experience. Losing their mother was bad enough, but to have to face the potential involvement of their father...

Polly took a deep breath. She'd been judging Mitch harshly, when he'd simply been doing the best he could do.

"Would you like some breakfast?" she said, straightening as she smiled at him. "Your brother thoughtfully provided a housekeeper to help with the cooking and such since apparently you hadn't had time to engage one. Lucy has just gone down to get some more milk, but I think you'll be pleased with her."

Mitch nodded slowly, then sat at the head of the table. "Thank you. I guess I hadn't realized what a mess I'd left behind."

He spoke slowly, as though the remorse for the difficult position he'd left everyone in had finally dawned on him.

"We made it through just fine," Polly said, handing him a plate. "Now we need to move forward as best as we can."

She'd have liked to have told him that she was sorry for her accusations the previous night. The five accusing glances, even from little Isabella, must have weighed incredibly heavily on him. He didn't need the additional pressure from her.

The back door opened, and Lucy bustled in. "There's a crowd gathered out front, and they were asking me all sorts of questions."

Mitch had just raised a forkful of eggs to his lips but hadn't taken a bite yet. The fork clattered to the table as he jumped up and went to the front window.

He muttered something indistinguishable as he turned back toward the kitchen area. "Reporters."

"Like when Mummy has a show?" Clara asked, her eyes lighting up momentarily, then dimming. "They don't know she is gone?"

"No, you dolt. It's because Mummy is dead. They all want to know how we feel about losing her." Louisa's face darkened, but fire filled her eyes. "Why won't they leave us alone?"

Mitch looked over at Polly, his eyes locking with hers. A silent reminder that the children didn't know the circumstances that hung over him.

How were they supposed to carry on with their lives with the reporters hanging about? One ill-placed question, and Mitch would have a great deal of explaining to do.

"Let's forget about them and enjoy our breakfasts, shall we?" Polly tried to sound cheerful, but as the sullen children stared at their congealing eggs, she found she didn't have much of an appetite either.

Isabella, however, was too innocent to understand the darkness surrounding her family, and she devoured her meal. At least one of her charges was eating.

Mitch made a show of finishing his breakfast. "It was delicious. Thank you, Lucy."

He acknowledged their housekeeper with a smile, but his eyes weren't in it.

How had Polly come to take such an interest in him? To notice his moods and his features? She shook her head. Just part of the job. Of course she had to be sensitive to Mitch's moods—for the children's sakes.

"I suppose we could start our lessons." Once again, Polly tried to sound cheerful, but she was met with dull expressions. Typically, the suggestion of lessons would have elicited a few groans, or some argument. But with the mention of their beloved mummy, their grief came back up again, swallowing them into a pit of mourning that left them incapable of feeling anything else.

"Or, I was thinking, we could go to the parsonage and take our lessons with the children there today."

"Wif Nugget?" Isabella's big dark eyes brightened as she hopped off her chair and bounded toward Polly.

In the days Mitch had been gone, the children had spent a good deal of time with the parsonage children. Partially because it was easier than keeping them cooped up in the tiny apartment when they were clearly used to living in a larger home. But also because Polly had seen how much the children needed to be around others their own age. Nugget had taken a shine to Isabella and relished finally having a child younger than herself to mother.

Oddly enough, Isabella seemed to relish the attention just as much.

"Yes, my sweet. With Nugget." She ruffled the little girl's hair, then looked over at Mitch. "With your father's approval, of course. It might provide a nice distraction."

Mitch gave her a warm smile. "Yes, that would be nice. Thank you." Then he looked over at Lucy. "Had anyone followed you to the back?"

"No, sir. It's not a well-used entrance, and the only reason I knew of it was because the other Mr. Taylor suggested it to avoid the reporters."

Then he turned his attention to Polly. "Let's go now, before anyone discovers it."

Madness. That's what the whole situation was. He would take the children out of the apartment now, so they wouldn't see the people standing in front of the building holding signs that said Murderer, but what then? Eventually, they'd have to come home, and those people, as well as the reporters, would still be there.

Everyone thought he'd killed Hattie. The newspapers in Denver already blasted the headline that he'd killed her in a fit of passion. Passion. Ha! He hadn't experienced passion toward Hattie in so long, he couldn't even remember what it felt like. But the sensational headlines sold papers, and convicting him of Hattie's murder would get the sheriff reelected. No one cared about the truth.

Had it not been for his lawyer calling in a favor with the governor, who'd called in a favor with the judge to allow Mitch to be released on bail until his trial, Mitch would still be sitting in a jail cell.

He appreciated the way Polly bundled up the children and hurried them out the back door.

"Let's be as quiet as we can," she said softly, putting

a finger to her lips. "We're hiding from those people, and we don't want them upsetting you further."

Five heads nodded at her.

"Lucy, you take the older two and meet us at the parsonage. If they see a woman and two children walking down the street, they won't realize it's us. I'll go with the younger three, and Mitch, you may follow in a few minutes."

Efficient. Strong. And yet, there was a tenderness to her voice that made him think she really did care for the children and sparing their feelings.

Then she looked at him, piercing him with those blue eyes. "I'm assuming you know your way around town enough not to take a direct route? No sense in leading them there, though I know Uncle Frank will do his best to shield everyone."

Mitch nodded slowly. "You've thought of everything."

Polly shrugged. "We've had to deal with our share of reporters over the years. Don't worry, your children are safe."

The tension seemed to evaporate from his chest, and suddenly, he felt like he could breathe again. Polly had very easily managed everything in his absence, and for the first time in a long time, he could almost believe that everything would be all right.

"Thank you, Polly. I'll see you all there soon." He kissed each of his children as they passed and almost bent to kiss Polly as well. Then he shook his head. Where was he coming up with all this ridiculousness?

Habit, of course. He just kissed every head that passed, especially now, knowing how very precious each moment with them was.

Polly seemed to sense his hesitation because she

ducked her head away, but not before he caught the pink tingeing her cheeks.

As he exited, Mitch was pleased to note that none of the reporters or people carrying the horrible signs had discovered the service entrance. Perhaps it was because the rear stairs led to the storeroom of the Mercantile, then out the back door of the Mercantile. People probably didn't even realize the two were connected. He could only hope that the commotion didn't hurt his brother's business too much. Iris was expecting another child, and they'd just built a nice house down the road.

Though no one had seemed to notice Mitch's departure, he still carefully wound his way through town, taking alleys, backtracking and going the most unlikely routes possible. When he finally arrived at the parsonage, he could hear laughter coming from the backyard.

Polly opened the front door before he could knock. "Good. You made it. Everyone is waiting for you in the parlor."

Everyone? "I thought I told you to keep my family business private."

"And I have," she said, looking him so firmly in the eye that if he were one of the children, he'd obey her immediately. "However, if you think that you're going to be able to continue to shelter your children from the reporters and those people with the awful signs, then you can't keep them at the apartment. Uncle Frank has said that we can all stay here until the furor dies down."

He should be angry with her. Had every right to be angry with her. Polly MacDonald was so efficient at managing everything around her that she'd forgotten that he was an adult, perfectly capable of managing himself.

Except in this instance, she was right.

If they went back to the apartment, the children were bound to see the signs. Were bound to ask questions like, "Did you kill our mummy?" just as Polly had.

"Thank you," he finally said. "But I don't see why everyone needs to be gathered in the parlor over all of this."

"Because you're in a serious situation," a deep voice behind him said.

Mitch turned to see a tall man younger than he sporting a badge prominently on his vest.

"Will Lawson," he said, holding out his hand as he examined Mitch.

Mitch shook, wondering what this lawman was going to do in the situation. Polly had mentioned a close family friend being a lawman, but that didn't mean the man was going to be on his side. None of the lawmen in Denver seemed to care about the truth. Why would this guy be any different?

"Mitch Taylor, but I suppose you already know that."

"Seems to me you're in a bit of a pickle."

"My lawyer is handling things."

"Fair enough. But I'm happy to do some investigating of my own."

What would Will find that the deputies in Denver hadn't already found? Supposedly, they'd exhausted every lead, and everything seemed to point right back to Mitch. The last thing he needed was more evidence suggesting he was guilty.

Back in Denver, Mitch had hired an investigator of his own, a man who promised he'd find something on the real killer. That man now worked for the deputies, claiming there was nothing that said Mitch didn't do it.

Mitch swallowed the lump in his throat. "Thank you, but I believe my lawyer has everything in hand.

I'd hate to take you from your important work here in Leadville."

"It's no trouble," Will said, obviously not accepting the easy way out that Mitch had given him.

What was the other man's agenda?

"All the same, I think we'll be just fine."

Actually, they weren't. That was the trouble. So much evidence was stacked against him, or at least that's the way it seemed. It didn't appear to matter that they couldn't prove that Mitch had been at the murder scene, or that Mitch had any connection to whatever had been used to bludgeon Hattie to death. But that's what happened when all they really wanted was someone to take the fall so the sheriff looked like a hero.

Mitch turned to Polly. "I believe you said people were waiting on me."

Her brows furrowed as she pursed her lips, but she didn't argue with him. She meant well, he knew, but Polly didn't understand what he was up against. What he'd always been up against. People were constantly trying to be his friend, hoping to gain access to the amazing Hattie Winston. And now that she was gone, every charlatan in town was offering "help" with the case, only their motives weren't so pure. Whether it was to prove his guilt, or get the inside scoop for the latest newspaper, all the supposed offers of help never had Mitch's best interests in mind.

Did Will have Mitch's best interests in mind? He had no idea. He'd barely met the man, and while Polly's recommendation might mean something to some people, Mitch had too much at stake to trust just anyone.

Polly led him into the parlor, where Pastor Lassiter, Gertie and Maddie sat waiting. Before Mitch could speak, Pastor Lassiter stood.

"Now I know you object to receiving help, but I have to say that in this instance, you are going to accept what we offer. Those children of yours need protection, and if they're staying with us, no one is going to know who they are. Folks around here are used to us having all sorts of children running around, and not one will question who these children are. Pride isn't going to keep your children safe."

Mitch nodded slowly. "Thank you. I am grateful for the offer. In fact, I was afraid of what would happen if I had to take them back home. They don't need to be subjected to the scandal."

The older man looked at him solemnly. "Now, Polly assures me that you're innocent, but I need to hear it from you. I won't harbor a murderer in my home."

The ever-present lump in Mitch's throat threatened to cut off his airway. It seemed like all he ever did was proclaim his innocence, but no one ever listened.

"I didn't kill Hattie."

There. The words were his own, but he hardly recognized his voice. He had children who were grieving a lost mother, and rather than focusing on them, he had to continually defend himself.

"Where are my children?"

Polly smiled at him. "They're playing in the yard. We're letting them get their wiggles out before we start lessons."

Once again, Mitch nodded slowly, trying to process the information. Laughter drifted toward him, and somewhere in there, he thought he recognized the sound of his own children. Pastor Lassiter walked over to him and put a hand on his shoulder.

"I believe you, son. But from what I've seen in the

papers, you're going to need to do a lot more than what you've been doing to get the rest of society to believe it."

Mitch's body went cold as he looked around the room. "You've seen the papers? Are they here? I don't want the children—"

"They've already been burned in the stove," Maddie said, rising. "What do you take us for? Fools?"

Once again, he felt his body relax at the knowledge that someone else was thinking through all the details that plagued him.

"Thank you." Mitch looked around the room. "I'm not used to people wanting to help me like this, and I'm not sure what to do with it. To be honest, I don't understand why."

The hand that rested on his shoulder squeezed it, spreading warmth through his body. "Because we serve a Lord who has taught us to love the least of his children and fight for justice for those for whom no justice comes."

Mitch wanted to believe him, but he'd spent so much time listening to the church people standing in front of his house, his store and every other place he went telling him how undeserving he was because of all his sin.

And, if Mitch were honest with himself, all those people were probably right. He'd committed a good number of sins in his life. The trouble was, he wasn't guilty of any of the sins people accused him of.

So when was the real agenda of these people going to come out? Mitch would like to think they were who they said they were, but he'd had too much experience with life teaching him otherwise. Still, he had to admit that this was the safest place for his family right now, and while he wasn't sure how long this hospitality would last, for the children's sake, he'd accept it.

Chapter Six

Polly tucked the blankets around Isabella, pleased that the children were settling in so well. Their father, however, was another story. Why was Mitch being so obstinate about accepting help? Yes, he was letting the children stay at the parsonage, but how did that help exonerate him? How did that ensure that the children would continue to have a father?

She turned to leave, but the little girl sat up in bed. "You didn't say my pwayers wif me."

Warmth radiated through Polly's chest. With so many things about the situation bothering her, at least something was going right. This sweet little girl, who'd clearly not known the Lord before meeting Polly, asking for prayer. Louisa still sullenly ignored her, and the other children seemed to tolerate it, but at least Isabella seemed to love Polly's nighttime prayer.

"I'm sorry, I thought you were sleeping and I didn't want to wake you."

A drowsy smile filled the girl's face. "I sweep better wif my pwayers."

Polly knelt beside the bed and recited the prayer she said every night. Before the "amen" was out of her mouth, Isabella had drifted back to sleep. She'd join the little one in bed later, but she still had other things to do before retiring.

As she exited the room, she nearly ran into something hard, firm and warm—Mitch's well-built chest. "Oh!"

He smelled fresh, clean and with just a hint of the pine-scented soap she'd helped Maddie make over the summer. She hadn't thought of soap being so…intimate… and yet Polly recognized the feeling of attraction almost immediately.

With a quick step to the right, Polly got out of his way, trying not to notice how handsome he looked with his still-damp hair. The butterflies fluttering in her stomach had no business there. She was meant to do a job, not ogle her employer.

"Sorry," he said slowly. "I didn't mean to be spying on you. It's just that…" His voice caught, and for a moment, Polly thought she spied tears glistening in Mitch's eyes.

"I don't think Isabella has ever known such tenderness and love before."

Polly's heartbeat returned to its original state. At least Mitch hadn't noticed her foolishness over him. And instead, he'd brought her focus back to where it should have been in the first place—his children. "I imagine it's been hard, having so many nannies, and with her mother now gone, love is all the little dear needs. And I'm happy to provide it."

But Mitch didn't return the expression. Instead, his eyes looked haunted, his brow furrowed. "I don't think she even had that before." He rubbed his forehead, then shook his head slowly. "How could I have missed it, all this time?"

"Missed what?" Polly reached forward and touched his arm tenderly. Oh, if he were only a little boy like Rory or Thomas, she could take him in her arms and hold him. But Mitch wasn't a boy, and the longing in her heart felt different from how she felt toward his sons. But it didn't change her wish to somehow make whatever was going on in his mind better.

"They're so easy to love. But why couldn't the nannies? Why couldn't she have loved them?"

"She?"

In the dim corridor, Polly couldn't read his expression. But when he spoke, his voice cracked, and the ache in Polly's heart deepened.

"Hattie."

Their mother. "I'm sure she loved them. Of course she loved them."

Mitch shook his head slowly, his brow twisted momentarily, though he was trying to figure out a puzzle. Just as quickly, the expression disappeared, then he spoke. "I'm sorry, I don't know what came over me. I've just never seen a woman tuck my children in and say prayers with them. Hattie wasn't the motherly sort, and the nannies were more interested in discipline than love."

Something in Mitch's mood had shifted, and it seemed better to lighten the atmosphere. "Perhaps you just don't know what to look for in a nanny," she said, giving him a wink.

"I hired you, didn't I?" The light had returned to his eyes, and Polly thought she caught the hint of a smile at the corners of his lips.

"Then I suppose there's hope for you, after all. You've finally learned from all of your mistakes."

Mitch chuckled, a sound she hadn't heard before,

and from the awkward way it creaked out in the beginning, something he probably hadn't done in a while. Which, of course, he wouldn't have, given that he'd just buried his wife and was dealing with accusations of her murder.

"You have been good for my family, that I will admit." Then he composed himself and said with his usual solemnity, "Thank you. I know the situation has been difficult for you, and I've made it even more challenging. But what you've done for the children means the world to me."

It seemed unnecessarily cruel to bring up the fact that it would make her job a lot easier if he would just open up to her, to her family and let them help. The emotional admissions he'd given her just now seemed to be hard-won, and if she pushed, it could take them backward rather than forward.

"You're welcome. I meant what I said about your children being easy to love. I know the other nannies had difficulties with them, but it's only because the children have had such instability in their lives. They need to know they are loved unconditionally and that no matter how badly they behave, they are still loved."

"What about discipline? The other nannies seemed to think that was the real problem with the children."

Polly frowned. "Discipline is important, certainly. But it's absolutely useless if it's not given in the context of love. A child will obey out of fear if the source of fear is present. But what happens when the child is on his own? If the discipline has been given in love, then the child wants to obey, even when the child is left to his own devices."

Funny how her mouth spoke her own mother's words so easily. She'd been blessed with a mother who taught her about love and never disciplined out of anger. Ma might not have been the best example in terms of romance, but if Polly could be half the mother she'd been… Polly shook her head. She was never going to be a mother. But at least she could impart that same loving wisdom on any children who were in her care.

"You make it sound so simple." Mitch rubbed his forehead again. "I'll be honest. They can try my patience even on the best of days. I've often wondered if the other nannies were right. If I wasn't hard enough on them."

Then he peered into the room at his sleeping daughter. "But how can I not love that sweet girl? How could I possibly be harsh with her?"

"Discipline, if done in the right way, is love. You've just never known a loving way of doing it."

A screech sounded from the bottom of the stairs, and then the blur of two children ran past them, yelling as they climbed the stairs into the attic room.

"Give it to me," Clara wailed.

"It's mine," Rory shouted.

Polly let out a long sigh.

Mitch grinned. "About that loving discipline you were just telling me about?"

"Follow me."

She led Mitch into the large attic all the children shared as a bedroom. Uncle Frank had built several sets of cozy bunk beds lining each side of the attic—one for girls, and one for boys, divided by a large sheet across the room. It gave them plenty of space for the MacDonald children, the Taylor children and any other children who happened to need a bed for the night.

Clara and Rory rolled around on the floor, hitting each other.

"That is enough," Polly said in a quiet but firm voice as she stood over them.

The children stopped, midswing, and stared at her.

"Now, would you please tell me what is going on?"

"She started it!"

"No, he did!"

Polly shook her head. "I didn't ask who started it, I asked what was going on."

She could feel Mitch's presence, even without seeing him. He stood just to her left, close enough to witness what was happening, but not so close as to interfere. And yet, having him so close, it was somewhat hard to focus.

What would he think of her methods in caring for his children? He'd approved of how loving she'd been to Isabella, but what of her handling of the other children?

And then, there was the very…nearness…of him. Oh why, oh why, did she have to be attracted to this man when it was absolutely the most wrong thing in the world? She had plans for her life that didn't involve men, and he—he'd just lost a wife and had all these children to raise.

"Rory took the last biscuit!"

"Maddie said I could have it."

"But I'm hungry," Clara wailed. "You just asked Maddie if you could have it to be mean. You heard me tell Louisa I was going to ask if I could have that biscuit, and so you took it before I could."

"Maybe I was hungry, too." Rory smirked, and by the way he casually held the biscuit in his hand, Polly thought Clara probably had a point.

"So you're both hungry," Polly said casually, looking at the children.

"Yes," they said in unison.

"Good. Give me the biscuit please."

Rory handed her the biscuit. Polly neatly broke it in half and handed a piece to each child.

"There. Now you each have a little something in your stomachs so you can sleep well tonight. In the morning, I'll have some chores for the two of you to do together. You'll do chores for as long as it takes for you to get along."

The children looked puzzled, but that was all right. They'd find out soon enough about their punishment.

"Now off to bed, both of you." Polly shooed each child to their own side of the attic, then turned to Mitch. "Want to help me tuck them in?"

He nodded slowly. "Thank you. I believe I do."

Though he answered in the affirmative, his voice was unsteady, like this was the most unnatural request anyone had ever made of him.

"You've never tucked in your children?"

"The nannies said it would spoil them."

Polly looked up at him, wishing she could erase the doubt from his cloudy blue eyes.

"Well, this nanny says it's time for them to learn just how much their father loves them."

The sound of footsteps on the stairs indicated the other children had come up to bed as well. Louisa held Thomas by the hand, and Polly smiled at the older girl.

"Thank you for bringing up your brother. I appreciate all of your helpfulness."

Louisa scowled. "I'm only doing this to prove I can take care of them. Then we can get rid of you."

"And I will be delighted when that happens," Polly said, still smiling. "That means I will have done my job."

The scowl didn't leave Louisa's face as she turned

to get ready for bed. Polly looked around the attic and saw that Rory was already in bed and Thomas was scrambling to join him.

"Come on, Mitch. Let's tuck in the boys, then we can come back for the girls."

She tucked in the boys, giving them a squeeze, then motioned for Mitch to do the same. Her chest tightened as she watched him awkwardly bend down and kiss them on their foreheads. Though the action was clearly one he wasn't used to performing, the backs of Polly's eyes prickled with tears when she heard the catch in his voice as he wished the boys a good night. Anyone with a heart could see that Mitch loved his children deeply, and yet something inside him seemed to struggle with showing it.

Mitch turned to her. "Now what?"

"Now we say our prayers."

She knelt by the bed and began to pray over the boys, just as she'd done every night since they'd been in her care. After pressing a final kiss to the tops of each of their heads, she motioned for Mitch to follow her to tuck in the girls.

Mitch quietly walked behind Polly, marveling at what he'd just witnessed. No, been a part of. He'd never been invited to assist in putting his children to bed, but he couldn't imagine that it had ever looked like this when the other nannies had done it. Polly clearly cared for his children, and just when he'd thought he'd finished marveling at that fact, she'd gone and done something else to make him marvel at it anew.

He watched as Polly knelt beside Louisa's bed and attempted to tuck her in, but his daughter recoiled and rolled away.

"Don't bother," Louisa said, her voice harsh.

"Well, good night then, Louisa. I love you." Polly brushed the back of his daughter's hair, then turned away.

Louisa didn't answer, and it made Mitch's heart ache. As the eldest, she'd been deprived of love the longest. He hated himself for missing just how desperate his children had been for love. He could see that now.

Mitch knelt in front of Louisa's bed. "My turn," he said softly.

Louisa didn't turn to face him, so he rubbed her back gently. "I love you, Louisa, and I'm sorry you haven't been told that often enough. I know you don't like having a nanny, but right now, we need Polly to help us."

His daughter turned to him, her eyes full of tears. "So that's what this is about. You're being nice to me so I'll be nice to Polly."

The knife in his gut wouldn't have hurt so much had it not been well deserved. He'd neglected his daughter for so long that naturally she wasn't going to be able to accept his love so easily. His throat tightened with the tears he wanted to cry but couldn't.

"No. I'm being nice to you because I love you. And because until Polly came into our lives, I hadn't realized what a poor job I'd done of showing it. So I'm trying to do better."

A tear trickled down Louisa's cheek. Mitch leaned forward and pulled his daughter into his arms. "I love you, Louisa. And I'm so, so sorry that you haven't been shown that love until now."

Louisa clung to him as though she was holding on for dear life. Her tears soaked his shirt. He kissed the top of her head, repeating "I love you" over and over.

Why had he listened to all of the nannies who'd

told him that to lavish his children with love and attention was to spoil them? Holding his sobbing daughter seemed to be the most natural thing in the world. He'd wasted years of listening to the so-called experts on how to best raise his children, when all along, the answer came in the form of a tiny spitfire named Polly MacDonald.

He turned his head slightly to see that she was sitting on her sister Caitlin's bed, talking to her softly.

It wasn't just that Polly had a knack for dealing with his children, but she seemed to be able to love all children. All people. She had a special love power in her that seemed to radiate love to all the lives she touched.

Caitlin hugged Polly, and Polly got up, just as Louisa's sobs subsided. Mitch turned his attention back to his daughter.

"Good night, my love. Sleep well." He thought he should pray with her, except he didn't remember the words to the prayer Polly had said, and he didn't know any others.

As he stood, Polly joined them. "Did you say your prayers?"

Louisa made a noise. Though their time hugging and crying had done them both good, she still wasn't going to be cooperative. But they'd made progress, and that was enough.

"No. I was just thinking about that, and how I liked what you said."

She smiled, and even in the dimly lit room, Mitch could see how it lit up her face. Beautiful. If only she didn't have other plans for her life, Polly MacDonald would be...

Mitch shook his head. No. He was absolutely not going to go down that road again. Falling in love had cost him too much, though he'd willingly paid the price, given that he'd ended up with five incredible children. Now that he had no need for additional children, the cost of romance was too high for him to consider again. It was just as well that Polly had no interest in that direction either.

"I always say the prayer Ma said with us, but you don't have to be that formal. Just say whatever is in your heart."

But then, as if she understood his hesitation, Polly knelt and said the prayer he'd heard her utter just a few minutes before. Would God protect his children the way she'd asked? He supposed it didn't hurt to try, but he'd spent too many years being told by church folk that his family was unfit for God's mercy. Frank had told him otherwise, but who was right?

At Polly's gentle "amen" Mitch could only hope, no, pray, that Frank Lassiter was right.

Mitch followed Polly out of the attic room, trying not to notice the way her hair was falling out of its bun in the back, sending tendrils of reddish-blond hair in all directions. It would have been ungentlemanly to point it out, but Mitch loved the wild look to her hair. It seemed to match its rather unconventional owner.

"Thank you for letting me help tuck them in," Mitch said once they were on the landing and out of hearing range of smaller ears.

"Of course." Polly smiled, and Mitch thought he caught sight of a tiny dimple in her cheek. "You're their father. You should be tucking them in every night."

Her words weren't meant as a chastisement, he could tell from her gentle tone. But his heart felt as though she'd sent a thousand tiny daggers into it.

"I suppose your father tucked you in every night."

She let out a long sigh. "Well, no. But Pa's different. He's been too busy with other pursuits to pay us much mind. Ma, on the other hand, she always made sure to give us a good tucking, a good praying and a good loving to send us off to sleep."

Basically, the same situation his children were in, only reversed. Except that until tonight, he hadn't realized just how much his children needed him to put them to bed at night.

Gertie appeared at the top of the steps from the main level, making the small hallway a bit crowded.

"I was just coming up to tuck Caitlin in. See if the others need anything."

"We just finished," Polly said, giving her mother a tender look. "I think Caitlin is feeling a little sad now that Nugget has moved down the street into Joseph and Annabelle's place."

"Oh, the poor dear. I should have known she'd be feeling lonesome. I suppose a roomful of children doesn't make a lick of difference when you're missing your best friend."

"No, it doesn't," Polly agreed. "I offered to let her sleep in with me and Isabella, but she didn't want anyone to think she was a baby."

"I'll see to her, then. Don't stay up too late yourself? I know you just got that new book you're dying to read, but you'll be absolutely worthless tomorrow if you're up all night reading."

"Yes, Ma," Polly said, then hugged her mother goodnight.

The interaction was probably commonplace in this household, yet Mitch marveled at it. How many times had he wished for his children to have such an easy relationship with their mother? Had Hattie ever hugged them like that? He shook his head. It didn't matter now, since Hattie was gone.

"Sorry about that." Polly gave him a sheepish look, then beckoned at the floor below. "Once a mother, always a mother, even when your baby is grown. Would you care to join me for a cup of tea before bed? Maddie grows the herbs herself."

"I think it's wonderful to have such a caring mother," Mitch said. "You'd told me only a little of your father, but I suspect that your father and Hattie had a lot in common. It's nice to see such a good relationship between parent and children. Makes me hopeful that I can have the same with mine."

He followed her down the stairs into the parlor, where Maddie had left a pot of tea on the side table.

"Were you expecting me to come down?" Mitch looked at Polly as she sat.

"No, not at all. But it's my custom to have a cup of tea before bed, and Maddie knows it. She spoils us, and I'm so very grateful for her."

Polly poured a cup of tea and handed it to him. "Here. This will help you relax and sleep better."

He took the tea and sniffed it. Definitely a lot of herbs, and almost medicine-y. But he wouldn't hurt Polly's feelings by refusing. He took a sip, delighted when he discovered that despite the medicinal smell, the tea had a pleasant, sweet flavor with just a hint of mint.

"My second night in a real bed? I doubt I'll have trouble sleeping, but I appreciate the sentiment."

Mitch leaned back against the chair and closed his eyes, finding it hard to believe so much had changed in his life in twenty-four hours.

"Was it so bad, then?"

He opened his eyes to look at Polly. "Jail?" With a

quick shake of his head, he remembered what they'd just been doing. "No, not really. It was quieter than at home, and I spent a lot of my time thinking."

"Thinking?" Polly stared at him over her teacup.

"Yes. I wondered what would become of my children if I couldn't get out of jail. I knew you would care for them, of course, but what then? As much as Andrew loves me, he's already said that if I end up being convicted, he and Iris can't take the children. The last time my children and his children were left alone together, my children shaved his daughter Augusta bald."

Polly tried to hide a giggle, but Mitch still caught it. There was something endearing about the way she covered her mouth with her hand to hide her smile, but her twinkling eyes gave her away.

"What's so funny?"

"I'm sorry. I shouldn't be so irreverent while you're pouring your heart out. I'm just wondering what Augusta did to deserve such punishment."

He wasn't sure what he found more attractive, her stifled giggle or her automatic assumption that his children weren't entirely at fault.

"The children called her a horrid little toad who needed to be taught some manners."

Polly gave a tiny snort as the giggle she'd been trying to hold in burst out. "I'm sorry," she said, wiping tears from her eyes. "I shouldn't laugh, but that's too precious. I suppose I should feel sorry for poor Augusta."

Could Polly find her way into his heart any deeper? Her laugh was like a balm to the scars he thought would never heal. No one had ever told him his children were anything but awful, and here, with her taking their side in a situation that nearly caused a rift between him and his brother, it was almost too much for his heart to bear. Why had it taken him so long to find her?

"Augusta was fine," Mitch told her with a smile. "They actually didn't shave her entire head, but she did have to wear her hair just so for a while so that no one could tell."

He took a deep breath, feeling much lighter now that they'd both had a good laugh. "Still, it is a sobering thought to realize that you are the only person on this earth who wants my children. If something happened to me, they'd go to an orphanage. And then what? Louisa would be sent off to work somewhere, with Clara and Rory not far behind. I suppose a good family would want to adopt Thomas, since he's young."

Then his heart tightened as he looked at Polly. "But what of Isabella? It's obvious she's of mixed race. When she was born, people told me I should get rid of her. But who would do that to a child? To his own child?"

Mitch's chest thudded so loudly, he thought it would wake the whole house up. "I don't care what anyone says. Isabella is my daughter."

Polly leaned forward, breaching the space between the two chairs, and took his hand. "Of course she is. And she has an amazing father who will do anything for her. Which is why we have to find a way to prove your innocence."

"We?" Mitch wanted to pull his hand away, but the warmth of hers in his was too tempting. Especially with the way her eyes mesmerized him.

"I love your children too much to see them deprived of another parent. And I love justice too much to allow an innocent man to be convicted of a crime he didn't commit."

She was close enough that if he leaned forward just

a little bit, he could kiss her. He wanted to kiss her, and he hadn't wanted to kiss anyone in almost twelve years. Had it been that long?

Mitch's head snapped up and he pulled his hand away as he realized what he'd been about to do. He could not, would not, kiss another woman whose plans for life didn't involve sticking around and seeing everything through. Besides, Polly was his employee, a young woman, and he couldn't take advantage of her like that.

But as Polly gazed at him and said, "Please, Mitch. Let me and my family help prove your innocence," he wondered if kissing her would have been the easier route. She had no idea what he was up against, and he couldn't have more lives ruined for his sake.

"It's not that simple," he said, trying to avoid those eyes of hers that seemed to get him to open up to her even when he didn't want to. "I can't put people through any more scandal."

"Scandal?" Polly set her teacup on the table with a clatter. "You could be hanged, and you're worried about a scandal?"

"I won't have my children treated worse than they already are. People stand outside my brother's store, demanding to know why he's harboring a murderer, and I know it's hurting business. If your family gets involved, what will happen to them?"

The ease he'd felt in his chest left him, being replaced by what had to be vises squeezing him this way and that. Frank Lassiter had taken him in, and until now, Mitch hadn't thought about what that might end up costing the good preacher. People who needed to hear his message wouldn't want to go to a church plagued by scandal.

"I'm sorry, Polly." Mitch looked down at his hands and stood. "I've only ever tried to do the right thing, and I fear it's hurting the ones I love the most."

If only there was a way to keep his children safe without involving these good people.

Chapter Seven

The next morning Polly sat in the parlor, enjoying the calm before everyone woke up and hurried about their day. Maddie was in the kitchen, preparing breakfast, but she'd shooed Polly out, saying she could handle the meal just fine. Arguing seemed to be a bad idea, though Polly really had wanted something to keep occupied to distract herself from her thoughts of Mitch.

There seemed to be a connection between them she couldn't explain, and sometimes, it felt downright dangerous, the way she wanted to take him in her arms and let him know everything was going to be all right. Mostly, though, she wanted to kiss him senseless, which meant she hadn't learned a thing in all of the lessons she'd been taught about men.

She sighed. If only kissing weren't such a pleasant pastime, and if only it didn't mean a commitment she wasn't willing to make. Besides, she knew better than to act on any attraction she felt. Attraction was the easy part. It was the living with the bad choices a person made in the throes of it that was hard.

A shadow fell across the doorway, and Polly looked up. Will.

"I thought I'd stop in to see if you all needed anything before I headed out."

Will and Mary had finally moved in to their own home, just a few houses down, but they came and went so often that it still felt like they lived in the parsonage. In the months since Will had come into their life, he'd become like an older brother to her. Well, she did have older brothers, of course, but they'd always been so busy working in the mines that Polly had never developed a close relationship with them. Even now, they spent their days in the mining camp and not in town.

A sigh escaped Polly's lips, and Will entered the room. "Sounds like you have a lot on your mind."

"I just wish Mitch wasn't being so stubborn. He thinks that if we help him, that we're going to face trouble because of it."

Will nodded slowly. "We've had to disperse the crowds gathering in front of his brother's store several times now."

"But if someone doesn't help him, he might well be convicted."

The sound Will made didn't make Polly feel any better. Especially when he followed it up with words. "Not might. Will. I did some asking around, and it isn't looking good. Are you sure he didn't do it?"

Polly's heart fell to the pit of her stomach, where it churned and ached. "Would I take up for him otherwise?"

"Of course not." Will reached forward and ruffled her hair. "But you have to understand, everyone I've talked to is convinced he did it."

"That doesn't mean he did."

A long silence filled the room, and Polly knew it meant Will was considering her words. Above all, Will

Lawson was a fair man, and he wouldn't want to see an innocent man convicted of a crime he didn't commit.

Will rubbed his chin, then finally looked at Polly. "I admit there are a few things about the case that have been troubling me."

Those were the words Polly had been hoping to hear. Anything, really, to give Mitch a fighting chance.

"Like what?"

"As far as I can tell, the only suspect they've even looked at is Mitch. It's been conveniently pinned on him, but all of their evidence is circumstantial. I know Sheriff Conley is in a tight race to be reelected, so a high-profile murder conviction would help his cause. Easy enough to prove the husband is guilty, so why investigate further?"

Polly nodded. "Mitch said the same thing."

"I never liked Conley much," Will admitted. "He was more interested in the notches on his belt for putting people away than he was in justice. I understand that's what he thinks the public expects of him, but I never could stomach the idea of working for a man like that."

Then he shook his head, as though he realized he was probably speaking out of turn. "I suppose none of that matters, though, with Mitch being the only suspect."

"Do you think he really is the only suspect?"

Will shrugged. "There's usually at least a dozen or so folk who want a person dead, especially if we're talking about someone like Hattie Winston. I imagine she made a lot of enemies over the years, not just her husband."

More hope swirled in Polly as she realized the potential for proving Mitch's innocence. Surely Mitch could identify some of Hattie's enemies, and then they could…

Polly shook her head. If only they could get Mitch to cooperate.

She looked back up at Will. "So what you're saying is that there's a good chance her husband didn't do it."

"Most times, it ends up being the husband, I hate to say. I know you believe in Mitch's innocence, but what I've learned over the years says otherwise. Still, there's something not right about the situation, and I'll do my best to find out what it is."

A sound echoed in the hallway, and Polly looked up at the doorway to see Louisa hiding in the shadows.

"Louisa, is that you?"

"You're talking about my mother's murder, aren't you?" Dark eyes stared at her accusingly, making Polly want to shrivel up in her seat. Mitch had specifically asked her to keep the children in the dark about the situation and here they were, talking about it where Louisa had overheard.

"I didn't mean…" Polly could barely get the words out; her vocal cords seemed paralyzed as punishment for speaking out of turn.

"Papa wants to think we don't know anything, but it's hard not to notice the crowds calling him a murderer and holding up signs."

The matter-of-fact way the young girl spoke made Polly's heart feel raw, aching at the realization of just how much this girl's childhood had been stolen from her.

"You weren't meant to see any of that," Polly said quietly.

"Well, you did do a better job than Mrs. Abernathy," Louisa said as she finally entered the room. She picked up the teapot, then poured herself a cup of tea as if to prove she was older and more mature, and perfectly capable of running her family.

"Mrs. Abernathy said we were heathens, and she said we were going to end up dead in a hotel, just like our mother."

Louisa took a sip of tea and looked at Polly over the rim of her teacup, daring her to react.

Oh, how she wanted to react. She wanted to scream and wail, and do that very thing to the horrid nanny who would tell children such a terrible thing.

"What kind of monster would—"

Louisa made a noise. "My father isn't here for you to impress with your defense of us. I've heard enough talk to know that however she died, it was in a horrible way. And she deserved it."

"Louisa!" The word came out shriller then Polly intended, but she couldn't imagine a child saying that about her own mother. Even as poor of a father as her own father was, Polly had never wished for his death.

"It's true." The girl sat with so much composure, and wisdom in her eyes, that for a moment Polly had a hard time seeing her as just a child. "My mother was a horrible person and a horrible mother. But if we didn't say otherwise, we were punished."

Something cold settled in the pit of Polly's stomach. "Your father?"

"Of course not. Mother came round once in a while and made sure the nannies understood how things were. Poor Papa..." Louisa looked down at her tea, and Polly felt a kinship with the other girl, having also been forced to grow up too soon. "He just wanted us to be kind to her and love her because she was our mother. But I don't think he understood that we were like props in her plays. Everyone loved Hattie Winston's darling family, but when no one was looking, Hattie Winston never cared."

Louisa's eyes were filled with tears, and Polly tried to reach out to touch the girl's hand but she jerked away. Will made a noise, and once again, she felt the gentle pressure of his hand telling her to let it go.

"Mummy used to tell us that Papa wasn't even our father. She said all kinds of horrible things when he wasn't around, and she told us that if we said anything to him, she would send us away. We all hated her, but we had to pretend she was wonderful, because none of us wanted to go to the places she said she'd send us to."

This time, as a sob wracked the young girl's body, Polly couldn't help but reach for her. To hold and comfort a little girl who should have known a mother's love, not this disdain.

Louisa jerked away. "I don't need your pity. I'm only telling you this so you understand that my father had every right to kill her. I heard them fight the night she died. He told her he could kill her, and she laughed. The next morning, she was dead."

It was as if the young girl, holding Polly's heart out for the world to see, had just crumbled it to dust. Yet she was powerless to do anything about it as tears streamed down Louisa's face. "He can't go to jail, he just can't. You have to get them to understand that she deserved it."

"What is going on in here?" Mitch's voice roared from the hallway, sending Polly's eardrums crashing against her already crumbling heart.

"We were just—"

"Talking to my daughter about the case, when I explicitly told you not to?"

If she'd thought the shame at Louisa overhearing

them was bad, she'd had no concept of the emotion, not really, until she saw the look of betrayal in Mitch's eyes.

"You're right," she said, her voice quivering. "Louisa overheard us talking, and we shouldn't have been so indiscreet."

The trouble with being caught in bad behavior was that no matter how much you tried to justify your actions, they were still wrong. She'd only been trying to help, but she'd gone against Mitch's wishes and now it had made everything a mess.

"I'm so sorry," Polly said, knowing that no amount of sorries could erase what Mitch had heard. How much he'd heard, she didn't know, but from the fire in his eyes, and the despair sagging his face, she knew he had to at least know that his own daughter thought him capable of the crime.

Could words ever erase that kind of pain?

Mitch had thought that being arrested for Hattie's murder was the worst thing that could ever happen. Now, even if he were convicted, the very worst thing had just happened.

His brain refused to process the words he'd just heard coming out of Louisa's mouth. Except they echoed in his mind like a bad headache that no amount of pain powder could cure.

His own daughter thought him a murderer.

"I…" Mitch couldn't even come up with another sentence.

"Why don't we go outside for a walk?" Will clapped a hand on his shoulder and started to lead him out of the room.

Mitch brushed him off. "Why? Do you think I'm going to kill them, too?"

"No." Will spoke quietly while gesturing toward the door. "But I imagine you're hurting pretty badly right about now, and I've found that a little fresh air does a world of wonders."

Fresh air? His daughter thought he'd killed her mother, and Will thought fresh air was going to fix it. Mitch's stomach rolled, like he was going to be sick. Suddenly, it felt too hot in the room, as if he couldn't breathe. Maybe some air would do him good. It had to be better than looking at the horrified expression on Polly's face, and...well, he didn't know what he saw on Louisa's face, but if he had to guess, he'd think that someone had just killed her favorite pet. Only no one had been killed here. He'd merely been accused of being a murderer.

Mitch followed Will outside, pausing when Will stopped at a bench behind the church.

"Let's sit," he said, pointing to the seat.

"I'd rather stand."

"Suit yourself," Will said casually, sitting. "I haven't had my coffee yet, since Mary still hasn't gotten the knack of fixing it the way I like, and Maddie's is perfect, so you're going to have to bear with me."

"I didn't ask for your interference." Mitch still felt warm, but he'd admit that the early-morning cool air was helping. Not so much as to fix the rest of his life, but at least his head was no longer going to explode.

"If you want to stay out of jail, then you're going to have to accept it. I don't know how much of our conversation you heard, but here is the gist of the case against you. As far as anyone is concerned, you're the only person with motive. So you'd better think about who else would want Hattie dead, and let me start investigating."

Something boiled in the pit of Mitch's stomach,

shooting to the top of his head in a searing pain. "What good will that do? My own daughter thinks I'm guilty."

Will stood. "And she thinks you were justified in doing it. Didn't you hear her begging me to make sure you didn't go to jail?"

The boiling pain reduced to a simmer. "I don't suppose I did."

"Apparently, everyone thinks you have good reason. But that's not going to win your case. If she was as horrible as Louisa said she was, someone else has to think so, too."

Mitch ran his hand over his face, wishing he could wake up from this nightmare. "Louisa loved her mother."

"Apparently, not as much as you think."

Even if his stomach wasn't already rolling, Mitch wasn't sure he could digest those words.

"Why didn't they say anything?"

"The same reason you haven't told the children much about their mother's death. They wanted to protect you. As much as you think you've been protecting them, I suspect they know a lot more about everything than you realized. Your children aren't stupid. They can't be, if they take after you."

"They don't." The words hurt as they came out of his mouth, searing the inside of his throat. And yet, once they were out, his chest felt lighter than it had in years.

"Of course they do. Any fool can see that."

Mitch shook his head. He'd lived the lie for so long that no one could see the truth. Especially since in his own heart, the biology of the fact didn't matter to him. "None of them are mine."

Will coughed. "Well, sure, I mean, I suppose it's obvious that the little one didn't come from you, but..."

He coughed again, seeming to lack the capacity to understand.

"Hattie and I stopped having relations shortly after we were married."

The first time he'd ever spoken the truth out loud. Oh, when Hattie needed to look good for the papers, she'd cozy up to him and playfully try to kiss him, but he'd always turned away. Everyone thought he was shy, but the real truth was, he stopped being able to stand Hattie years ago.

"I...don't understand." Will looked him up and down. "Hattie was a beautiful woman, she was..."

"With every other man who paid her the slightest bit of attention in the form of money or jewels."

The ever-present rolling in his stomach had started to ease. What had felt like an imminent explosion in his head had become a dull roar. No one, not even his brother, had known what being married to Hattie had cost him. Pretending the truth didn't exist had been the only way he'd been able to look at himself in the mirror.

"I'm sorry," Will said quietly. "That must have been difficult for you."

He looked down at the other man, whose expression was not of the disgust Mitch had felt for himself over the years, but of deep compassion.

Before he could formulate any kind of response, he heard the crunch of footsteps on the ground. Mitch turned and saw Polly approaching.

"I can tell her to leave if you're not ready to talk to her yet," Will said, and for the first time since the suggestion of having Will help him on the case, Mitch understood him to be an ally. He'd never really known what it was like to have someone on his side, but Will's willingness to stand up for him against Polly meant there was action behind his words of compassion.

"No." Mitch swallowed, feeling the scratchiness that had begun when he'd first started speaking of the situation ease. "She needs to hear this. Polly deserves to hear the truth."

And again, the nausea that had been threatening since the awful moment in the parlor eased up. His head, almost clear. It was as though the closer he got to the truth, and to sharing it, his entire body could finally relax.

Chapter Eight

"Mitch?" Polly's voice quivered, and as much as Mitch could still feel the sting of betrayal from them talking behind his back, he felt something else.

Guilt.

"It's all right." The words came out hard, like rocks, but once they were out, he felt better, as though he'd purged one more thing from his irritated system.

"I am so, so sorry."

He could hear the tears in her voice. Deeper than the own pain of his feelings of betrayal was the pain of a woman who felt like she'd disappointed someone she cared about.

"I know." The backs of his eyes prickled with an unfamiliar damp sensation. He'd not cried in all of this nightmare with Hattie, and yet... Mitch shook his head. Now was not the time.

He swallowed back the emotion and turned to look at her. "I imagine it must be difficult to want to help someone and have that someone be as stubborn as I am. I should have accepted your help."

Then he gestured to the bench. "You should sit.

There's a lot you both need to know, if you're still agreeable to helping me."

Those clear blue eyes glistened at him. "What made you change your mind?"

Mitch looked down at Will, who wore the same compassionate expression that had given him so much confidence earlier. "A few things, I suppose. One, the reason people think I killed Hattie is I've done a good job of hiding the truth over the years. Two, everything I've ever done has been to protect my children. If protecting them means letting you help me, then that's what I'm going to do."

He turned his gaze down, looking at the ground, then examining his hands. "But mostly, because I told Will the truth about a lot of things just now, and I can't believe how free it makes me feel."

His hands seemed worn, weary, just as he was. Was it because of all the burdens he'd been trying to carry on his own for so long?

Mitch could feel Polly's gaze on him, and he turned to meet her eyes. Warmth shone in them, and he wished he'd allowed himself to realize it before. It had been too long since he'd trusted in the kindness of strangers, and even now, it was almost hard to believe that any of this was real. Except the depth in her gaze assured him of it.

"I've never had allies in my life before. My brother, I suppose, but he's always looked up to me. How could I let him down by telling him how bad things were? I've had countless so-called friends in my life, but not one of them cared about my best interests. They all just wanted the inside scoop on Hattie."

He looked from Polly to Mitch, then back at Polly. "But you're different, aren't you? You really do…care."

As hard as it was to get the word out, it was harder to decipher the puzzled expressions on their faces.

"Of course we do. Why would you..." Polly started, then stopped, as if what he'd said finally made sense in her mind. "I'm sorry that you were so mistreated. And I'm sorry that my going behind your back to talk to Will made it seem like I had my own agenda. I truly wanted to help, and I'm willing to do whatever you need."

"I know."

And as he said those words, he did know. Even better, he had the feeling that everything would actually be all right. But he still had much to tell them.

"When Hattie and I married, I was a green youth, barely a man. I was flattered that someone so beautiful and sophisticated as Hattie would even pay attention to me."

Looking back, he wanted to throttle his younger self for being so easily taken advantage of. "She said we should run away and get married. I was so caught up in the moment that I agreed. And we did."

Mitch shook his head, wishing he didn't have to admit just how easily taken in he'd been, but with each word that came out, deep in his soul, he knew that this confession was exactly what he needed.

"My family was horrified and said I'd made a huge mistake. But we were married, so what could they do? Hattie and I had a beautiful, passionate month of marriage. I thought I had struck the biggest vein of gold ever to be discovered. And then she told me she was expecting."

Mitch could sense that Polly had shifted but didn't realize what was happening until he felt her hand in his, leading him to the bench.

"Sit. It's all right. You're safe."

Her gentle words were a balm to all the wounds he was ripping open. Safe. He hadn't felt that way in a long time. But it was enough that he knew he could finish his story, without judgment, or the condemnation he'd seen in his family's eyes as they watched the situation with Hattie play out. Of all things he'd felt around Polly, judgment was not one of them.

Mitch took a deep breath and continued. "Once Hattie told me she was expecting, she grew distant. Everyone said that some women got moody when they were expecting, and I assumed that was the case."

Polly's hand squeezed his, and more warmth shot through his body. How long had it been since he'd received compassion from another human being?

"After Louisa was born, Hattie remained distant. Louisa would be in her cradle, screaming all day, and Hattie would ignore her. I finally hired a nanny to take care of Louisa because I knew Hattie wouldn't, and I had a store to run. The only thing that ever made Hattie even smile was an expensive gift, and I had to work hard to provide them. I kept thinking that if I just worked harder, the old Hattie would be back."

His heart ached for the earnest young man he'd been. "When I wasn't working, I was with Louisa, caring for her to give the nanny a break, but also because I loved my daughter and I wanted her to receive at least some parental affection."

The memory of Louisa sobbing against him last night, combined with her words this morning, collided against his skull, and he couldn't make sense of them, not as he remembered all the time he'd spent with her and her sweet baby scent nestled up against him. Polly murmured and patted his hand again, once more reminding him that he wasn't alone.

Drawing on Polly's strength, Mitch continued his story. "And then one day, Hattie informed me that she was offered a part in a traveling theater group and if I wanted her to be better, this was the way to do it."

Even now, he wasn't sure what the right answer had been. "What was a man to do? I let her go."

He looked over at Polly, then at Will. Would they understand? The choice between having a wife who spent all day in bed and a woman who finally had the strength to walk around and live normally?

"After she left, I started hearing the rumors. Hattie had been having an affair with a married man, and he refused to leave his wife for her. When she became pregnant, he told her it was her problem, so she decided to marry me to give the baby a name. Our romance was all an act, and once I was convinced I could be Louisa's father, she started back up with the man again. His wife finally got fed up, and they arranged for her to get a part with a traveling theater troupe to get her out of the way."

Their wide eyes told him what he'd thought when he'd first heard the stories. It was too incredible to believe.

"Hattie didn't come home for over a year. When she did, her belly was slightly rounded with another pregnancy, and she tried to seduce me. I knew it was so she could try to convince me that this baby was mine as well, so I confronted her with the rumors and she confirmed they were true."

Polly's indrawn breath gave Mitch a chance to pause, to take a deep breath of his own, and to try to ignore the expression of outrage on Will's face. This was why he never told anyone. Because no man should have to put up with what Hattie put him through.

"Why didn't you ask her to leave?" Polly's voice was gentle, and it was the same question he'd asked himself over and over. The question that bore the judgment of his mistake and why he'd let Hattie continue to use him.

"Because she was going to take Louisa away." Mitch brought his gaze back to his feeble, worn hands. The ones that had worked so hard for everything he had, and had done everything he could to hold his life together.

"Louisa was nearly two years old, and I loved her. Until that day, I believed her to be my natural daughter, despite the rumors. Hattie would have taken her out of spite, and I'd seen how Hattie had ignored her before. She might not have been my blood, but Louisa was my child."

With that, he locked his eyes on Polly's. "I would do anything for my children. Try as I might, every time Hattie came home with another baby in her belly, I couldn't keep myself from giving that child the love it deserved. I played Hattie's game because the only way I could keep my children was to do so. Otherwise, she'd have been on the next train to who knows where, and I'd have been helpless to do anything about it."

Polly nodded slowly. "Do you think she would have?"

"She tried to, once. But the train broke down, and I caught up with them, only to be told by the lawman she called to protect herself from me that if the children weren't mine, there wasn't anything I could do."

Mitch sighed. "So I did what I had to do to keep them. I begged Hattie to come home, and I would agree to whatever arrangement she wanted."

And that had been his life. Dancing to Hattie's tune because otherwise, she'd take his children, and because

Hattie Winston was everyone's darling, and an exceptional actress, he'd be unable to stop her.

Polly squeezed his hand again, and part of him wished he could have met her before he'd been so irrevocably broken. And part of him would have gone through everything all over again if it meant getting to have the five delightful children he had in his life.

Then he looked over at Will. "I know people think that the fact that Isabella is obviously not my child is why I killed Hattie. That's one of the things the investigators asked me about over and over."

"Maybe you got tired of dancing to her tune, so you finished it," Will said, scratching his jaw.

"Do you think that?"

"No, but it's what the investigators think, so you'd better have a good answer."

Mitch let out another long breath. "I was hoping it wouldn't come to that. None of the children know, and I won't have them thinking I love them any less because of Hattie's ill deeds."

Polly gave his hand another encouraging squeeze. "I can't imagine they'd think that. It's obvious to everyone how much you love them, so the truth—"

"Isn't going to help him as much as you think." Will looked pensive as he stared at Mitch. "Who was Hattie's current lover?"

Mitch returned to examining his hands again. "I don't know. That was what our last fight was about. She was leaving me for good this time, because she was expecting again, and the father needed a son. I begged her to wait, to be sure that this man would accept responsibility, since now the children were of an age to hear gossip if her plan backfired, but she just laughed."

Swallowing the lump in his throat and wishing he

didn't have to describe the mother of his children as being so callous, he looked back up at Will. "She said that if I cooperated, I could keep the others. Otherwise, she'd take them, too."

He closed his eyes and took a deep breath. "And that's when I said I'd kill her."

Looking at them to see their reaction was almost too much, but he forced his eyes open and looked from Will to Polly. "I didn't mean it, honest. I was angry because I was tired of her games, and I knew that whoever this man was, rich as Hattie claimed, there was no way he was going to marry her. She was so reckless, and it made me angry to see her doing it again."

Mitch shook his head, realizing through the tears he hadn't sensed were coming, that neither Polly nor Will appeared to be disappointed in him.

"I didn't kill Hattie. I couldn't. How could I work so hard to protect the children, then throw it all away like that?"

"I believe you." Polly's voice was soft as she gave his hand another squeeze.

"I believe you, too," Will said, standing. "But there's a big difference between convincing us and convincing a jury. I need you to give me a list of all of Hattie's friends and associates so I can start looking into who her lover might have been."

Then Will gave him a serious look. "I've got to head down to Denver on some other business. I'm going to grab some breakfast, then run by the sheriff's office before I leave town. I'll be back midmorning for that list and any other sources you think would be good for me to check out. Don't leave anyone off the list. Protecting people is what got you arrested to begin with."

Mitch's collar tightened around his throat. He didn't

need Will to tell him how serious things really were. But at least now there was someone on his side.

"You can count on it."

Polly hated seeing how torn up Mitch was in telling his story. In every other situation, she'd been able to do something to fix whatever was wrong in the other person's life. But here, with Mitch, all she could do was listen.

"We should go in to breakfast, too," Polly said, giving Mitch's hand a final squeeze as they watched Will head into the house against the dim light of the rising sun. "I'm sure the children are all up by now, and while I know Ma and Maddie don't mind watching them for a few minutes, they are my responsibility."

She started to stand but felt the reluctance in Mitch's hand to let go. "It will be all right," she said softly. "If anyone can find out who Hattie's lover was, it's Will. I've heard many folk talk about how he's the best lawman around."

Mitch didn't respond but still wore the same intense expression that he'd borne through their entire conversation. She supposed it was simplistic of her to try to reassure him when he seemed to be collapsing under the weight of the situation.

She took a deep breath. "I know it was hard to tell us about the children and the pain of knowing they aren't yours. But as I mentioned to you last night regarding Isabella, your love for them is obvious, as is her parentage."

For a moment, she hesitated, knowing it was a sensitive subject but also knowing that while they were doling out truths, Mitch needed to face some himself.

"You should talk to the children. Tell them your

truth. About how much you love them and how much you've sacrificed for them."

Mitch jerked his hand away, then stood. "Didn't you hear a word I've said? I don't want them to know. They need to know that they are my children, that I love them and that's that."

Part of Polly hated herself for forcing him to see the truth when Mitch had already been forced to face so much. But he had to know the things Louisa told her. The wounds that only Mitch's truths could heal.

"Apparently, Hattie already told the children that they aren't yours. According to Louisa, she mistreated them and threatened them if they told you anything. Louisa felt that Hattie deserved to die."

His face turned white as she spoke, and it felt like Polly was sticking daggers in her own heart as she revealed her conversation with Louisa. But too many secrets and too much pain had already divided this family, and it was time to end it.

"You owe them your side of the story, and to let them know how very much you love them."

Polly felt her own eyes grow misty. "That is the message they need more than anything right now. The truth, and that you have loved them all along. Your children are not bad, but they are suffering from spending their childhood hearing mixed messages and not knowing how deeply loved they are. That's something you can change for them."

He nodded slowly. "How could I have missed it?"

"Because you loved them and believed in them. You thought that they would come to you if there was a problem, but you had no idea the lies Hattie told when you weren't around."

He looked as though he was seeing right through her.

Polly sighed. Yet again, he was lost in his own agenda and not willing to listen to anyone else or let anyone else in. It shouldn't bother her so much, except she'd seen how these precious children were hurting.

Then, because she didn't think he was listening anyway, Polly said softly, "I wish you'd just told me the truth from the beginning."

"How could I?" His voice was raspy. "Do you know what it's like to have no one to trust? Nowhere to turn? And feel like everyone is out to get you?"

"Fair enough," Polly conceded. "But even after all that we've been through, all that we've talked about, and how you've seen that Nugget, despite her illegitimacy, is still a beloved family member, how could you put us in that category?"

Mitch shook his head slowly. "I don't know. The pressure of everything, it's been too much."

The deflated expression on his face made Polly regret even asking him about it. Her hurt feelings over his lack of trust were nothing compared to what he must be going through.

"But things will be different moving forward, won't they?" Polly looked at him expectantly. "Now that Will is on the case, and we're united in finding the real killer, you don't have to hide."

Mitch nodded slowly. "I can't give you the answers you want regarding the children. I'll talk to them myself, and I'd prefer you not share any of this with them."

Polly didn't like it, not one bit, but she could hardly keep arguing when Mitch had already given so much ground. She had to remind herself that even as quickly as Leadville had gone from tiny mining camp to thriving city, it still hadn't happened overnight.

"Of course." She nodded, then gestured toward the

house. "We really should be getting in. Well, at least I should. I suppose if you need some time alone, then you can stay."

"I would, thank you. I'll be in shortly, though. I'd like to spend some time with the children this afternoon, once I've given Will the information he needs. Perhaps you can come up with an activity that will keep us out of the public view."

The small smile he gave her was an inkling of why Polly found herself trusting him, even before she'd known the truth. There was something deeply good lurking in Mitch's heart, and his desire to raise five children not his own, and to make them feel as deeply loved as would his own flesh and blood, made him as noble as a man could be. Even now, with his own reputation— and his very freedom—on the line, his biggest concern was for his children.

Polly meandered into the house, knowing she shouldn't dawdle but needing to find some way of calming her racing heart. Mitch Taylor provoked so many emotions in her, conflicting emotions, and they all seemed to do battle at the most inconvenient of times. She could find herself falling in love with a man like Mitch, but of course, that was just plain silliness.

Chapter Nine

Mitch watched as Will rode off, papers neatly tucked in his saddlebag. For a moment, he'd been tempted to ask the deputy to allow him to come, but he knew that his presence would make many of those listed unwilling to talk. Besides, he'd been away from his children long enough.

"Papa!" Clara ran out the front door, clutching a blanket in her hands. "Polly says you're taking us on a picnic!"

He corralled the little girl in his arms. "Yes, my darling, we're going to spend the afternoon together, but that's only if you don't crack your head open falling off the porch."

"Oh, I won't!" A wide grin stretched from ear to ear, and the freckles on her nose seemed to jump for joy. "I'm s'posed to be bringing Polly this here blanket, but I just had to come find out for myself. Louisa says you're too busy for such nonsense, but I told her that ever since we got Polly, everything's different now. And it is, isn't it? Polly's come to make everything all better, hasn't she?"

He ruffled his daughter's hair and smiled in spite of

her fanciful musings. "Now, you know she can't make everything better, but I will say that Polly is the best nanny you've ever had."

Privately, he'd admit that she had made an incredible difference in their lives. Though he sometimes found her pushing him highly annoying, he couldn't argue that things were, in fact, better.

"I love Polly," Clara sighed. "I hope she never goes away."

And then, just like that, all the turbulence in his stomach from earlier today returned. As much as Polly was making a difference in his family, it wasn't going to be forever. Polly wanted a chance to get out in the world, to live her own life. How long would they have before she made the decision to leave?

Even though he knew Polly was nothing like Hattie, he couldn't help make the comparison anyway. Hattie had wanted to make her own way as well, and she'd left the first chance she'd got. While Polly was of better character than Hattie, Mitch had to find a way to keep their hearts from being too entangled when she left.

"Nothing lasts forever, my sweet. Someday, Polly will have to leave us, and then..." Mitch couldn't bring himself to finish the sentence. Even now, he wasn't quite sure what he'd do without her.

"Oh, Papa," Clara said, sighing deeply. "You just have to use your 'magination. Anything can happen, if you just believe."

He put his arm around her, wishing that life were as simple as the childhood musings of a little girl who spent too much time reading her books, then trying to make them come to life. "Let's go see what Polly has prepared for our picnic, shall we?"

Clara skipped on ahead of him, and for the first time,

he realized that his little girl seemed happy. Usually, when she came to him, it was to complain about Rory, or the nanny or some other terrible catastrophe that had befallen her, like someone took her favorite book.

He watched as Clara skipped right into Polly's arms, and the little girl received a warm hug. It shouldn't be a marvel to see his children receiving affection, but he couldn't think of the last time he'd witnessed it from anyone other than Polly.

Polly released Clara, then sent her in the direction of the kitchen, smiling as she waved at Mitch before taking Thomas by the hand and following Clara.

Joy.

That was the element missing from his family all this time. Love, too, he supposed, but he'd always thought his love had been enough. It seemed, after mulling over Polly's words from earlier in the morning, his love hadn't been enough.

He spied Louisa coming down the stairs. Would she tell him the things she'd told Polly?

"Louisa? May I have a word with you in the parlor?"

Fear darted in his daughter's eyes as he realized that he should have found a more loving way to approach the subject. But as he followed her into the other room, he told himself that he'd be able to convey that love anyway.

"I wanted to talk to you about the conversation I overheard you having with Polly this morning."

Louisa gave him a dark look. "I suppose you're going to punish me for saying I thought you killed Mummy." She sighed. "So what's it going to be? Missing the picnic? Being locked in my room? No supper?"

Her defiance didn't hurt him so much as her automatic expectation of punishment. "When have I ever punished you?"

"I..." She looked at the floor. "I don't suppose you have." Then she looked up. "Well, you have sent me to my room before, but you weren't being mean."

"I have no intention of ever being mean to you," Mitch said softly, looking down at his daughter. "But you did say some things that troubled me. And I'd like to hear more about them so I can understand what's been going on."

Louisa sighed. "I shouldn't have said what I did about you killing Mummy. I'm sorry."

He knew that apology. One she made often, and he'd always doubted her sincerity when she did. But he wasn't ready to question it. Not yet.

"Thank you. I want you to know that I did not kill her. I was angry with her, yes, but I would never have killed her."

Louisa nodded. "Is that all? Polly said she needed help with the children."

A lie, but again, it didn't seem right to call her on it. "In a moment. She won't be mad if it's because you're with me. You said your mother deserved to die. I'm curious to know why you thought that."

"I shouldn't..." Louisa turned away.

"She's dead. She can't hurt you anymore."

Tears rolled down Louisa's face. "Polly told you everything, didn't she?"

"No." Even though Louisa's mention of "everything" made him wish Polly had, he was grateful that she could be seen as maintaining trust in the relationship. "But you did say your mother deserved to die, and I need to know why."

Louisa shook her head as tears continued to flow.

"It could keep me from going to prison."

She sniffed and wiped her nose with the back of her sleeve. "It will just make you angry."

"And what have I ever done to make you think that you should be afraid of my being angry? I love you, Louisa, and nothing will change that."

He took her in his arms as sobs shook her body. "I can't. It's too terrible."

Mitch took a deep breath and realized that Polly had been right. His family had suffered too long under the secrets they all bore. In Louisa's case, they were secrets no child should have to carry.

"I understand your mother might have told you that I'm not your father," he said gently. "Are you afraid that I would be hurt if I knew?"

Louisa looked up at him and nodded.

He kissed the top of her head. "It's true that I'm not your natural father, but I have never viewed you otherwise. I've always known, and I've always loved you. You are one hundred percent my daughter, and nothing your mother said or did will change that. Do you understand?"

"You knew?" Louisa sniffled loudly.

"I knew."

"She said you would throw us all out if you found out, so we had to keep it a secret."

Mitch took a deep breath, trying not to give in to the boiling heat that filled him at the knowledge of his wife's deception. "She lied."

Louisa sobbed, soaking the front of his shirt as he continued to hold her, just as he had the night before.

"I love you, Louisa, and nothing will change that or make me send you away."

He looked up to see Polly poking her head into the

room, then motioning that she'd come back. Mitch shook his head and waved her in.

"Polly's here," Mitch said softly. "I'm sure she wants to know that you're all right."

Louisa looked up at Polly. "She lied." Then a new set of tears streamed down her face.

"I know, and it is an awful thing to lie to your children like that. I hope you know that she lied because she was a bad person, not because you are. You're an incredible young lady, and her actions have no reflection on you."

Mitch wished he could have the kind of love and grace that Polly seemed to have as she addressed his daughter. Wished he'd thought to speak those words of love over her.

"Papa says he loves me."

Polly nodded. "And he does. I've never met a man who loved his children more. Trust in that love, not the lies your mother told."

Louisa disengaged from Mitch's embrace and went to Polly, wrapping her arms around her. "I'm sorry I've been so difficult."

"You were only protecting your family. I imagine you thought that if you got rid of the nannies, you could get rid of your mother's threats."

"How did you know?" Louisa looked up at her. "I didn't tell you that."

"No, but you said that your mother told tales to the nannies. It's not hard to come up with the rest."

Once again, Mitch felt sick at the realization that the very people he'd hired to care for his children were the ones keeping them in fear. No wonder they'd been so badly behaved. Polly had been saying all along that the children weren't misbehaving because they were bad children. Now he understood why.

"Thank you," he mouthed to Polly as she looked up at him. She had given him a precious gift that he could never repay.

Polly marveled at having Louisa's arms wrapped around her. The young girl had been so difficult, so unwilling to give Polly even the smallest courtesy. It was like something had broken open in her, and as she sobbed, for the first time, Polly realized how deeply wounded Louisa had been. She hadn't just been trying to keep her family together and protect her siblings from a horde of evil nannies, but she'd also been living under her mother's threats. She'd been protecting a father she dearly loved.

"There, now," Polly said gently. "It's going to be all right. We've cleared things up between us, you and I, and there will be no more secrets, yes?"

Louisa looked up at her. "Yes."

"If there is anything else your father needs to know, you'll tell him, right?"

Louisa nodded, then looked at her father. "I was afraid, but I'm not afraid anymore."

Polly smoothed Louisa's hair. Before long, Louisa would be as tall as she was. Though that wasn't saying much, considering Polly was the shortest woman she knew. Still, Louisa was nearly a young woman, and despite all of their attempts to make sure Louisa enjoyed as much of her childhood as possible, there wasn't much left. Even now, in the mature glance Louisa gave her, Polly knew there was a wisdom to the young girl that she'd gained from this experience.

"I'm proud of you, Louisa," Mitch said, his voice sounding hoarse.

The poor man had dealt with a lot over the past few hours, let alone days, and she could see the lines in his forehead as he strained to hold the emotion back.

Giving Louisa another squeeze, Polly said, "Let's give your father a few minutes, and we'll go make sure the rest of the preparations are in order."

Louisa nodded slowly, her eyes still red with tears.

"But first, go by the pump outside and wash your face." Polly touched her cheek gently. "After all, this is a happy picnic, and you're going to have a marvelous time."

As Polly turned to follow Louisa out, Mitch said, "Wait."

Polly stopped and looked at him. "I really do have to get back in there. Your children might have come a long way with their behavior, but left unsupervised too long, they're bound to start a riot."

Mitch grinned, the smile lighting his eyes. She'd missed that expression on his face. Of course, none of them had much to smile about these days.

Unless you counted the breakthrough they'd just had with Louisa.

"You saw through their tantrums."

Polly shrugged. "I've had a lot of practice."

Suddenly, as much as she thought she missed not having a childhood of her own, she found herself grateful for all the time she'd spent taking care of her siblings and minding the rest of the children in the mining camps. She'd seen a variety of children, and she'd learned that much of what people considered misbehavior often pointed to something else going on in the child's life. Still, she'd never anticipated the depth of what had been troubling the Taylor children.

"No, it's more than that." Mitch reached out and lightly touched her arm. "You see them for who they are as people. You see me."

Even though she wore a long-sleeved gown, his fingers nearly seared her flesh with their warmth. No, *seared* was the wrong word. Because where that one spot was warm, it had begun to spread through the rest of her body.

"Anyone would do the same," she said, trying to turn away.

Once again, Mitch stopped her. "No, anyone would not. I've had enough people try to take advantage of me to know that. Your love and compassion for others is unlike anything I've ever seen."

Then he shook his head. "No, that's not true. I suppose I've seen it here. In this house. This place. I don't understand."

Polly took a deep breath. Now that she could explain. As much as Mitch saw this in her, it wasn't about her. "It's God's love. It's what Uncle Frank teaches us about at church, but mostly in how he lives his life. He's not perfect, but we've learned to love and forgive each other just the same."

Mitch's eyes twinkled. "I don't know, I'm starting to think you're all pretty perfect."

"Me? Perfect?" Polly frowned. "You mentioned earlier that I can be pushy at times, and that's true. Sometimes it's a good thing, but as my friends and family will tell you, there are times when my speaking without thinking has gotten me into trouble."

She glanced over at a photograph from Annabelle and Joseph's wedding. "Annabelle Lassiter Stone was my best friend, but out of anger and spite, I said things to her that hurt her deeply. We've mended things between us, but there was a time when I wondered if we'd ever be friends again. I felt like I'd lost a limb."

"And I felt the same way." Annabelle's voice made Polly turn, and she saw her friend standing in the doorway.

"Sorry, I shouldn't have been eavesdropping, but you were talking about me."

"What are you doing here?" Polly went over and gave her friend a hug. "It's been too long since I've seen you."

"Only a few days." Annabelle rubbed her stomach and sighed. "I've been wanting to come by, but I've been having pains at night, so Joseph's been making me rest during the day. Gertie says it's not time yet, and I have to stay off my feet as much as possible."

Then she let out another long sigh. "But I'm bored, bored, bored. No one lets me do anything, and if Mary tries to get me to knit another bootie, I think I'll go mad."

Polly giggled at her friend's mock hysteria. "You see, Mitch. We aren't perfect at all. Poor Annabelle's on the verge of madness."

"Oh, you laugh now," Annabelle said, looking forlornly at her swollen stomach. "Just wait until it's your turn. Then we'll see how you feel, being stuck at home all day with nothing to do but wait."

"Well, I can ease your mind on that account." Polly shook her head as she looked over at Mitch. "They all suffer under the delusion that I'm going to meet some wonderful man who will sweep me off my feet and change my mind. But mark my words. I shall never marry, and I shall certainly never have children."

A screech from the kitchen seemed to echo Polly's words. "You see? I suppose I should go find out what that is all about."

As Polly passed her friend on the way to the kitchen, she gave her another hug. "But I am deliriously happy for you, and soon enough, you will be holding the most beautiful babe the world has ever seen, and it will all be worth it."

They were the same words Polly had been using to comfort her friend for weeks now, but as she entered the kitchen and saw little Isabella sitting in the middle of the floor, covered in what appeared to be batter, something in her speech felt off.

"It was a accident," Thomas said, looking guilty. "I tripped."

"And I told you to wait for a grown up to help you." Maddie picked up Isabella and handed her to Polly. "I'll let you get this one cleaned off while I get the others to mopping the floor."

Maddie sent a stern look to Thomas. "It may have been an accident, but in my kitchen, if you make a mess, you clean it up."

Holding the dripping little girl as far from her as possible, Polly sighed. All she'd ever wanted was to leave this chaos, yet there was something dearly familiar about it all. For all her bravado, could she leave?

Though she'd told Mitch there was truly nothing special about this place, other than their faith, Polly had to wonder—if she did get what she wanted, would the love be as strong?

Chapter Ten

Never marry and have children. Polly's pronouncement to Annabelle shouldn't have surprised Mitch, but
hearing the strength of her conviction made his heart
ache. Polly really was going to leave them.

"Don't mind her," Annabelle said. "She's always
been a stubborn one, that Polly. But that's why we love
her. As stubborn as she is in resisting things, she's also
stubborn in clinging to her love. Which is why she's so
good for your children."

"I'm certainly grateful for her influence on them,"
Mitch said slowly, trying to ignore the twinkle in Annabelle's eyes. It might have been more than a few years
since he'd played victim to someone else's matchmaking, but he could see where Annabelle's thoughts were
headed.

"I think it's admirable that Polly doesn't want to
marry and instead wants to devote her life to helping children. It's good for a person to know what they
want out of life."

Annabelle snorted. A very unladylike noise for
someone who looked like the advertisements in his
catalogs of all that a lady should be. "The last thing

on earth Polly wants is to be a teacher. She might say that's what she wants, but just wait until she has to live under those rules for a while. Honestly, what Polly really needs is—"

"A friend who doesn't meddle," Polly said, poking her head into the room. "I've just come to tell Mitch that we're ready to leave on our picnic."

Then she turned to Annabelle. "As for you, it's all well and good that you've found happiness with Joseph. But it's not the life for me. And I'll thank you to remember that before you start concocting plans in your head. Now you'd best go put your feet up before that husband of yours comes round the corner and sees you."

Mitch hid his grin with a well-placed cough behind his hand. He had nothing to complain about with his own family growing up, but it had lacked the friendship and warmth he'd seen at the Lassiter house. Even among those not related by blood, he saw a kinship that almost made him envious. Except that they seemed to be pulling him in to that same kinship.

Their good-natured teasing, and even Annabelle's attempt at meddling, all spoke of love and caring for one another. He hoped, at the very least, he could help his children have that same bond.

As Annabelle sniffed and hurried to the chair and footstool where she'd most likely spend the rest of the afternoon, she winked at Mitch. She wasn't giving up on her matchmaking anytime soon. Though he thought, like Polly, that Annabelle was wasting her time, part of him was flattered that she wanted to make his inclusion into their family official.

"Shall we?" Polly gestured toward the door. "Uncle Frank has the wagon all loaded up. "I hope you don't mind, but he's asked us to drop off some supplies at a nearby mining camp. They have a nice place to picnic there, so I didn't see any harm in combining the trips."

"No, it will be nice to see some of the countryside." Mitch hadn't taken the time to enjoy much of the view as they traveled to Leadville.

The ride to the mining camp was pleasant, and he appreciated Polly's chatter as she pointed out landmarks and places of interest. When they arrived, Polly led them to a picturesque stream in the midst of a sunny meadow that seemed far removed from the bustle of town and the industry of the mines. Here, he felt a peace he hadn't known in…well, he couldn't remember when he'd felt this peaceful. But more than that, he noticed a camaraderie amongst his children he'd not seen before. Isabella sat, cuddled in Polly's lap, and Polly seemed to act as though having a three-year-old attached to her was the most natural thing in the world. Louisa braided Clara's hair in a fancy new way she'd just learned. And the boys, Rory and Thomas, were whittling sticks. Whittling!

Mitch paused for a moment as he realized he'd never given his boys knives.

"What do you have there?" he asked them, looking at Polly.

"Maddie gave 'em to us," Rory said, sticking out his chin in the defiant way Mitch was accustomed to. "She said she doesn't want us using the pastor's good silver for making arrows."

Polly gave him an amused look. "Maddie is quite particular about her housekeeping, as you know. The boys saw Nugget and Caitlin playing with their bows and arrows, and they wanted some, too. It's quite clever, really, how they came up with the idea of making their own."

Clever. No one had ever called his sons clever. Devious, certainly, and they'd never been praised for their creativity.

He caught Polly's warm smile as she looked at the boys. "Rory asked Nugget if he might borrow one of her arrows so he could fashion one similar. I know you said they've never really had friends before, so you should be quite proud of how well they're getting along with the other children."

"That's remarkable. Well done, Rory and Thomas." Mitch smiled at his sons, and the expressions of pure joy on their faces made his heart shatter into dozens of tiny pieces. How long had it been since he'd had cause to praise his sons? He'd spent so much time tearing his hair out trying to get them to behave that he'd never taken the time to see what Polly was so clearly showing him.

Thomas clambered over to Mitch and sat on his lap.

"See mine? Rory says it won't fly because I used the wrong feathers, but I liked the feathers from Mrs. Bates's chicken better, so I chased it, and I catched it and I got a whole handful of feathers. I think it makes my arrow look real pretty, dontcha think?"

Polly let out a long sigh. "I thought I told you to leave Mrs. Bates's poor chickens alone. Maddie was saving you some feathers she had, and all you had to do was ask her."

"But they weren't pretty feathers!" Thomas's lower lip quivered in a pout, and Mitch wanted to laugh at the ridiculousness of it, but he knew it would crush his son. And yet, he had disobeyed Polly's request.

"Still, you should have listened to Polly," Mitch told his son, picking up the arrow, then looking at Polly. "What do you think we should do with this?"

Polly sighed and turned her attention to Thomas. "Well, I don't suppose we can glue the feathers back on the chicken, now can we?"

Thomas shook his head furiously.

"But I do think that we'll have to keep this arrow until you've properly apologized to Mrs. Bates for disturbing her chickens and she says it's all right for you to have your arrow back."

"But that's mean," Thomas wailed.

"How would you feel if someone much larger than you pulled out a bunch of your hair to make some arrows?" Polly's voice was gentle, tender, but Thomas looked terrified as he put his hands over his head.

"Don't pull out my hair!"

Polly gently rested her hands on top of his, stroking them. "I would never do that. You're a handsome boy, and I wouldn't want to spoil it. I'm just asking you to think about how that poor chicken must feel."

"I just wanted pretty feathers." Thomas sniffed as he removed his hands from under hers to wipe his nose.

"Next time, let's think of a different solution that doesn't involve hurting Mrs. Bates's poor chickens."

"All right," Thomas said, hopping off Mitch's lap. Immediately, he missed the warmth of his son, even though it was a nice day. Suddenly, he understood the appeal of Polly constantly holding Isabella.

"Thomas?" Mitch called after his son.

Thomas turned to look at him.

"I love you."

Thomas stared at him, as Mitch realized that he hadn't said those words nearly often enough with any of his children. But then the boy broke out into a grin.

"I love you, too, Papa."

And if his heart hadn't already burst into pieces

"FAST FIVE" READER SURVEY

Your participation entitles you to:
* 4 Thank-You Gifts Worth Over $20!

Complete the survey in minutes.

Get 2 FREE Books

See inside for details.

Dear Reader,

Since you are a lover of our books, your opinions are important to us... and so is your time.

That's why we made sure your **"FAST FIVE" READER SURVEY** can be completed in just a few minutes. Your answers to the five questions will help us remain at the forefront of women's fiction.

And, as a thank-you for participating, we'd like to send you **4 FREE THANK-YOU GIFTS!**

Enjoy your gifts with our appreciation,

Pam Powers

To get your
4 FREE THANK-YOU GIFTS:

✳ Quickly complete the "Fast Five" Reader Survey
and return the insert.

"FAST FIVE" READER SURVEY

1 Do you sometimes read a book a second or third time? ○ Yes ○ No

2 Do you often choose reading over other forms of entertainment such as television? ○ Yes ○ No

3 When you were a child, did someone regularly read aloud to you? ○ Yes ○ No

4 Do you sometimes take a book with you when you travel outside the home? ○ Yes ○ No

5 In addition to books, do you regularly read newspapers and magazines? ○ Yes ○ No

YES! I have completed the above Reader Survey. Please send me my 4 FREE GIFTS (gifts worth over $20 retail). I understand that I am under no obligation to buy anything, as explained on the back of this card.

102/302 IDL GLDK

FIRST NAME	LAST NAME

ADDRESS

APT.#   CITY

STATE/PROV.   ZIP/POSTAL CODE

HLI-816-SFF15

too tiny to put together, it would have melted. Thomas skipped off to rejoin his brother, completely oblivious to how his words had impacted his father.

"They all do, you know," Polly said quietly, smiling at him as she adjusted Isabella in her arms.

"Did she fall asleep?"

Isabella turned her head to look at him. "No, Papa. I's not asweep. I's watching dem butterfwies."

Her chubby little finger pointed at a spot in the grass where, sure enough, a couple of butterflies flitted about.

Louisa must have overheard them talking because she approached them. "They're beautiful butterflies, aren't they? Want to see if we can catch them?"

"Oh, yes!" Isabella's curls bobbed up and down as she nodded her head furiously. "We will be vewy gentle with dem so's they don't get hurt."

Mitch started to tell her that if she caught a butterfly, it would hurt the creature, but Polly put her hand on his leg, speaking softly when the girls were out of earshot. "Don't spoil it for her. She's too clumsy to catch one, but it will make her happy to think she can."

He stared at her. "How do you do it?"

"Do what?" She moved a stray curl that had fallen down over her face and tucked it neatly behind her ear. Beautiful. So innocent and without any of the artifice he'd come to despise in women. Polly's beauty wasn't the sort that had men falling over themselves to escort her on the town. Rather, it shone from within, and it seemed to make everything around her even more beautiful.

But that was fancy talking again, and as delighted as he was by her presence, he had to remind himself that it wouldn't last.

"It amazes me how well you know the children. How you talk to them."

Polly shrugged. "Experience. I told you that."

"It's more than experience," Mitch said, willing himself to not try counting all the freckles on her nose. He'd sold many a cream to help women rid themselves of the scourge, but in Polly's case, he hoped not a one disappeared.

Argh. He was doing it again. Why was he acting like a youth in the throes of his first crush? Polly was his nanny, not someone to romance.

"All of the other nannies I hired, they came with more experience than you. But you see my children with your heart, not your eyes. And I see the difference in them. They behave far better than they ever have."

Polly sighed. "Not completely. I'm not looking forward to my conversation with Mrs. Bates tomorrow. She loves those chickens like they were her children, and I'm sure she's going to have something to say about the emotional distress her chickens have suffered."

Mitch couldn't help but laugh. "Emotional distress? For a chicken?"

"Laugh all you want, but you haven't seen how she treats those chickens. They were one of the few flocks to survive last winter, and when one of the miners came over with an axe to see if she could spare one, I thought she was going to use it on him! Needless to say, none of her birds have graced anyone's stew pot."

Polly's description of the woman and her defense of her chickens had him laughing all the more, until finally she joined in with a few giggles of her own.

"You're too much to resist, you know that?" Polly's eyes shone as their laughter died down. "I know you haven't had much to laugh about, but you have one of the best laughs I've heard. It makes me happy just to hear your joy."

Everything in him felt lighter. He wished he could express it to Polly, but he wasn't sure even how to explain it to himself. The world seemed different when he was with her, and the longer they were in that world together, the harder it was for him to imagine life without her.

"I should go see where Rory has gotten off to," Mitch said, standing. "I haven't spent much time with him since we arrived."

He hated the way Polly's face fell at his words. Clearly, she was enjoying their interlude just as much as he. But she had no idea the pain of becoming attached to someone who had no intention of reciprocating that attachment.

Moments like this, he thought that perhaps he should let her go now, while losing her would still be bearable. But he honestly didn't know how he was going to cope with finding Hattie's killer, potentially going through a trial and raising his children without her. Was it selfish of him to cling to her, knowing that in the end, it would result in heartbreak for them all?

Unfortunately, there were no clear answers, but as he approached his son, and saw the way Rory beamed up at him, he knew that above all, he had to find out what was best for his children.

Polly couldn't fault Mitch for going to be with Rory. After all, that's what the whole point of their outing had been. And yet, they'd shared a moment, connected on an important level and for once Polly felt...she shook her head. Whatever she'd been feeling, it was entirely inappropriate to be feeling about one's employer.

The three girls came running up to her, their hands filled with flowers. "Look what we found," they chorused.

"They're lovely. We can bring some home to Maddie. They'd be beautiful on the dinner table."

"Or you could give them to Papa," Clara said. "He would like that."

Louisa nudged her. "Girls don't give flowers to boys. It's the other way around, silly."

"Oh! Then we should give them to Papa, and he can give them to Polly." Clara beamed as Louisa made an exasperated noise.

"Fwowers!" Isabella held up a matted handful of wildflowers, barely salvageable after being mangled in her tiny fist.

"They're lovely," Polly said, ignoring the interchange between Louisa and Clara. It was only natural that they would want to start matchmaking, but obviously, there was no match to be made. She just had to find some gentle way of breaking it to the girls.

Isabella beamed, then climbed up into her lap. "I yuv you, Polly." The warmth of the little girl's lips pressed against her cheek spread through Polly's entire body, down to her very toes. In all the years she'd been helping care for her family, for the children in Pastor Lassiter's ministry and all the children in the mining camps, Polly had never felt this level of deep satisfaction.

"Me, too!" Clara ran up alongside Polly and sat on the blanket beside her. "Promise you'll never leave us."

Polly tried to speak, then tried to swallow, but her throat seemed to be paralyzed. This wasn't meant to be a place where Polly spent the rest of her life, merely a stopover until she was free to live on her own.

But what then?

Polly sighed. As a teacher, she'd never truly be alone,

and she couldn't help but remember the words she'd overheard Annabelle confidently tell Mitch. She would still be under the kind of restrictive life she'd always wanted to get out of.

"Polly said she'll be leaving as soon as I've proven my worth in taking care of you all," Louisa said, putting on the airs of a much older girl. "I imagine it won't be long now, since I'm almost all grown up."

At twelve, Louisa was hardly almost all grown up. And once again, Polly couldn't help but think of the unfairness of having to act as such when she'd needed the time to be a child.

Polly had never gotten to be a child, and from the way Louisa hung back, and the conversation they'd had earlier in the day, neither had Louisa.

Would it be so bad to stay with Mitch until the children were grown? Isabella had rested her head against Polly's chest, contentedly plucking the petals off her flowers.

Polly looked up at Louisa. "We shall see. You still have a long way to go, and in the meantime, I'd like for you to enjoy your life."

Farther down the meadow, Mitch was gathering the boys to take them fishing. "Perhaps you could start by going fishing with your father."

"Fishing!" Clara jumped up. "Oh! I've always wanted to go fishing. I've read about it in books, and it sounds fantastic! Louisa, come! You must try it!"

Louisa made a noise. "Fishing is for babies."

"Not at all." Polly smiled at the younger girl. "I still go fishing with my brothers, as well as the other children from the parsonage. Both Maddie and my mother love cooking fresh fish for supper, and I'm sure that if we all try, there will be plenty for tonight. In fact, given that she knows we've gone up here, I'm certain that she's counting on us."

That might have been a slight stretch of the truth. Whenever they came up here, Maddie always hoped they'd bring back enough fish for supper. But sometimes they returned empty-handed, and Maddie still had plenty on the table for all.

"I fish?" Isabella looked up at her.

"Certainly. I'll help you."

Isabella jumped up and tugged at Polly's hand. "Come!"

Polly looked over at Louisa, who appeared doubtful. "I don't know how to fish. It's not ladylike."

Polly sighed. On one hand, Louisa did have a point. Fishing was not the most ladylike pastime. But here, in Leadville, it didn't matter so much what made a lady. Though many put on airs and tried to seem more important than they were, the truth was, life in Leadville was rough. Yes, it was the largest city in Colorado and boasted many of the refinements of cities back east, but it was still a wild land, untamed, and sometimes survival was more important than upholding the ladylike ideal.

"Perhaps it's not something one does in high-society drawing rooms, but if you're ever in a situation where you might be forced to go hungry otherwise, fishing is a good skill to have. Besides…" Polly grinned. "Fishing is loads of fun. My good friend Annabelle and I used to go fishing all the time."

A small pang filled Polly's heart as she remembered the girlhood joy they'd had at going fishing, before their lives and friendship had grown complicated. Before Annabelle's mother died. Catherine Lassiter had taught Polly so much about what it meant to be a lady in this rough town. Polly's mother had taught her all about what it took to survive, but Catherine's lessons had been equally important. Especially in the importance of what it meant to be a child.

"I'm sorry," Louisa said softly, "I didn't mean to make you sad."

Polly looked up at her, shaking her head. "Oh, no, not at all. I'm sorry. I was just lost in my memories. We had some good times here, growing up."

"But it made you cry." Louisa pointed to Polly's cheek.

Reaching up, Polly felt the damp spot where a tear had fallen. "I hadn't noticed."

"What made you so sad?"

Polly took a deep breath. "I just remembered what it was like to be taught how to be a child." She smiled at Louisa, who wore a puzzled expression.

"I know you want to help your father and prove that you're an adult. But don't miss out on the joys of being a child. The grown-up responsibilities will come soon enough."

Polly pointed to the stream where Clara and Rory were more intent on splashing each other than on listening to their father's instructions on fishing. "I was forced to grow up too fast, taking care of my siblings and the other children in camp. But the things that I remember the most were times like those, where I was allowed to be a child and have fun. The tear you saw was of regret, of not having more of those moments."

The puzzled expression didn't leave Louisa's face, and it probably wouldn't. Not until years later, when Louisa remembered how, instead of participating in the fun, she'd stood to the side and tried to do all the work that wasn't hers, to be the parent it wasn't her responsibility to be. Louisa would stand by her conviction now, but years later, when it was too late, she'd regret giving up her childhood so easily.

Having done the same herself, Polly wasn't about to allow that to happen for Louisa.

"Polly!" Isabella tugged at her hand. "Come! They get all the fish wifout us."

Polly grinned. "Come on, Louisa. Join us. I'm not going to be convinced of your ability to help with the others unless you're also willing to join in and be a child yourself."

Louisa sighed, but she followed them over to the stream, where the sound of laughter greeted them. The only lines Polly spied on Mitch's face were the laugh lines crinkling his eyes.

And his laugh…it sparked joy in every cell in Polly's body, listening to him as he and Thomas chased a fish thrashing on the banks.

"Allow me," Polly said, grinning.

She helped them catch the slippery fish, impressed by its large size.

"Papa helped," Thomas exclaimed with pride, "but I mostly did it all by myself."

Mitch beamed as he looked at her. "Only in bringing it in. It's been so long since I've taken a day to fish, I nearly forgot myself."

"I got more worms!" Rory rushed toward them, a fistful of worms dangling from his fingers.

"Ew!" Louisa exclaimed. "That's disgusting!"

"Not as disgusting as you, birdbrain!" Rory flung one of the worms at his sister.

Louisa squealed as she jumped out of the way of the writhing creature.

"Rory." Polly kept her voice calm and as modulated as possible. "That wasn't very nice."

"But worms aren't disgusting, they're wonderful."

She smiled at the boy, who'd opened his hands to show off his prize. "True, but Louisa doesn't know that. Perhaps instead of trying to upset her, you should educate her on all the reasons worms are so wonderful."

Rory frowned for a moment, but then his eyes lit up. "They make gardens grow, and the birds and the fish eat them, and so we can use them to help us fish because the fish want to eat the worm, and then we can catch the fish, then we get to eat the fish."

He turned to Polly. "We do get to eat the fish, right?"

"We do. Maddie fries up the most delicious fish you've ever tasted. But we'll have to do much better than this to make sure there's enough for everyone. Uncle Frank loves to eat fish."

"All right!" Rory raced toward the edge of the stream and dumped the worms in his pail, then began preparing his pole to catch more fish.

Mitch smiled warmly at her. "I don't think I've done this since I was a boy."

"Then I'm glad to have afforded you the opportunity. Perhaps you can take the children again. I'm sure they'd enjoy it."

The look he gave her made her hot and cold all at once. "We will definitely be taking them again."

We. Because somehow in all this crazy mess, they'd become a team. Mitch wanted to be a part of raising his children as much as Polly was working to help him. She'd never doubted his role in the process, but as she was learning, he hadn't ever known how to truly be a father to them. Or, as she recalled from their earlier conversation, perhaps he hadn't been allowed.

Working together, things were different. But as his gaze seared her skin, Polly had to wonder how different they were going to continue to be. Oh, she meant for things to be long-term between them, at least as far as the children were concerned, but was there another implication? Everyone seemed to be pushing them together as a couple, and while she found Mitch far more attractive than she should…

Polly shook her head. Enough of this nonsense. Being saddled with Mitch meant exploring places of her heart that she wasn't willing to explore.

She turned to the children. "Who else has caught a fish?"

Thomas gave a gleeful shout. Clara still seemed happy enough playing at the edge of the stream, occasionally sending splashes in Rory's direction. Rory scowled at his sister.

"Stop scaring away the fish!"

"Come on, Clara. Rather than bothering with Rory, perhaps we should see if you can catch one of your own."

Clara stuck her tongue out at Rory before coming toward Polly. "You mean it? You think I can catch a fish? Rory says fishing's not for girls."

"Of course it's for girls." Then she turned to Mitch with a grin. "Why don't we make it a competition? Boys against girls. Whoever catches the most fish will be the winners, and the losers will have to gut all the fish."

"That's not fair," Rory said. "There are more girls than boys."

"Isabella doesn't count," Clara said, pointing at her sister.

Isabella sat in the mud, poking it with a stick. "I catch fish!"

"She has a point," Mitch said, smiling. "I don't think Isabella's going to catch much of anything. Besides, I think we can still beat them."

Polly turned to Louisa. "Do you hear that? We'll need your help if we're going to win."

Louisa let out a long sigh. "I suppose. But you're going to have to show me what to do."

"This is going to be easy." Rory let out a guffaw and turned back to where he'd been fishing.

Polly handed out poles, and the girls found spots along the bank. Soon, everyone was fishing, and Polly was grateful to have found a small bend in the stream where Isabella could poke her stick in the mud and Polly could still tend her line.

"Something's on my line!" Louisa's voice was a mixture of panic and elation. "What do I do?"

Mitch was closest to her, and before Polly could react to Louisa's statements, he was already moving in his daughter's direction.

"Let me help."

Polly watched as Mitch put his arms around his daughter and helped her bring the fish in. He leaned in to whisper something in Louisa's ear, and Louisa beamed. Polly's insides turned to the consistency of the mud Isabella played in as she watched the father and daughter bond. This was more than the conversation they'd had earlier. Mitch and Louisa were cementing a connection they'd both been desperate for without realizing it.

Polly closed her eyes and prayed. *Lord, please help this family. They're finally finding their way together. Keep Mitch safe and free from the charges dogging him. His children need him, and he needs them.*

She wanted to say something about her own role in

the process, but she wasn't even sure what that would look like at this point. What she wanted it to be, and if what God wanted it to be looked different, would she be able to handle the results?

Louisa squealed as they pulled a writhing fish out of the water. "We did it!"

She dropped her pole and threw her arms around her father, who was still struggling to get control of the fish. And yet, fish or no fish, he let go of what he was doing and wrapped his arms around Louisa.

"Yes, we did."

Polly thought her heart was going to explode with the joy of having witnessed this precious moment between father and daughter.

"You lost the pole and the fish, you dolts," Rory said, irritation in his voice.

Polly turned her gaze from the father-daughter pair and saw the pole drifting toward them. "I'll get it," she said.

She trudged through the water and grabbed the pole. It slipped in her grasp, but she managed to keep hold of it.

"Fish!" Isabella's baby voice called out.

"Yes, I know, fish." Polly sighed, realizing that while she'd tied up her skirts to keep them dry while she fished at the edge of the bank, her excursion into the water had loosened them and as she dragged the pole out with her, she was also dragging behind soggy, wet fabric.

"Fish!" Isabella cried out again, this time louder and more urgently.

Polly threw the pole onto the bank, then turned to the little girl, who was holding the pole Polly had discarded to rescue the remains of Louisa's fishing attempt.

Bent wildly, it was clear the pole held a fish at the other end.

"Oh, my!" Polly reached to help the little girl pull in the fish. They struggled for several minutes trying to bring it in. Finally, she felt strong arms come around behind her.

"Let me help." The soft, warm whisper against her ear sent a chill down her spine.

With a final tug, they gained control of the fish. As they brought it out of the water and onto the bank, Polly noticed that it was the largest fish she'd ever caught.

"I catched a fish," Isabella declared.

"It's lovely," Polly said, breathless. Mitch hadn't released his hold on her, and as he murmured his agreement, his breath was warm against her neck. Too warm. Too…

Polly stepped away, immediately feeling a chill as she moved out of Mitch's arms.

"You're soaked through," he said as they stepped onto the bank.

"I had to rescue Louisa's pole."

He bent and brushed the stray hairs that had fallen around her face. "You're something else, you know that?"

She gave a soft murmur of agreement as she turned away. This effect he had on her, it made her feel as giddy as she had during her previous failed romances. But unlike with those other men, there was something different about Mitch.

Everyone had thought her heartbreaks had been so deep because she'd given too much of herself. Allowed herself to love too intensely. But what no one had understood, had been able to see, was that Polly had always held something back. Kept herself from giving her all to someone who would ultimately betray her trust. So far, she'd been completely right in doing so.

But with Mitch, holding back wouldn't be an option. If she allowed herself to love him, she'd be forced to love him with her whole heart, and if she loved him with her whole heart, how could she ever find the strength to leave?

She was met at the top of the bank by a mournful-looking Louisa. "I lost the fish."

Polly nodded. "You did."

"I got distracted." Louisa let out a long sigh.

Putting her arm around the girl, Polly smiled. "It happens to the best of us sometimes. But in your case, I think the distraction was worth it."

Louisa beamed. "I did have fun."

"Then that's all that matters." Polly gave the girl another squeeze as the wind picked up and the breeze chilled her.

"Thanks for going in to get my pole."

"You're welcome."

Rory rushed up to them, holding a string of four fish. "Look what we got! Me and Thomas. I don't know what Papa caught, but I think we have to be the winners."

"I caught a fish, but we lost it," Louisa said, a sulk in her voice.

"Then it doesn't count." Rory looked entirely too self-satisfied as he stared at his sister.

Mitch joined the group, carrying Isabella's fish. "Well, you may have caught more fish, but Isabella certainly brought in the biggest. Look at this guy."

He held it up as they all marveled at the fish's size.

"And don't forget about me," Clara said, sounding a bit too smug for her own good. "I caught three fish, all by myself. And…" She held up a string containing four fish. "I managed to snag Louisa's fish with my net. Three plus one, plus Isabella's large fish, that's five. So we win."

"You said Isabella wasn't going to catch any," Rory whined.

"She didn't." Clara stared at her brother, hands on her hips. "She was holding Polly's pole, and Polly and Papa brought it in together. So it was Polly's fish."

"Well if Papa helped bring it in, then it was part Papa's fish. And since Papa helped with Louisa's fish, that's part Papa's fish, too. So we win."

Rory squared off with his sister, eyes flashing. It always amused Polly to see how the largest sibling rivalry occurred between the twins, but having no experience with twins herself, she had no idea if it was normal or if this rivalry was different.

She was about to step in when Mitch spoke up. "Actually, I helped Louisa lose the fish, and Clara got it, so credit rightly belongs to the girls. As for the fish I helped Polly bring in, I think we can consider it a joint effort, therefore our fish competition is a tie."

Mitch looked at Polly and gave her a smile that melted her clear to her toes. "No winners, no losers."

That might be true, but somehow Polly felt as though the greater battle was yet to come. And she wasn't talking about fish but about the funny flutter in the pit of her stomach. She was committed to these children, but how could she maintain a professional distance when even the simplest look from Mitch sent her insides into a tailspin?

Chapter Eleven

Something had changed in Polly since their time fishing. Mitch couldn't put his finger on it, but where he'd once been entirely too aware of the warmth emanating from her, he sensed a new coolness, a distance that hadn't been there before.

He passed her in the hallway as he was about to go tuck the children in.

"Sorry," she murmured, then started to move in the other direction.

"No, it's all right. I was just going to…um…" Was he intruding in her territory by taking on more of the parental duties?

Polly smiled. "I'm sure they'll be glad. I just wanted to get another hot brick for the girls' bed. It's chilly tonight. You go on ahead, and I'll be there shortly."

The words were polite, but something in her tone sounded forced.

"Are you sure everything's all right?"

"Of course."

She didn't look in his direction as she continued down the hall.

What had changed between them?

He paused at the door to his room. It was ajar, and he was certain he'd closed it before going down to dinner.

Mitch looked inside and saw a note on his pillow. He picked up the paper and stared at its contents. *I love and adore you, and I wish we could be together forever.*

The note wasn't signed, but as if to indicate the sincerity of the sentiment, a large heart was drawn around it.

Mitch refolded the note, then stared at it. Was this the reason for Polly's awkwardness? She'd just declared her love for him and was afraid that he'd reject her?

Mitch sighed. He would reject her, of course. It was the only right thing to do. After all, he was Polly's employer, and anything between them was inappropriate. Besides…he let out another long sigh. While Polly was attractive in so many ways, there was one way in which they were completely incompatible. Eventually, she would leave. And Mitch was neither inclined to make her stay against her will, nor was he going to give his heart to someone who would take it with her when she went.

Because the truth was, as much as he had gotten to know her, he was beginning to care for her. She was a delightful woman who was opening his heart to so many possibilities, and bringing so much joy to his family. He was certainly grateful to her, but the feelings she stirred in him…he couldn't act on them. Nor could he be responsible for her acting on hers.

For a woman as young as Polly, what was happening between them was mere infatuation, and as the other romances her family had alluded to had passed, so, too, would this. Polly was right in judging herself too young to settle down. She didn't know her own heart yet, and he couldn't afford to give his to someone in that position.

Tucking the note in his pocket, he resolved to speak with her before her infatuation got too out of hand. She had a job to do, and she couldn't be distracted from caring for his children.

He made his way up the stairs to the attic, where the children were already in their beds.

"Polly went to get us a brick," Clara said, reaching up to hug him. "She's so thoughtful like that."

"Yes, she is," Mitch said, returning the hug.

"She's done so much for us."

"Yes, she has."

Clara let out a long sigh. "She would make a lovely mother, don't you think?"

Mitch tried not to groan. Hopefully, Polly hadn't been letting the children in on her romantic notions.

"I'm sure she would, but it's a long time before she needs to be thinking about that." He gave her a kiss on the top of her head. "But until then, she's doing a wonderful job of taking care of us."

"She could be our mother." Clara looked up at him with such hope in her big brown eyes, it nearly broke his heart.

"Polly is your nanny. Nannies aren't mothers."

"She could be, if you married her."

This time, Mitch couldn't help the groan that escaped his lips. "That's not going to happen, sweetheart."

"But why? We like her the very best."

Mitch closed his eyes. How could he explain the adult feelings that needed to happen between them for romance, let alone a marriage, to work? And how could he explain the utter impossibility of such things happening?

"Because Polly intends to leave at some point and make a life for herself. We can't keep her forever."

Clara wrapped her arms around him. "Then we should go with her."

"We can't."

Again, more adult ideas that his daughter couldn't possibly understand.

"How do we make her stay?"

The helplessness in his daughter's voice broke his heart. His children were experts at making people leave. They could drive away the most strong-willed nanny. He'd seen them break even the hardest of women. But giving someone with every intention of leaving a reason to stay?

Impossible.

Mitch had learned that the hard way.

And that was a lesson he couldn't share with his children. They'd already been hurt too much by their mother's actions. They knew that devastation all too well. But they didn't know, didn't understand, that in the beginning, Mitch had done everything he could to make Hattie stay. He'd tried all he could to make her so happy she wouldn't want to leave. For a long time, he'd thought it his own failure. But now he knew better. There was nothing that could keep a person chained to a life she didn't want.

And frankly, though he was trying not to care for Polly in that way, he cared for her too much to even try.

"We can't make her stay," Mitch told Clara softly. "But we can enjoy the time we have with her and be grateful for all she does for us for as long as we have her."

Clara squeezed him tighter. "But this feels different in my heart."

This felt different in his heart, too. But no matter what he felt in his heart, he couldn't control what Polly felt in hers.

Mitch pressed another kiss to her head. "Just remember that no matter what, we'll always have each other."

He pulled away, then walked toward Louisa's bed, not wanting to continue the conversation further or to be forced to think about the things he wasn't ready to confront. He couldn't make Polly love them, nor could he make her stay. He'd experienced the futility in that.

But the note he'd found on his pillow burned in his pocket. What if she did feel that way? What if those feelings were real?

Mitch sighed. As easy as it would be to think those feelings were real, love wasn't something that came of a short time together, as they'd only had. He'd seen the damage mistaking infatuation for real love could do. And while this, as Clara said, felt different in his heart, it didn't feel right to tread on such unsteady ground.

As he sat on Louisa's bed, she turned toward him. "I hate to say it, but Clara's right."

"What do you mean, Clara's right?"

"You should marry Polly."

Had someone come and replaced his daughter with someone who only looked like Louisa?

"What makes you say that? I thought you wanted to get rid of her."

Louisa turned to her side and propped herself up on her elbows facing him. "She's good for us. The others aren't fighting as much, and you're spending more time with us than you ever have. Polly's the first person I've thought actually cared about us."

Then she let out a long sigh. "I thought she was just

playing a game, making us think she cared. But it's not. It's real."

Louisa's voice quivered, and in the dim light, Mitch thought he saw tears in her eyes. "How did she do it? All this time, I thought…"

She took a deep breath, and he could see her whole body shake with it. "I thought you would never want us, could never love us, but because of Polly, I learned it was a lie. I know you're mad at her for interfering, but all she wants is the best for us and for us to see the truth."

Tears ran down his daughter's cheeks. "Why did we believe the lies for so long? Today was the best day ever."

He gathered his daughter in his arms. "It's just the best day so far. We're going to have many more good days like today, and there will be some bad ones, too. But together, we're going to make a lot of wonderful memories to make all those bad ones worth it."

Louisa squeezed him hard. "I would listen to Mother say all those horrible things a thousand times over if it meant having another day like today."

He squeezed her back, then pulled away. "Why do you call her Mother now? You used to call her Mummy."

She gave an exasperated sigh. "Because that's what she wanted to be called. She thought it sounded grander and more sophisticated. I wish I didn't even have to call her Mother, because she was never really a mother to us."

It was Mitch's turn to let out a long breath. "I know that right now you're feeling the hurt of everything she did to you. But remember that she is the one who gave you life. Without her, you wouldn't be here, and I wouldn't have you. I'm grateful for my time with Hattie because without it, we wouldn't have our family. Despite everything, I would go through it all over again to be your father."

Louisa stared at him. "You love us that much? But she was horrible, and we all had to pretend otherwise."

"But she gave me five wonderful gifts, who are worth everything I had to go through to get them."

He sensed Polly behind him, even before she was near enough to make her presence known.

"I'm sorry for intruding, but I have a brick for Louisa, and I don't want to drop it."

Mitch moved to let Polly do the work she needed. "It's all right. I should go see to the boys."

He kissed Louisa on top of the head. "Good night, sweetheart. I love you."

As he passed Polly, the light was too dim for him to accurately read the expression on her face, but he thought he spied a twinkle in her eyes. He tried not to groan. Did Polly find this amusing?

His children thought they should get married, and she... Once again, he thought of the note. Did she think this was a fun game? Young as she was, she probably didn't understand the serious implications of romance and of what declaring one's romantic feelings meant. No wonder she'd had her heart badly broken. If she went chasing after other men in this manner, they were bound to take advantage of her heart being laid bare.

Mitch shook his head. What was he thinking? Surely Polly wasn't that sort of girl. She'd already made clear her desire not to marry, so of course she wouldn't easily and readily declare her love for someone.

Mitch bent to tuck Rory in and kiss him good-night.

"Good night, Papa. Clara's right, you know. Polly would make a fine mother for us all."

Madness. That's what this all was. Perhaps it was one of the children's many pranks.

Which was why, as he stared down at his innocent-looking son, who'd just agreed with his nemesis on something, Mitch had a funny feeling that something far different than romance was in the air.

He knelt beside Rory's bed. "Since when did you agree with Clara on anything?"

"Since we met Polly," Rory said. "She's loads of fun. No one's ever taken us fishing before, and she didn't even scream when I threw fish guts at her. Did you see the way she caught them?"

Actually, it had been pretty impressive. Rory had thrown fish guts at Polly to protest her pronouncement that they'd all be getting baths when they returned home. Polly caught them midair, then casually put them in her bag, saying that they'd be a wonderful addition to Maddie's compost pile.

So what game were the children about now?

"I will admit she did a mighty fine job," Mitch said, trying to sound like he was being an ally to his son. Perhaps he could ferret out what they were up to.

"And Wheezy isn't so mean to us anymore. She isn't so bossy."

Mitch glared at his son. "You know she doesn't like it when you call her that."

"Well she is mean and bossy."

"I would hate to have to tell Polly that instead of play time, you're going to have to sit inside writing sentences about loving and respecting your elder sister."

Rory let out a long sigh. "Fine. I'm sorry I called Louisa Wheezy."

The exasperated tone indicated he wasn't sorry at all, except in that he would potentially be punished for it. Typical Rory, and Mitch wasn't sure exactly how to deal with it. Polly would have an idea.

And just as quickly as the thought floated through his mind, Mitch wanted to snatch it away. She'd been in their lives such a short time, and yet he'd come to depend on her. To rely on her as an ally and for sound advice.

Mitch gave a quick shake of his head. Now was not the time to analyze his feelings about their nanny. However, he did need to disabuse his son of any notion that Polly's place in their lives was going to be permanent.

"All right, then." Mitch tucked the covers around his son. "But just so you understand, I am not marrying Polly. She's going to go off to school to learn how to be a teacher and find her own way in this world. She's only with us for a short time."

Rory snorted. "Shows how much you know. Polly doesn't need to go to school to learn how to be a teacher. She's already the best teacher we've had. Last week, we got to bake cookies. She said it was a math lesson. I say it was a delicious lesson."

Mitch had to hold in the laugh at his throat. No wonder Rory wanted to keep Polly. If he'd had baking lessons instead of math, he'd have enjoyed school far more himself. Her creative approach to the children's lessons was one of the things he appreciated about Polly. But clearly one of the reasons his children were going to be reluctant to let her go.

"Well, good night, then," Mitch said awkwardly as he bent to kiss his son. He'd lost this round, but eventually, he'd convince the children that keeping Polly wasn't going to involve matrimony.

Thomas was already asleep when Mitch went to tuck him in. But Mitch kissed him on top of his head anyway. He was really enjoying this bedtime ritual, one more thing he could thank Polly for.

But as he saw Polly and Louisa, heads together, whispering about something, Mitch had to hope that it wasn't about his marital prospects. One wife had been plenty for him. Whatever attraction he felt for Polly, and she for him, it was a temporary emotion, and once it wore off, Polly's dreams of living her own life would override any romantic notions she might have had.

He retreated downstairs to the parlor, where he took the note he'd found out of his pocket and tossed it into the fire. Whether it had been from Polly or a trick set up by the children, it didn't matter. For now, he'd pretend he hadn't received it. If the children were behind this whole nonsense, they'd see their effort as a failure. If it was Polly, his lack of response would hopefully be all the answer she needed.

Polly woke with a start. The sun shone brightly in her room, and Isabella was no longer snuggled beside her. How long had she slept?

She dressed hurriedly, then, as she ran down the stairs, quickly rebraided her hair so she could easily tuck it up into a more serviceable style. She'd never been one to oversleep, but she'd spent most of the night tossing and turning. When she'd returned from tucking the children in, she'd found a note from Mitch on her pillow.

You are so beautiful, it had said. *I've never met a woman as wonderful as you. I love you.*

All right, it hadn't been signed from Mitch, but who else could it be from? No wonder he'd acted so awkwardly toward her last night when they'd tucked the children in. She'd been trying to put distance between them, afraid that the strange attraction she felt for him would somehow be noticed and he'd think her incapable of doing her job.

And all this time, he was in love with her!

This would never do. Polly took a deep breath as she entered the kitchen. What if Mitch was there? What was she supposed to say? *Mitch, I got your note, and, against my better judgment, I am finding myself very attracted to you, but I cannot imagine how a romance between us would work?*

Preposterous. That's what it was. How could she even consider falling in love with a man who would keep her tied down to a family that...

"Good morning, Polly!" Five cheerful voices greeted her as she entered the kitchen. They were all seated at the kitchen table, working on their...lessons?

Isabella held up a slate. "I wite name!"

Someone had clearly written Isabella on her slate, and underneath, Isabella had scribbled.

"I've already done my spelling," Louisa said. "And the other children are still working on theirs, but we should be ready for the rest of our lessons soon."

Then she held up a book. "Pastor, er, Uncle Frank said it was all right to borrow something from his study. I thought this looked interesting."

Robinson Crusoe. Not something Polly would have picked for the girl, but if she wanted to read it...

"That sounds just fine."

Polly looked around the spotless kitchen. "Where's Maddie?"

Maddie came in the back door, drying her hands on her apron. "Just out finishing up a few things. I don't know what you did to these children, but they've been well behaved all morning. Said they wanted you to get your rest and helped me with the washing up, then got right to their lessons."

Polly stared at them. "Really?"

"Oh, yes," Clara said, her smile filling her face. "We like you best of all of our nannies, and since the other ones left because we were so bad, we decided that we would be extra good so that you would never leave us."

Of course. That's what this was all about. She'd heard some whispering between Mitch and Clara the previous night about Clara not wanting Polly to leave. The poor children had never had a positive female influence in their lives before, so of course they were eager to keep her.

"Oh, dear one." Polly walked over and put her arms around the other girl. "I loved you even when you didn't behave. I won't love you any more or any less based on your behavior. Love is something you can't earn."

"But will you stay?" Big brown eyes looked up at her.

"Who said I was leaving?"

"Papa," four voices chorused. And then, not to be left out, Isabella chimed in with a "Papa" of her own.

As if he knew they were talking about him, Mitch walked in, Uncle Frank by his side.

"What's this about me?" Mitch wore a smile, and Polly couldn't help but notice that he looked particularly handsome that morning. Freshly shaven, his cheeks were clear of stubble and rosy from whatever they'd been doing outside.

Polly squeezed her eyes shut, willing herself not to see him as an attractive man, but as her employer. Then she opened them and smiled. "Apparently, the children think I'm leaving."

"Well." He took off his hat and held it in his hands.

"They seem to want you to stay forever, and as I told them, you have your own life to live. There's going to be a time when you'll be moving on. I just want them to understand that forever isn't possible."

She watched as he fiddled with his hat, not making eye contact with her or the children.

Was he afraid that she was going to reject him after his note? Well, she was, of course, but it wasn't because she didn't care for him. After all, he was an incredible father who sacrificed so much for his children. But he was also a secretive man who seemed to dole out the truth at his leisure. Mitch claimed that he'd shared all his secrets, but what if there were more? What else was he hiding? And what would he hide from her if they did end up married?

Polly shook her head. It didn't matter. They weren't going down a romantic road. Attraction faded, and then what?

But perhaps… The children all looked at her wistfully. Was that what Mitch's note was really about? Not leaving the children?

With a smile, she turned to the children. "I've already told you. I'll stay as long as I'm needed. I have no definite plans for the future. You don't have to go to extraordinary lengths to keep me."

She gave Mitch a long, hard look. Did he understand that? He needn't feel obligated to romance her simply to keep her from leaving. Then she turned her attention back to the children.

"But I do appreciate how hard you've worked on your lessons today. If you keep applying yourselves with such diligence, I think we can organize another outing like we had yesterday very soon."

"Wahoo!" Rory's grin nearly split his face in two.

The rest of the children also looked pleased, but it was the freckle-faced boy's joy that warmed Polly's heart the most.

Mitch's sister-in-law, Iris, had warned Polly that Rory was the most difficult to handle. But the more time she spent with the boy, the more Polly realized that he simply had a great deal of exuberance to work out of his system, and an innate curiosity about nature's creatures. Iris had not been delighted with all of the insects, small creatures and the occasional snake Rory found, but once Polly had directed all that energy toward exploration and science, Rory seemed to blossom. He liked being outdoors, and Polly did what she could to encourage that love of nature.

"Can we go fishing again?" Rory's eyes sparkled. Usually, those sparks meant mischief, but Polly could see the genuine interest in them.

"If you can behave yourself and get all your schoolwork done this week." Polly smiled at him, then bent to look at his slate.

The handwriting was sloppy, but much more readable than what it had been when she'd first met him a few weeks ago. "Nice work," she said, handing it back to him, then giving a quick glance to the other children's work.

She looked up at Mitch, who stood in the doorway with Uncle Frank. "You should be very proud of them. Iris had told me the children were behind on their studies, but they are catching up quickly and I imagine that before long, you should have no trouble registering them to go to school."

"School?" Four voices sounded their horror in unison.

"Oh, no, we can't go to school," Clara said. "They don't like us at school."

"Isabella is too young for school," Louisa stated calmly, "and I'm too old."

"They don't let me bring these to school." Rory pulled a toad out of his pocket and held it up.

Polly grinned. "Of course Isabella won't go to school." She pointed at the slate, where Isabella had scribbled her name.

She looked over at the scowling Louisa. "And I know that you think you're too old for school, but Ma made us do our lessons until we were sixteen years old. It's a rough world we live in, and a woman needs to know how to read, write and do her arithmetic so she's not cheated dealing with the merchants out there. Not everyone is as honest as your father."

Her conscience nagged her as she said those last words. Though she spoke with confidence that Mitch was honest in his dealings, a part of her did doubt. Not that he'd lied to her, but once again, his reticence, though he'd tried to justify it, bothered her.

And that was why she wanted Louisa not to have to focus on raising her siblings but on being a child and getting an education. She needed to learn to think for herself, to do all the things a productive citizen did, so that when everything in her life fell apart, she had her own skills to fall back on.

Polly sighed. Her mother had worked too hard, for too long, but she'd always admired how Ma had the skills needed to support her family when her father couldn't. She didn't know what the future held for Louisa, but at least Polly would see her prepared.

"I'm not ready to send them to school yet," Mitch said slowly. "I wouldn't want them to receive any undue attention. If you can keep up with their studies, then I'm satisfied with the current arrangement."

"Of course I can." Polly relaxed slightly, not realizing how tense her shoulders had become. Of course Louisa would have an education. Mitch would see to that. She supposed her tension and stress had more to do with her own situation than worries about Louisa. A woman's lot in this world was hard, and respectability seemed to come at the price of one's freedom. But at least a woman could be equipped with a strong mind to carry her through.

"And she is quite capable," Uncle Frank chimed in. "I know they just opened a fine school here in Leadville, but I'm of the opinion that Polly will do just as good of a job, if not better, than those teachers."

Polly looked over to the doorway, where Uncle Frank still stood. She'd forgotten he'd come in with Mitch, and he stood expectantly, like his conversation with Mitch wasn't finished. Hopefully, it was good news about Mitch's case.

"She seems to be doing admirably with my children," Mitch said. "You'll be an asset to whichever school you end up at."

What was he talking about? How did a man leave a woman a love note one day, and the next, seem to be almost desperate to get rid of her?

"As I mentioned, I have no definite plans," Polly said smoothly. "However, even when all the children are old enough for school, if you decide to send them to school, I'm still here if you need me."

Then she looked at the children, her gaze resting on each of their faces for a moment, before moving on to the next. "I will always be there for you, no matter what. Even if we're in different places, you can write me letters, and visit, and anything you need, I am willing to do for you."

Her heart gave a funny dip as she turned back to face Mitch. "I mean that. I love the children dearly, and I wouldn't dream of abandoning them. No matter where life takes any of us, we're still family."

Then she looked over at Uncle Frank. "You taught me that. And I hope I've adequately passed that love on to the Taylor family as well."

"Indeed you have." Uncle Frank smiled broadly. "It's just as I was telling Mitch as we walked. Under God, we are all part of the same family, and we are obligated to love one another because we are all beloved children of God."

"God doesn't love us," Rory said, the defiant look returning to his face. "Nanny Peters said we were abominations, and she should know, because she grew up in a convent."

Polly wanted to call Nanny Peters an abomination, but she knew that Uncle Frank wouldn't like it. He'd have some comment about the nasty woman needing God's love just like the rest of us, but what Polly really wanted to do was slap her silly for making children believe such horrible things about themselves.

"Nanny Peters was wrong," Polly said quietly. "You are not abominations but children of God, and He loves you."

"Why would she say it if it wasn't true?" Rory stood, crossing his arms in front of him.

Mitch came around Polly and put his arm around her. "Because sometimes, we think we know things about God, and we think they're true, but they're not."

Keeping one arm around the back of Polly, Mitch pointed at Rory's slate. "See there? You've spelled friend *f-r-e-i-n-d*. You have the *e* and the *i* switched. You haven't properly learned how to spell it, so if your sister asked you, you'd tell her the incorrect spelling. But now that you know the correct spelling, you can give her the correct information. It's the same with God."

Uncle Frank laughed. "So true. And even I some-times misspell the things of God. I don't think any man can learn all of God's truth in his lifetime. But I sup-pose that's why we have eternity to spend it with Him."

Then Uncle Frank walked over to Rory and put his arm around him. "I'm so sorry that your former nanny told you something so hurtful about God. Sometimes the things we get wrong end up hurting others, and that makes God sad. But now that you know the truth, God is happy indeed."

Rory's brow furrowed. "But why would God love me? I'm bad. Everyone says so. Naughty Rory, the worst of the Taylor Terrors. That's what they all call me."

Polly's heart twisted as it squeezed her insides so tight she could barely breathe. Oh, she'd heard all the horrible things the children had been called, and how they saw themselves, but she thought they were mak-ing progress. She'd had no idea that all those names had formed their very identities.

"And even though they say he's the evil twin, they say I'm not much better," Clara said softly.

Louisa nodded. "We're all terrible. We did go to school for a while, but the mothers wouldn't let their children talk to us because they didn't want them to be influenced by our badness."

How could Polly's heart take any more? "You're not terrible. They just didn't understand."

Uncle Frank nodded and hugged Rory tighter to him. "God loves you, no matter how naughty you are. Any-one who says otherwise doesn't really know God."

Bending down so he was eye to eye with Rory, he said, "You're staying in my house, and I've watched you. And I'm telling you, anyone who says that you are terrible does not know who you are. You are not Naughty Rory, or the Taylor Terrors, but Rory of the Terrific Taylors and God loves you."

Beside her, Mitch sniffled, and Polly looked over to see he was weeping. She caught Uncle Frank's eye, and he nodded. Gently, Polly took Mitch by the hand and led him into Uncle Frank's study.

"I thought you might…need to talk." Polly looked at him, her heart aching at the tears running down his cheeks.

"How could I not know the kind of pain my children were in?"

"The same reason you didn't know what was going on with their mother. They thought they were protecting you."

He looked so lost, so despondent, that Polly couldn't help but put her arms around him. She held him as he sobbed, and she realized that the man before her, the man she was trying so desperately not to love, was absolutely broken. And the only way to make him, to make his family, whole again, was to give them all the love she had in her heart.

But how was she supposed to love him without falling in love with him?

Chapter Twelve

What was he thinking, coming unglued like that in Polly's arms? How had he turned into a weeping babe so easily?

God.

Mitch thought about how he'd spent the morning talking with Frank. There were so many things he hadn't understood about God's love, and yet, it didn't seem to matter. Not when he saw the impact it was having on his children. They hadn't needed to understand it to experience it, and, were Mitch to be so bold, be transformed by it.

He pulled away and looked at Polly, who wore such an expression of gentleness, he thought he might weep all over again.

"You've done the best you could," she said softly. "And now that you know what they've been through, you can do even better. The children love you, and you love them and that's all that matters."

"Thank you," he said, looking in her eyes and realizing that here, with her, was one of the safest places he'd ever known.

How could he be letting his guard down for someone

bound to leave? It didn't matter that she said she'd stay as long as she was needed. Ten months, ten years, it didn't matter. The point was, she was leaving. And even if she wasn't, Polly had made it perfectly clear that she had no intention of ever marrying or having children.

Perhaps the safest-feeling place was the most terrifying of all.

"You're welcome." She smiled at him, her expression lighting her face, making her more beautiful than Hattie at her finest.

The purity and innocence he saw in Polly was unlike anything he'd ever known. She was jaded, yes, but underneath, there was something else and it made her seem all the more beautiful.

Mitch shook his head. He couldn't keep thinking of her like this. Above all, he had to maintain his professional distance. Thoughts of the note he'd found on his bed last night drifted back to him. There'd been another one in his coat pocket this morning.

I love you was all it said.

Theoretically, it could have come from one of the children.

He took a deep breath. He should say something. But Polly seemed so happy, so…

It seemed like so much was going well with his family, and everyone was finally healing. Talking to Polly about the notes seemed premature at this stage, especially since he wasn't fully certain that she'd been the one sending them. Why stir things up when it wasn't necessary?

Sounds of a scuffle came from the kitchen. Polly let out a long sigh. "I should be getting back to the children. Will you be all right?"

"Yes. Your job is to take care of them, not me."

He used a more forceful tone than he'd intended, as the expression on Polly's face looked like he'd just thrown a glass of cold water at her.

"I was just trying to be a friend," she said stiffly, then turned to leave.

Mitch was about to stop her when he realized that if he did so, she might have reason to think that he had feelings for her beyond friendship. He shook his head. But he couldn't have her feeling hurt either.

"Of course you were," he said as she retreated. "But the children are more important."

She gave a quick nod, the only acknowledgment of his words as her pale blue skirt swished behind her as she left.

"You're doing just fine, son." Frank's voice came from the hallway, then he entered the room.

Doing just fine? Did Frank have any idea how much he struggled with his feelings for Polly? In doing the right thing, when he couldn't even be certain what the right thing was?

Mitch wasn't even sure how to answer that as the other man came over and clapped him on the shoulder. "You've been in a difficult situation, and I can't imagine how coping with your late wife's circumstances has burdened you. It's no surprise that even despite your best efforts, your children have suffered under that weight as well."

His circumstances. Mitch exhaled slowly. Frank wasn't talking about Polly at all. Clearly, Mitch's mind had been on the wrong things. Frank was right in drawing his attention back to the children. He'd allowed himself to get distracted, which wasn't a good thing when he had so much at stake.

The children were only a part of Mitch's larger worries.

"Do you know when Will is due back?"

The question was a deliberate change of subject, and recognition of that fact dawned across Frank's face.

"I haven't heard. Even with him taking the train, it's liable to be a few more days. But rest assured that he will do his best."

Frank shrugged. "We still have the power of prayer, and the Lord's will shall prevail. I know things seem hopeless right now, but I've been praying for you and your situation. We serve a big God Who can do mighty things."

Over the years, he'd had ladies come in to his store telling him that they'd pray for him for this and that, and usually he thought it was a nice sentiment that wouldn't do him any good, even though the women meant well. Hearing it come out of Frank's mouth, Mitch almost believed praying might actually get him results.

"Thank you," he said quietly. "I suppose I'm willing to accept God's help, should the Lord be willing to provide."

Frank clapped him on the back again. "And that's all we can do. Sometimes the reason we don't see the Lord in action is because we aren't open to receiving. So don't let worry over the situation trouble you. Will will return in good time, and then we can create a plan of action."

Mitch nodded slowly, hopeful that even though things didn't necessarily look the way he wanted them to, there was still the chance they would work out. Will was doing what he could, the children were progressing and for the first time in his life, Mitch felt like he had God on his side.

An eruption of laughter came from the kitchen, far

different from the conflict that had interrupted him and Polly earlier.

Frank grinned. "Ah, now that is a sound I always hope to have in my home. Laughter is so good for us all. Let's see what tomfoolery they've all gotten into. Perhaps we can join in."

The men walked into the kitchen, where they saw Polly standing in front of the children with a pot on her head.

"What is this about?" Frank chuckled as Polly turned to face them.

She grinned. "I was pretending to be a fine gentleman so they knew how to address me."

"Maddie won't like you using her pot," Frank said as she removed it from her head.

"I know, but we won't tell her, will we?" She winked as she put the pot back on the counter. "But now that we do have some fine gentlemen in the room, let's all practice how we will greet them, shall we?"

"Good day, sirs," the children chorused, sounding every bit as proper as those educated in the finest schools. The Taylor Terrors were no more.

Mitch looked over each of his children, one by one. The boys had their hair neatly combed, and the girls wore theirs in proper braids, with nary a strand out of place. They were clean, and their clothes all properly arranged, with no tears, misbuttoned buttons or anything amiss. Both Clara and Rory used to scream as though they were being murdered when forced to take a bath. And to get any of them to brush their hair?

Surely if his children could be so transformed, then so, too, could his life. The idea of being exonerated didn't seem so hopeless anymore. In only a few weeks, he'd seen enough positive change in his family that he could believe anything was possible.

Polly clapped her hands. "That was well done, everyone. I think you've all worked hard enough for now. Let's take a break. It's a nice day outside, so you may all go out and play. Just stay in the yard."

The children needed no further encouragement, as they got up from their seats and quietly walked to the door. Before Mitch could say anything, they were outside, laughing and carrying on. Once again, he marveled at how happy they sounded. The squabbling he'd resigned himself to had all but disappeared.

"How do you do it?" he asked, looking at Polly.

She'd gone over to the stove and was holding up a tea kettle. "Make tea? It's quite simple, really, and incredibly convenient on the Lassiters' stove. I quite despair of having to go back to a place without one."

Her eyes twinkled, and as he was about to protest, he realized she was teasing him.

"I'm assuming you mean the orderly way they left the room," Polly said with a grin. "That's simple. We've had several days where they did not leave in an orderly fashion, and they forfeited their time outside."

Then she came and sat at the table. "The children have spent years suffering punishments that don't fit the crime. I know how hard that can be, and I do my best to be kind and fair. They don't always like how things work out, but they know that in the end, I'm going to be just."

How could so many other nannies have not seen this? Not chosen to act in the children's best interests?

He stared at Polly. "Why weren't the other nannies able to do this for them?"

She shrugged. "Everyone has different philosophies

in raising children. Besides, in the past, the nannies were also acting on Hattie's instructions. You've given me freedom to care for them as I see fit."

Frank joined them at the table. "Now that is wisdom I needed to hear." He placed his hands over Polly's and looked at her with all the love of a father, even though he wasn't her father.

"I couldn't understand why you've been wanting to leave us, but now I do. You've been telling us all along that you want your freedom to make your own decisions. We thought we'd given you that, but I can see how we've been asking you to do it in the context of how we want things done. Mitch's children have blossomed. And I credit that to you, and using that freedom wisely."

Frank turned his gaze toward Mitch. "Thank you for giving Polly this opportunity. It's helped me see her far better than I ever have."

Polly's eyes welled up with tears as Frank brought his attention back to her. "You are an amazing woman, and I'm so proud of you. I'm sorry I wasn't giving you enough freedom in your obligations here."

Feeling like an intruder, Mitch started to push back in his chair to leave.

"Don't go," Frank said. "I know you and Polly have much to discuss."

Then he gave Mitch that same fatherly look. "You're struggling with the mistakes you've made with your children, but I want to be an example to you that we can't always get it right. All you can do is acknowledge where you've gone wrong and do your best to make it right."

Mitch nodded slowly, wishing he could wipe away

all the wasted years. The hurting years. He'd thought he'd done the right thing by his children, only…

"You've got to forgive yourself," Frank said, as if he was reading Mitch's thoughts.

As Polly got up, she touched Mitch's shoulder gently. "Uncle Frank is right. It's the only way to move on."

Passing Frank, she stopped and pressed a kiss to the top of his head. "And of course I forgive you. You were only looking out for my best interests. How can I fault you for that?"

Mitch watched as Polly went to the stove and retrieved the kettle of boiling water to make the tea. Her skilled hands mesmerized him. Though it was a common, everyday activity, Polly moved with such grace and fluidity, watching her was a pleasure.

"She is too good to me," Frank said, smiling. "I don't know what I would have done without her and Gertie after my Catherine died. I did the best I could to keep the ministry going, but Gertie's tireless efforts, along with Polly's assistance, helped me carry on. Annabelle was lost in her grief, and I couldn't reach her."

"There now," Polly said, setting the teapot on the table, along with a plate of sugar cookies. "We only did for you what you did for us. We had nothing when you and Catherine first came to the camps. But because of you, I could continue my education, and Ma found meaningful work that kept food on the table during lean times. We look out for each other, and when times are bad for one, the other picks up the slack. It's how it's done."

As she handed out the cups, she looked at Mitch. "The hospitality we show you is only the hospitality shown to us. I know you've felt guilty about taking so much, but we've been on the receiving end, just like you."

Her smile filled him with a sense of peace as he put Frank's words together with hers. They'd created a real community amongst themselves—a family. And somehow, Mitch had found himself adopted into it, even before he'd known how desperately he'd needed them.

The only trouble was, when Polly's hands brushed his while she poured the tea, he didn't think of her as a sister.

Polly tried to relax as they sat in the kitchen, enjoying their tea. But with Mitch, she felt on edge. Uncertain as to how to behave. There'd been another note in her apron pocket, one that said, "You're beautiful."

He was staring at her again, with that funny look on his face. Was he thinking about how beautiful he thought she was? She ought to say something, but what?

Polly sipped her tea, trying to focus on the delicate flavor rather than these troubling thoughts. Her conversation with Mitch had been all about encouraging him as a father and letting him know that the welcome he received here was the welcome they'd give anyone.

If only her heart raced like this for everyone.

Oh, how she wished she could find something to make them joke and smile about. Something to ease this strange tension in the room.

Was it wrong to hope the children would come inside and need her for something?

Uncle Frank watched her like he knew there was something on her mind but wasn't sure if he should ask her about it. If he did, she could hardly tell him the truth. But she also couldn't lie.

"Well," he said slowly. "I suppose I have a sermon

to prepare. They don't write themselves. I'm sure you two have plenty to discuss."

Polly stared at him. "Do we? That's the second time you've referenced Mitch and me needing to discuss something."

Then she turned her attention to Mitch. "Unless there's something I don't know about."

The blank expression on his face made Polly feel a little better, especially when she caught the sheepish look on Uncle Frank's face. Surely he wasn't in matchmaking mode.

Uncle Frank coughed. "No, I just thought, you know…it's always good to have a chance to talk without the children around."

"I'm fairly certain we've covered everything we need to," Polly said, settling into her chair with her cup of tea. A quick glance at the clock told her that she only had a few more minutes of peace before she'd need to gather the children again. She'd promised them they could help Maddie bake cookies, and Maddie would be home from helping at the mission soon.

She settled back and closed her eyes, enjoying the sweet silence, knowing it wouldn't last long. The squeak of the floorboards told her that Uncle Frank had gone to his office to catch up on his sermon preparation. Though she could feel Mitch's presence, he remained silent, seemingly content to enjoy the stillness as she did.

Polly could have fallen asleep but for the soft ticking of the clock reminding her that there wasn't much time left in her short break. She opened her eyes to see Mitch staring at her.

"Sorry. Is something amiss?"

"Not at all." He smiled easily, almost rakishly, sending a tiny jolt to Polly's heart. "You just looked so peaceful sitting there, and I realized that the children have kept you incredibly busy. You haven't had any time off since you took the post."

Naturally. Polly blinked several times to clear the sleep out of her eyes and the fog out of her brain. The notes she'd been finding were clearly addling her mind. Mitch was thinking of her merely as an employee, of caring for her, of doing the right thing. As a human being, not a suitor.

But if he'd been leaving the notes...

She searched his face for any sign of his feeling something more. Of wanting there to be more between them. She found none.

"I haven't minded. Extenuating circumstances and all that. I'm sure when your situation has calmed down, we can make up for it." She adopted as pleasant of an expression as she could muster, ignoring the odd pang in her heart over his focus on his duty.

"Still, it's not right. You may not mind, but I've taken advantage of you dreadfully. Tomorrow you'll have a day off."

She stared at him. "But what about the children? Who will mind them?"

Mitch shrugged. "I will. It will do us some good to spend time together as a family."

How could she argue with his logic? And yet, being parted from the children, even for one day, didn't feel right.

"Are you sure you can manage?"

He gave a small chuckle. "Yes, I think I can manage. I've learned a lot in a few days, and even if I don't get everything exactly right, everything will be all right."

And then he stopped. Looked as though he were in

deep thought. Then smiled, a long satisfied expression spreading across his face.

"Yes. I do believe everything will be all right."

Turning his gaze to Polly, he said, "Thanks to you and Frank, I'm confident that no matter what happens, everything really will be all right. You have no idea how much this means to me."

His sincerity made Polly feel guilty for even suspecting him of having ulterior motives. Mitch was just trying to deal with a bad situation and was appreciative of all the help he'd received from Polly. Nothing more.

All the more reason for her to keep focused on the children, not the way the light from the window shone against his blond hair. Handsome is as handsome does, her mother used to tell her, and right about now, she had to keep that advice in mind. The trouble was, Mitch was just as handsome on the inside as he was on the outside.

The back door banged open.

"Papa! You're still here!" Clara ran into the room and jumped onto her father's lap.

Rory and Thomas soon followed, and Polly's heart delighted in seeing the children with their father.

"Why haven't you gone to work at Uncle Andrew's store?" Rory asked, his question not trying to get rid of his father so much as it was finding out why he was home.

In an earlier conversation, Mitch had told Polly that he often worked long hours. He'd left his own store in the care of trusted employees in Denver, but even upon coming to Leadville, he'd found solace in working in his brother's store.

At least until crowds had gathered, wanting information on the accused murderer in their midst.

"As it turns out, Uncle Andrew doesn't need my help. And I'd much rather spend the time with you."

Polly caught the wistful expression in Mitch's eyes. He'd wanted to do something to help his brother out, but his presence had only made for bad business. She'd overheard Uncle Frank telling him that he'd see what he could do to encourage parishioners to visit Taylor's Mercantile and shop as they normally would to help detract from the unwanted attention.

But knowing that Mitch was an honorable man, it had to be hard to sit back and do nothing, which is exactly what both Uncle Frank and Will had told him. The fact that he listened to them, well, Polly had to admit that it raised her estimation of him. Wisdom and the ability to take advice was a rare thing in folks these days, so she admired Mitch having both.

Isabella had crawled into Polly's lap, her favorite place to be when she wasn't running around with the others. Absently, Polly rubbed the little girl's back, enjoying the rhythm. Isabella snuggled closer to her.

"She's really taken to you, hasn't she?" Mitch's voice rumbled over her, warm like the cup of tea she'd just finished, only it heated her to a depth that made everything feel right with the world.

"She has." Polly stroked the dark curls, untangling the mess that never seemed to behave. Isabella had already fallen asleep.

"It's a wonder—that girl can sleep anywhere."

Polly smiled as she looked down on the dark lashes resting against velvety skin. Her mother used to say that she loved her babies so much that she thought her heart would burst. So what did it mean when you felt that way about a little girl who wasn't even your own?

"She's had to learn." Polly looked up and smiled at

Louisa. "Louisa told me that none of the children have ever had regular nap times. To them, nap time was what the nannies gave them when they were fed up with the children's antics. To even suggest a nap to any of the children means that they've done something wrong."

Weaving her fingers through Isabella's hair to get out a few more tangles, Polly continued. "But the little ones need the sleep, and so with Isabella, she's learned to sleep whenever and wherever she feels tired. If you suggest a nap to her, she'll scream and throw a fit. But if you give her a safe and loving place to sleep, she'll drift off easily."

Polly had learned that one the hard way the first day she cared for the children. She'd tried to get Isabella to take a nap, and the little girl had screamed and thrown things every time Polly closed her in the room. She'd finally given up and let Isabella sit quietly with her. Isabella had fallen asleep within minutes.

"Mrs. Abernathy used to lock her in the closet to get her to nap," Louisa said, coming to stand behind Polly. "So I would find Isabella little places to hide. If Mrs. Abernathy found her, and she was asleep, she'd let Isabella stay there, and she wouldn't have to go to the closet."

Though Louisa had already apprised Polly of that fact, it didn't make the ache in her heart any less than the first time she'd heard it. Not just for poor little Isabella, who was the sweetest child imaginable, but also for Louisa, who'd had to search for creative ways to protect her siblings.

"I'm sorry," Mitch said quietly. "I didn't know. I wish you'd told me sooner."

He looked at Polly, then at Louisa, his face long and drawn. "I understand why you were afraid to tell me about the things your previous nannies did, but from now on, when something bad happens, you have to tell me right away. I won't tolerate any of you suffering further mistreatment."

Clearing his throat, he brought his attention to Polly. "No offense to you, of course. I'm sure you'd never mistreat my children, but I want them to feel safe in coming to me."

Before Polly could answer, Clara piped up. "Of course Polly wouldn't do anything to hurt us. That's why we want her to be our mother. Papa, you'd better marry her before someone else figures out what a great catch she is and snatches her away from us."

Polly clamped her free hand over her mouth to keep from laughing. A muffled sound escaped through her nose, but fortunately, the children were more focused on their father's response than hers.

"Yeah, Papa, you hafta marry Polly. Why, if you don't marry her, when I grow up, I will." Rory turned and gave Polly a huge grin and a wink.

After a refreshing deep breath, Polly smiled at her charges. "That's very sweet, and I appreciate the sentiment, but I don't want to get married."

"But Papa needs a wife, and we need a mother," Clara stated, squaring off with her hands on her hips.

Oh, dear. Clara, Rory and Thomas looked indignant that they were offering Polly the opportunity of a lifetime and she wasn't interested. Louisa remained silent, but she stared at Polly with those intense, dark eyes, enough that she knew the girl was very interested in Polly's response to the question.

"Your father isn't even out of mourning yet," Polly said carefully. "And as I've told you before, I'll always be here for you. I don't need to be your mother to love and care for you."

Clara's eyes flashed. "What happens when you do get married and have your own children? Then you won't love us anymore, now will you?"

Jealousy and possessiveness were good signs. They meant that the children were bonding to Polly and cared for her. Having not learned how to properly deal with emotions, it was understandable that they'd feel insecure. But that wasn't an explanation they'd understand.

"I will always love you," Polly said, pressing a kiss to the top of a still-sleeping Isabella's head. "As for my getting married and having children, I don't want to get married—ever. I promise you'll always have me here."

The back door opened, and Maddie entered, Polly's mother in tow.

"Is it time to bake cookies?" Rory asked, his stomach taking precedence over his heart.

"It certainly is," Maddie told him. "Now go wash up. All of you."

Then she looked at Polly. "Except you, of course. Seems to me you have a little one to put down for her nap. You take care of your business, and I'll deal with the children."

"Thank you." Polly stood, carefully balancing Isabella so she wouldn't wake. She cast a look over at Mitch to see how he was handling the children's desire for them to marry, but Thomas was already tugging at his hand to take him out back to the pump so they could wash.

It was just as well. They had the children to take care of, not their relationship to sort out. Even though the children had a marked interest in how things went, they would have to figure out together how to handle it, to put on a united front. Perhaps tonight, after the children went to bed.

Polly left the kitchen and started up the stairs.

"Polly?"

She turned to see that her mother had followed her. "Yes?"

Ma wore a concerned expression. "I'm worried that you keep saying you're never going to get married. Your heartbreak—"

"Has nothing to do with my decision." Polly shifted the sleeping child in her arms. "I know you all mean well, but the truth is, I'd decided not to marry long ago. For a moment, I found a beau who turned my head, yes, but he merely served to prove all the reasons why I didn't want to get married in the first place."

"What are you talking about? There are plenty of reasons for you to marry."

Polly sighed. "I've seen too many things go wrong in marriage for me to ever want that for myself."

Ma's brow furrowed in confusion. "Like what?"

Like all the things Polly didn't want to say to her mother and hurt her feelings.

"It doesn't matter." She shifted Isabella's weight again. "I need to put her down."

But Ma followed her up the stairs, waiting outside her bedroom door until Polly had put Isabella down. Polly's stomach twisted. She didn't want to have this conversation with her mother.

"It does matter," Ma said quietly. "I've let you rant about how you think men are worthless, and I've heard your comments about not respecting men and I've let them go, thinking you were speaking out of a broken heart. I'd hoped that you only needed some time to heal your wounds. So if that's not what's going on, then I'd like some answers. Because I did not raise you this way."

"Yes you did." Polly kept her voice low. "I've seen how Pa treated you. The whiskey on his breath, the perfume from cavorting with other women. And the women in camp, as well as the ones we've helped over the years. What tales do they have to tell? The same woe over and over. Men who drink, cheat and do all sorts of horrible things. I learned that men can't be trusted, and while there may be a few honorable men out there, it's a sin to gamble. I won't be risking my heart only to find several years later that he's just like all the rest."

Tears ran down her mother's cheeks. "Is that what you think of me, then?"

Polly shook her head. "Not you. You have been honorable and faithful and loving, even when he didn't deserve it. I respect that. But I will not find myself saddled with a man who is not honorable, faithful and loving to me."

"You don't understand… I never said a word against your father. Why would you think…"

"The walls are thin at camp. You don't think you and Pa woke us up at night with your arguing? And even when you didn't argue, I could smell him just as well as you. You didn't have to say a word to me. I already knew."

The ache in her heart deepened as she realized that her mother and Mitch probably had a lot in common. Both had remained silent about their suffering for years because they hadn't wanted to hurt their children.

"Oh, Polly…" More tears ran down her mother's face. "I wish you had told me. There's so much you don't understand."

"I understand plenty."

"No, you don't." Her mother shook her head, then dabbed at her face with her handkerchief.

"Yes, your father did have a drinking problem. But over the past few years, Frank has guided him in overcoming it with the Lord's help." Ma let out a long sigh. "And yes, your father strayed. It was the most difficult thing I'd ever experienced. I'm sorry you heard us fighting about it."

Ma's voice quivered, and Polly hated herself for even bringing it up. She'd been avoiding this topic precisely for that reason. She hadn't wanted to hurt her mother.

"As your father dealt with his problems, and as he let the Lord work in his heart, he repented of his sins. And we repaired our marriage. Caitlin was the result."

She smiled softly as she looked at Polly. "Didn't it ever occur to you as being odd that she was born so late in our marriage? So long after Angus? Things were better, and Caitlin came along."

Polly tried to look back and see the happiness that her mother alluded to, but there were still pieces of the story that didn't make sense. "He still came home reeking of perfume and drink. Why, he's even been fired for being drunk since Caitlin's birth."

She hated to call her mother a liar, but she also couldn't understand why her mother would cling to this fantasy.

"True, true," her mother said, sighing. "Your father has always fought his biggest battles against the bottle. But he's stayed sober the past couple of years, and for that I'm grateful."

Then her mother smiled. "As for the perfume, your father would go to places of ill repute, not for the sake of partaking in the services, but because he, along with

Frank, was trying to help the women find a way out. And, I think, to help the men see that there was a better way."

She gave a shrug, but concern still filled her face. "I wish you'd just talked to me about all of this. Your father would be terribly hurt to know you thought so little of him. He's made his mistakes, true, but he's also doing everything he can to help other men avoid them."

Polly found she couldn't even process her mother's words. She'd been wrong, all this time?

"How could I have not known?" she said slowly.

"You were young. Having fun with Annabelle. And then Catherine died, and things weren't the same. You were so caught up in your own world that you didn't notice all the other things happening around you."

Then her mother sighed again. "And to be honest, I was so busy taking care of things, and I didn't realize that's what you thought. I just assumed…"

Green eyes stared at Polly. "I suppose we both assumed a lot of things, and that we knew each other's minds and what was going on, when we should have talked about it. I'm sorry. But I hope, now that we've cleared things up, that you will rethink some of the vows you've made based on faulty information."

She hated the way it felt like her mother could see into her. Could tell how deeply Polly struggled with the knowledge that everything she'd believed to be true wasn't. Worse, she hated that the deeper kinship she felt with the Taylor children was all based on the same thing. They'd tried so desperately to protect a loved one but had only ended up hurting them instead.

"I'm sorry, too," Polly said quietly. "I truly never meant to hurt anyone."

"It seems you've mostly just hurt yourself." Ma paused, looking deep in thought for a few moments.

"But I think it would do you some good to spend some time getting to know your pa. He's a good man, and you've vilified him long enough in your own mind that I don't think you see it. He's not perfect, but then, none of us are. Still, despite all the bad times, all the sorrows, I'm glad that I married him."

Ma's words tore Polly's heart in two. She'd seen how the Taylor children had suffered, and she'd been able to relate. And yet, the situation was so different. Because now that Polly had found the courage to discuss the issues that had been bothering her, she'd found that she'd been wrong about her father all along. She'd fought for the Taylor children to have a strong relationship with their father because she'd wished she could have had a father she could have a relationship with.

The trouble was, it was Polly's own fault that it hadn't happened.

Chapter Thirteen

Polly's day off dawned the way the previous day had: realizing, with a start, that she'd slept later than she'd intended. Only today, there was no rush to tend the children. Which felt strangely empty.

Odd, since she'd spent a good portion of the night crying, praying and reading her Bible. Her mother's revelations had shaken Polly's entire foundation, and yet, when she read her Bible, she found it shaken even more. All this time, she'd been trusting herself and her instincts to guide her in life, and she hadn't bothered to trust in the Lord. Oh, she trusted Him in all sorts of other things, but in following the direction of her life, and in finding her life's calling, she'd boldly gone forward, figuring she knew best.

Only she hadn't known at all.

The bedroom door opened, and the sound of giggles greeted her before she saw their smiling faces.

"Good morning, Polly," Clara chimed, as the children walked in.

Louisa carried a tray with breakfast on it, and Isabella and the boys each held flowers.

"We wanted to do something special for you on your

day off, so you knew how much we appreciated you," Louisa said.

"Papa suggested we bring you breakfast." Rory grinned as he handed her the flowers.

Thomas gave a gap-toothed smile as he handed her another bouquet. "He didn't come up because he said it wouldn't be 'propriate."

"Thomas! You've lost a tooth!" Polly ruffled his hair as she accepted his gift.

"Rory helped me pull it out."

Polly couldn't help but smile as she imagined how that would have happened.

Isabella climbed onto the bed and snuggled against her, still holding tight to her flowers.

"Isabella," Clara said. "You're supposed to give those to Polly."

Isabella gave Clara a cross look.

"It's all right," Polly said, squeezing Isabella to her. "I have plenty. Let Isabella enjoy these."

Louisa set the tray in front of her. Simple fare, eggs, toast and a cup of tea, but it looked delicious.

"Thank you so much, everyone. And please thank your father for the lovely idea."

"Oh, but there's more," Clara said, pointing to an envelope on the tray. "You have a note."

Polly picked up the note and read it. *Join me for a picnic this afternoon. Maddie will watch the children.*

She closed her eyes. Mitch. A picnic. Alone. It was easy to tell herself that Mitch only wanted to discuss the children. But the hopeful looks in their eyes told her that it wasn't going to be so simple.

And how could it be simple? Yesterday she'd had good reasons for not giving in to the feelings she felt for

Mitch. She'd told herself that happiness wouldn't last, and that men ultimately showed their true colors, and…

Grief filled her chest once more.

How could she possibly begin to make up for all that she'd lost? All she'd missed out on?

Was she even ready to give in to her feelings, knowing how they'd already led her so far astray?

"Please say you're going," Clara said, earnest eyes staring brightly at her.

Lord, please help me. Of all the things Polly had learned over the past day, she was finished with relying on herself and trying to do it on her own.

What was the right thing to do in this situation?

"Papa will be terribly disappointed if you don't," Louisa said. She looked so poised and so much more than her twelve years would have indicated. Polly looked at her, wondering how her twelve-year-old self would have handled the situation.

If her pa had died, leaving her ma alone, would Polly have pushed her mother toward a more honorable man?

The difference was that Louisa's mother was everything Louisa had thought her to be, and more. Polly's father?

Polly sighed. At twelve, she'd thought it terribly unfair that her father would be gone for days on end, come home smelling of women and drink, and they'd been stuck in that tiny cabin with a fussy Caitlin.

And she'd been wrong, horribly wrong.

As she searched Louisa's face, Polly couldn't help but wonder what Louisa was thinking in all of this. How much was based in the maturity of life and how much in her own imagination?

"Please, Polly!" Now the boys had taken to begging.

The children wanted so desperately for her to become their new mother, but they barely knew her. And, it seemed, she barely knew herself.

Four pairs of earnest eyes stared at her, and if Polly looked down, she'd find a fifth.

It was just a picnic, she reminded herself.

Picnics didn't lead to marriage.

Nor did she have to decide her entire life based on one outing.

"Of course I'll go," she said slowly, hoping it was the right decision. Why couldn't God have written the answer in the note for her?

"Wonderful!" Louisa said, walking over to Polly's closet. "We must find you something beautiful to wear. Papa loves yellow, but I think it would be a dreadful color on you, but pink suits you. Where is that dress you wore to church on Sunday? I'm sure it will be suitable."

Clara and Louisa rifled through Polly's closet. The boys had already gotten bored and wandered off. It seemed all they'd needed for reassurance was Polly's agreement in the matter.

"Girls," Polly said slowly. "Your father and I aren't courting. It's lovely for you to think that I would make a good mother, but he and I haven't even discussed it. There's nothing romantic between us."

"But there could be," Louisa told her firmly as she held out Polly's new Sunday dress. "Wear this. If I learned anything from my mother, it's how to be irresistible to a man."

Polly shook her head. "I don't want to be irresistible to your father. He's a nice man, but he's also my employer. I'm sure this picnic is nothing more than him wanting to catch me up on things without little ears to hear."

"I've seen the way he looks at you. We used to go

to the theater with our mother for her to show us off, and men would fall all over themselves to be near my mother. That's how Papa looks at you."

Clara made an exasperated noise. "No he doesn't. He looks at her like she's chocolate cake. And everyone knows how much Papa loves chocolate cake."

Polly knew she probably shouldn't, but she giggled. Maddie had given them all chocolate cake one night as a treat for dessert, and Mitch had acted like a schoolboy on Christmas morning for all the joy it seemed to bring him. She'd made a mental note to be sure Maddie baked it for his birthday.

But now…to be compared to that same cake…her stomach fluttered. "I'm sure you misunderstood."

The two girls groaned, and Louisa shook the dress. "You should still wear this."

Isabella tugged at Polly's nightdress. "Pwetty," she said, pointing to the dress Louisa held up.

"Now," Clara said, sounding like a much older girl. "Finish your breakfast so we can get you ready for your big day."

Polly sighed. Even though she felt the children's previous nannies were too easily intimidated by them, she couldn't deny that the children knew how to make things happen—their way.

She managed to eat her breakfast and get dressed according to the children's plan, all the while trying to determine what God's plan was in all of this.

And even though she'd had time to read her Bible before heading out on her expedition, Polly still wasn't any closer to answers when she arrived at the livery to meet Mitch to go to the picnic spot. Mitch hadn't arrived yet, which should have given her time to collect herself, only it served to make the butterflies dance in her stomach even more.

What if Mitch didn't come?

What if this was one of the children's famous pranks? They'd only done minor things to Polly, and that was only in the first days. Once she'd earned their trust, they hadn't tried anything else. They'd even told her about their tricks to drive former nannies away.

Setting the nanny up romantically with their father? Now that was something the children hadn't done. And surely they wouldn't do such a thing, not in malice anyway.

But out of the misguided notion that they needed a new mother?

The trouble with sorting out her own heart in the matter was that it wasn't just about her and Mitch, but five other delicate hearts that had already been broken.

What was she to do?

Mitch strode into the livery, looking puzzled for a moment, but his face brightened when he saw Polly.

"What's this about a picnic? I thought today was your day off."

Polly stared at him. "I thought you invited me."

Then they looked at each other and laughed. "The children."

"Well, that settles that," Polly said, brushing her skirts. "I should have asked more questions about the mysterious note, but I'd taken it in good faith that they wouldn't..."

She sighed. "Well, all right. I had my suspicions. But it's so hard to know the right thing to do and not disappoint them."

Mitch grinned. "They are masters at the game. If I weren't trying to raise them to do the right thing in life, they would make excellent traveling salesmen, peddling wares of questionable origin."

"Mitch!"

"It's true, I'm afraid. They get that from their mother. She could sell a bear a new fur coat without even trying. Their persuasiveness can be a good thing, as long as they learn the difference between persuasion and manipulation."

He took off his hat and held it in his hands as he looked at her solemnly. "And in your case, I'm so sorry that they've manipulated you. I suppose none of us are impervious to their charms."

"It's not your fault. I should have just come to you when I started getting the notes. I just didn't want to embarrass anyone."

Or herself, but Polly didn't want to say that. Obviously, she'd been a fool for thinking that there was anything between her and Mitch. Or that Mitch could feel anything for her.

His cheeks colored slightly. "I guess we're both guilty, then, because I'd been getting notes as well. I didn't want to make things awkward by talking to you about them, so I just tossed them in the fire."

At least the mystery was solved. But Polly wanted to kick herself for letting the thought of those notes occupy so much of her time.

Mitch held up the picnic basket. "So what should we do with this, then?"

"I'm surprised you even brought it."

He shrugged. "I wasn't going to, but then I thought that perhaps you only wanted to meet so that we could talk about the children alone and the picnic was just an excuse."

Something warm shone in his eyes, and he gave her

a small smile. "Plus, I would have felt bad leaving you all alone. I'd been rehearsing a speech all the way here to let you down gently. I may not want to marry you, but I definitely value having you in my life."

Small comfort, she supposed, since she wasn't sure she wanted to marry him. Except she hadn't expected it to sting so much when he said he didn't want to marry her.

"The feeling is mutual." She gave a smile as if to show they were both on the same page, but it didn't feel right. It felt fake, forced and completely unlike what Polly felt inside.

Which was ridiculous, considering she hardly knew her own mind on matters these days, let alone what the Lord wanted for her. Clearly, based on Mitch's speech, a relationship with Mitch was not it.

Mitch lifted the end of the cloth covering the top of the basket. "It does smell good, though. It couldn't hurt to go on a picnic, could it? We could discuss how we're going to handle the situation with the children."

Then he paused, looking dejected. "I'm sorry, it's your day off. I shouldn't impose on your time. I'll go home and let the children know that their trick didn't work and that they need to get this ridiculous notion out of their minds."

And now it was Polly's turn to feel bad about the whole situation.

"No. I don't mind. I understand there are some of Maddie's tarts in that basket, and it would be a shame to let them go to waste. Besides," Polly said, smiling at him, "I didn't have any plans for the day beyond stopping by the mission and saying hello to everyone."

She had to remind herself that it meant nothing when Mitch's eyes lit up. Merely an employer being grateful that his children's antics hadn't spoiled everything, and that there were no hard feelings.

"Let me take that, and you can see to our buggy," Polly said, reaching for the basket.

Their hands met and for a moment, Polly caught a spark that traveled all the way up her arm and when she looked into Mitch's eyes, she could tell that he felt it too.

Or was that her mind playing tricks on her again?

Mitch tried telling himself that the spark he'd felt when he'd handed the basket off to Polly meant nothing. And as he took the reins of the horses, he forced himself to banish the image of the sparkle in her eyes from his mind.

At least he knew now that the notes hadn't been from her. More of the children's trickery, which he would deal with severely when he got home. He'd make sure they understood in no uncertain terms that people's hearts were not things to be trifled with.

Polly met him at the front of the livery, basket in her arms and a smile on her face. Truly, if he had been looking for a wife, he couldn't go wrong with Polly MacDonald. Except, of course, that she didn't want to be a wife, and that's where nothing romantic could ever happen between them.

She wore a pretty pink dress, with the lace edging the women in his store had gone mad to have, and unlike many of the women he saw sporting the fashion, he found it suited her. There was something very lovely about how the delicate lace trimming her collar framed her face. No one would suspect that underneath the exterior of the tiny woman with such gentle features, lay such an indomitable spirit.

Admiring Polly's outer beauty was no chore for the

eyes, but he found that the more he saw into her heart, the more difficult it was to keep his own heart from becoming entangled. The cliché of the things inside a person being what counted had never proven itself to be more true than with Polly.

How could he fault her for wanting to protect his feelings? For wanting to do right by his children. Everything about her oozed love, and her compassion made him want to...

Stop it, he told himself sternly. He'd come on this picnic to make things right between them, not make them more uncomfortable. Which is exactly what he'd be doing if he kept mooning over a woman he could never have.

He assisted Polly into the carriage, trying not to notice how much he enjoyed the feel of her hand in his, even if it was just for a moment.

These things were best not dwelled upon.

Once they were on their way, he said, "Do you have any ideas as to how we should deal with the children on this? I admit, my first reaction was anger, and I know that's the wrong thought."

He smiled at her. "But really! They shouldn't have trifled with your heart."

"Or yours," Polly said quietly. "But they're children, and they can't possibly understand the consequences of meddling with people's hearts. They think they know a good many things about love and romance, but in truth, they have no idea what real love is."

Good point, but Mitch wasn't even sure he knew what real love was. After all, he'd been duped into marriage and forced to remain in that marriage to protect his children. The only love he could rightly speak of was that of a father for his children, and even then, he felt woefully unable, given his inability to see what had been happening to them.

"So what do we do?"

He glanced at her, noting the thoughtful expression on her face and appreciating once more that Polly was a woman of depth and compassion.

Finally, she spoke. "I think we need to be honest with them. I've tried explaining to them that there isn't anything romantic between us and that I will always be there for them, but perhaps if we come to them together and let them know that we're on to them, they'll finally understand."

Polly's idea sounded so much more optimistic than the thoughts in his head. He'd reasoned with them multiple times over the years, but it seemed that when they got a thought into their heads, they wouldn't let go.

"I'm not so sure…" Mitch decided that sharing his experience was the best option. "If they're convinced that you're the one to be their new mother, nothing is going to stop them until they get their way."

Polly made a small noise in the back of her throat. Her expression was more thoughtful, and he decided it was best to give her a few moments to think. Besides, he needed to keep his focus on the horses. They were driving through a narrow canyon now, almost to the mining camp and the picnic spot Polly had brought them to before.

He glanced over at Polly, who seemed too lost in thought to pay much attention to the scenery. Thanks to her, one of his biggest problems—dealing with the children—seemed almost nonexistent. Sure, they still had to figure out how to keep the children's matchmaking machinations at bay, but that seemed simple compared to everything else he'd worried about with them.

If only his other problems were so easily solved.

As they pulled up to the picnic spot, Polly finally spoke. "I think the key to dissuading the children is for us to spend as little time together as possible. They seem to think there's something between us, and the more we're together, the more it makes think it's true."

Mitch frowned. "What makes you think that?"

"How much time did you spend interacting with the children while their previous nannies were present?"

As he thought about the answer, he understood her point. "Our picnic the other day was definitely not something I've ever done with another nanny."

"Exactly." She wore the same calm expression as she always did in working with the children, and part of him hated that she was using it on him now.

"Even though there are any number of reasons for the fact that you're spending more time with us than you have with other nannies, the only reason they can see is that it must be romantic."

"Are you saying I shouldn't spend time with my children, then?" The words stung in his mouth and pained him to even let them come out.

"No." She appeared to consider her words for a moment. "But I think we have to find some way of trading off. When you want to be with the children, then I'll go find something else to do. When it's time for their lessons, then you should make yourself scarce."

Her logic was sound, and yet he didn't like her words. He and Polly made a great team, allowing the children to have plenty of attention and love.

"We work so well together. You have a knack for keeping the younger children occupied while I spend time with the older children and vice versa."

Polly nodded slowly. "The children say you look at me like I'm chocolate cake."

Mitch closed his eyes. Had he been so obvious in his attraction to her?

"I meant no offense," he said carefully.

"I know. But the children aren't good at understanding subtleties and nuances, and what was probably a very innocent expression on your part, they took to be romantic."

"I see." Mitch parked the buggy, then helped Polly out.

She didn't say anything else, but she didn't need to. Her words had given him more than enough food for thought, and further conversation between them seemed to be almost pointless.

They shared their picnic lunch, carefully exchanging pleasantries as Polly updated him on the children's progress with their lessons. They were bright, all of them, but that didn't surprise Mitch in the least. What did surprise him, however, was that when Polly opened the container holding their desserts—two tarts and a large slab of chocolate cake—he found that the chocolate cake held no pleasure for him.

Well, that wasn't entirely true. He would have enjoyed the cake, savored it, even, had it not been for the fact that now, thanks to his children, he'd never be able to look at a piece of chocolate cake without thinking about how much he wished things could be different with Polly.

They didn't linger after they ate but quickly packed up and returned to town, a new distance between them. Mitch tried telling himself it was best for the children this way, but he found he couldn't swallow the lie. Even on the short ride home, he missed the easy camaraderie with Polly.

If he could say the one thing that had been missing from his courtship with Hattie, the one thing that, looking back, he wished he'd realized, it was how little he truly enjoyed her company. He'd been enamored of her, and yet, he couldn't say for certain that he'd ever actually liked her.

With Polly, it was different. He liked her. And the more time he spent with her, the more he liked her and the more attractive he found her.

Which was why the hopelessness of them ever being together seemed all the more cruel. He couldn't act on his feelings for her because it might scare her away. Or worse, she might choose to stay, and grow to resent him because of it.

When they arrived home, it was a blessing to leave the tension of being with her but not being able to be with her. They'd lost something very precious on the picnic, but Polly was right. For the sake of the children, it was the right thing to do. It wasn't fair to them to hold on to hopes of their marriage if such a thing were not possible.

But as soon as they walked up to the porch, the door flew open, and an excited chorus demanded, "So? Are you getting married?"

He didn't even have to look at Polly to know that her expression screamed "I told you so."

"No, we are not," Mitch said calmly, watching the excitement fizzle out of them like a fire doused with a bucket of water. "In fact, I am very disappointed in all of you for setting this whole thing up. There is nothing romantic between Polly and me, and there never will be. You must stop this nonsense of wanting her to be your mother immediately. If I find any more notes, there will be consequences."

Mitch had no idea what the consequences would be, and he wasn't sure if he was glad for it or not. The children delighted in finding ways around punishment, and they always tested the rules. But as he examined their crestfallen faces, he hoped that this was one situation they would not challenge.

He couldn't afford the heartbreak otherwise.

Chapter Fourteen

The children seemed to accept Mitch's edict about no more matchmaking, at least in terms of his not finding any more notes. However, they had taken to making sure that in every conversation, at least one of them mentioned needing a mother, or wanting Polly to be their mother. In fact, life at the Lassiter house had fallen into a neat routine. He and Polly were polite to each other, and though he missed the camaraderie they'd shared, the children also seemed to sense the distance between them.

Chocolate cake indeed.

Mitch was shaking his head as he exited the church, pleased that no one at the Sunday service seemed to know who he was, or anything about his scandal.

"Excuse me? Are you Mitch Taylor?"

Mitch sighed as he turned around. He shouldn't have even thought it.

A pretty young blonde, younger than Polly, with a bright smile greeted him.

"I'm Helena Jenkins. I help out in the Sunday school."

Mitch closed his eyes and said a quick prayer. At

least the poor girl didn't appear to be doused in anything.

She gnawed at her lip, as though she was struggling to come up with the right words to say.

"It's all right," Mitch said, giving her his most encouraging smile. "I'm sure that whatever you have to tell me about my children won't surprise me."

After all, there wasn't much worse they could do after that time they set a previous nanny on fire. Granted, it had been an accident, and the only damage was to the nanny's skirt, where the children had dropped a candle, but in the retelling amongst society, it had turned into something worse.

Helena's face scrunched up slightly and her shoulders rose and fell as she sighed. "I'm a little concerned about their prayer request."

Prayer request?

Mitch stared at her. "I don't understand."

"When we asked the class for prayer requests, they asked us all to pray that they would get a new mother. Now, I know it's none of my business, but…"

He smiled at her. "I appreciate you letting me know. The children recently lost their mother, and now they seem intent on getting a new one, even if it's only in their imaginations."

"Oh." Sympathy lined her face. "I will definitely be praying for your family, Mr. Taylor."

"Thank you," he told her, giving her another smile.

Her face brightened as she smiled. "You are most welcome. Such lovely children. Good day."

She turned and left, leaving Mitch to shake his head slowly. He should consider their church attendance progress. He'd never been anywhere where someone called his children lovely. That should make up for them and their hijinks. What were they thinking, telling people something like that?

He looked around the churchyard, spotting Polly talking to Mary, noticing that as always, Isabella clutched Polly's skirts. Rory, Clara and Thomas were playing tag with Nugget, Caitlin and some other children. Louisa… He scanned the area until he finally saw her. Standing with a couple other girls who appeared to be her age.

His children had never had friends. Mostly because none of the mothers were willing to allow their children to be under the influence of the Taylor Terrors, but also because other children were terrified of the kind of pranks that would be played on them. Here, there were no pranks, just good old-fashioned laughter.

"It was a good service, wasn't it?"

Mitch jumped at the sound of Will's voice. "When did you get back?"

"Early this morning. Spent some time in Denver with an old friend, a deputy I used to work with. He gave me some information on the case I think you'll be interested in hearing. Let's go talk in Frank's office, where we can have some privacy."

They started to walk toward the church, and Mitch glanced in Polly's direction. She and Mary were headed their way.

"Will it prove my innocence?"

"It's not a smoking gun, but it's good. Know anyone with the initials JB?"

JB… Mitch mentally went through the list of everyone in Hattie's world that he'd met. "No. Did any of her friends know?"

Will shook his head. "Nope. And none of them knew who she was seeing either. Said he was a high roller who sent her expensive gifts, but she was real secretive about it. Apparently, he was married."

"They always were," Mitch said, not trying to hide his disgust.

Polly and Mary joined them, and they went into Frank's office. As Will gave his wife a gentle kiss on the cheek, Mitch's stomach gave a weird start. Such tenderness between man and wife. He'd never known such a thing, and seeing it in action made him wish... Mitch shook his head. He'd wished for a lot of things, but wishing didn't make them come true. He stole a glance at Polly, whose expression had softened. She'd been touched by the romantic gesture as well.

"Anyway," Will said, barely breaking stride in the conversation after greeting his wife. "Despite this fellow being married, Hattie kept acting like her ship had come in. A lot of the other actresses were upset with her for putting on airs. They said she was full of herself because she was staying in a suite at the Orrington Grand, paid for by this lover."

Nothing Mitch didn't already know. "That sounds about right. But that doesn't tell us anything. None of them knew his name?"

"No, and I couldn't get the clerk at the hotel to tell me anything about the room. Apparently, it was registered to her, and there's no record of who paid."

"But you don't believe the clerk?" Polly asked, her brow wrinkled in thought.

"No. My friend said that he'd seen the room register, and the page had been torn out." Then Will looked around. "The only reason I have the initials is that apparently a bloody cuff link bearing those letters was found clenched in Hattie's hand. My friend was asked to dispose of it because the sheriff thought it might confuse the jury."

Destroying evidence. Mitch closed his eyes. He knew the sheriff would do just about anything to get reelected, but he hadn't realized how far he'd go.

"But your friend thinks it's important?" Mitch examined Will's face, hoping that there was some good news to come of the situation.

"Yes. I told him what I knew of Hattie's affairs, and he says it sounds like there was some kind of lover's quarrel. People in the room below complained because they'd heard shouting. My guess, and his, is that Hattie was trying to cash in on her baby news, and he didn't respond the way she thought he would."

None of them ever did, which was why Mitch had five children. But no one had ever been angry enough with Hattie over it to kill her.

"Did he talk to the sheriff? Let him know that obviously someone besides Mitch was involved?" Polly's voice was so earnest and sincere, Mitch wanted to be happy that he had someone like her on his side. But the more he felt appreciation for her, the more he had to face the difficulty of the fact that she would be leaving them.

How could he keep their lives from being so intertwined? She clearly cared about what happened to him, and that made him far happier than it should.

"The sheriff doesn't want to hear it. Until we have conclusive proof, and a name, it's not going to do us any good. The good news is, my friend thinks Mitch is innocent, and he's eager to help prove it."

Mitch stared at him. "He'd go against the sheriff? No one there would even talk to me."

"And they won't. This guy only talked to me because we're old friends, and on the condition that I not mention his name. No one's willing to cross the sheriff. He can make life miserable for a man who doesn't play the game his way."

The familiar old resignation sat in the pit of Mitch's stomach, like a long-lost enemy come to roost. "Is there any hope at all?"

"If we can find out who JB is, sure."

Mitch glanced out the window, noticing his children still outside playing. If they didn't find the answers they were looking for, he'd only have a few more weeks of enjoying them. And then…the enemy roosting in the pit of his stomach started to peck at his insides, taunting him with what his fate would be.

Polly hated seeing the discouragement return to Mitch's face. It had been nearly banished over the past few days, and it was a shame to see his handsome features marred.

"So how do we find out who this JB is? Do you think the owner of the hotel might know?"

Will nodded. "I've got a man looking into it. Seems the hotel ownership is tied up in some kind of trust, and we've got to be careful about how we go about things. When I was asking questions at the hotel, word got back to the sheriff, who paid me a visit. He didn't take kindly to my looking into things. I told him it was just curiosity because reading about the case in the papers fascinated me, but he still didn't like it."

Mary made the sound she always made when she was deep in thought. Polly had almost forgotten her friend was there. But now, she was glad for it.

"What are you thinking, Mary?" Polly asked.

"Seems like the sheriff is doing an awful lot of chasing people away from the truth. Why would he do that if there wasn't something to contradict the evidence he had for his easy conviction?"

Will planted a kiss on top of his wife's head, warming Polly's heart. She was glad for her friend finding someone like him, especially when she noticed how pink Mary's cheeks turned at the attention.

"And that, my love, is why I am so glad I married you. You have a way of confirming I'm on the right track with something, even when I just have my gut to go on."

"Well you've got mine, too," Polly said, looking at Mitch, who was gazing out the window. "There's something not right about how the sheriff is handling the case, and he's hiding something important. I can just feel it. Mitch, you are absolutely not allowed to lose hope."

His head jerked in her direction. "Who said I'm losing hope?"

"The crease in your brow says. And I will not have it, do you hear me?"

As he nodded slowly, Polly caught Mary stifling a giggle. She turned to her friend. "What's so funny?"

"You." She grinned, then cast Mitch a sympathetic look. "She can't help it, you know. She's been bossing people around most of her life, and the only reason we don't think she's completely insufferable is that she's usually right."

For the first time since they entered Uncle Frank's office, Mitch smiled. "Unfortunately so. But I think that's one of the things that makes her grow on you."

Polly should have been irritated that they were all picking on her, but with the way the mood lightened, she couldn't be mad.

"Just how much has she grown on you?" Will asked, suddenly looking almost menacing.

Polly forced herself not to smile. Watching Will take on a protective role was sweet. Unnecessary, but sweet. She looked over at Mary, who just shook her head.

Mitch seemed to understand, too. "Not so much as you seem to be asking. Trust me, I have enough problems in my life without adding romance to the equation."

"Romance comes whether you want it to or not." Will stared Mitch down the way Polly imagined he'd look at a criminal. "And just so we're clear, if you break Polly's heart—"

"Oh, now stop!" Polly gave Will a hard look of her own. "We've already been fighting off the matchmaking efforts of the children. Both Mitch and I understand where the other stands. There are no romantic notions between us. Save your heroic efforts for that little one you'll soon be raising."

Polly tossed a smile at her friend, who rubbed her stomach.

"Are you really clear on your relationship?" Mary asked. "The harder you fight it, the harder you fall."

Polly let out a long breath. These people were impossible. Every last one of them. She glanced over at Mitch, who was shaking his head. At least he understood where things stood between them.

"I can almost understand why Polly doesn't want to get married," Mitch said. "The way folks keep matching her up when she says she's not interested has to be frustrating."

Then he grinned. "Knowing Polly, she's apt to never marry just to spite you all."

"You *do* like her," Mary said, looking quite like she'd been given a tray of Maddie's tarts all to herself.

"I can like her all I want, but that doesn't mean I have to marry her." Then Mitch sobered. "Your teasing is just as futile as finding Hattie's killer seems to be. Actually, I'm starting to think that there's a greater chance of my marrying Polly than there is of finding Hattie's killer, and I am absolutely not interested in marrying her—or anyone else."

Well, that was a comfort. Even with his "or anyone else," it was a little insulting to hear the vehemence about not marrying her. Not that she wanted to marry him, of course, but it was the principle of the matter.

He gave Polly a sympathetic look. "It's nothing against you, but I'm sure you can understand where I'm coming from. Marriage has brought me nothing but trouble."

Then he let out a long sigh. "Although I would never change my decision to marry Hattie. I don't know what I'd do without the children."

Mary gave Will that sickeningly sweet look Polly was used to seeing her friends give their husbands. "Not all marriages are bad."

The same argument Mary, Annabelle and Emma Jane had been giving Polly the past few months. But what happened when the passion faded? When the newness of having that someone in their lives was gone? Her conversation with Ma fluttered back into her mind. She'd been wrong about her pa all these years. Could all these arguments Polly had been making against marriage be wrong?

It didn't matter, she told herself firmly. She and Mitch were not getting married. Mitch had just made his position quite clear, and hopefully everyone else would finally listen.

Polly cleared her throat. "Marriage may well have worked out for you, but discussing the merits or disadvantages to such a state isn't going to help Mitch stay out of jail. What we need now is a plan."

She mentally patted herself on the back for getting the conversation back on track. Especially since Mitch looked just as relieved to finally have the pressure taken off. He wanted to talk about marriage as little as Polly did, and it was frustrating to have everyone continually bring it up.

"I'm not sure what else we can do until we find out who the owner of the Orrington Grand is," Will said. "All of my leads have dried up, and unless we have someone come forward with the identity of JB, we're at a dead end. I was really hoping that Mitch would know."

A knock sounded at the door, and Uncle Frank poked his head into the room. "I just wanted to see if you were almost finished. I'm supposed to be meeting with a couple to discuss their wedding, but if you're going to be much longer, I can take them over to the house."

Will waved him in. "No, we're done. I was just updating them on what I found on my trip to Denver."

"Good news, I hope?" Uncle Frank sounded optimistic as always. Sometimes Polly envied him that ability. She'd never spoken to him of her doubts about marriage because his was one of the few truly happy marriages she'd witnessed. How could someone who'd had it so easy understand what it was like to fear the realities she'd known?

"Some promising information, but unfortunately, unless you know who owns the Orrington Grand, we've hit a dead end," Will said, looking regretfully in Mitch's direction.

"What's this about the Orrington Grand?" Eleanor Steele, a young lady Polly recognized from Bible study, entered the room followed by a gentleman Polly didn't recognize. Presumably, Eleanor's intended.

Eleanor paused briefly, but when no one volunteered information, she continued. "Mother and I stayed there when we went to Denver to do some shopping for the wedding. Not nearly as fine an establishment as the Rafferty, but it's not terrible. Take my advice, and if you stay there, don't get caught up in conversation with the proprietors. The wife is all right I suppose, but the husband is a dreadful bore."

"Who might they be?" Mary asked. "Do we know them?"

Eleanor sighed. "Not likely, though they are staying with us. Laura Haywood Booth is older than we are, and to my knowledge, she hasn't been to Leadville until now. James, her husband, was a nobody until he married her. Fortune hunter, you know. The family was so convinced that all he wanted was poor Laura's money that they tied everything up in a trust that he has no access to."

Polly, Mitch, Mary and Will all looked at each other.

"You said her husband is James Booth?" Will asked, sounding casual, even though Polly knew they were all hanging on the answer.

"You've heard of him?" Eleanor sounded incredulous. "He's of no consequence. The money is all from the Haywood family. I'm quite surprised really. As I said, he's a dreadful bore, and poor Laura is as timid as a mouse. I can't imagine what Mother was thinking, inviting them up, but you know how she is."

Eleanor let out a long sigh. "You can't imagine what

an imposition it's been hosting them. I had thought they were only staying for a few days, but Mother is constantly making plans for her and Laura. She says Laura is in desperate need of her help. For what, I'd like to know."

"They're staying at your house?" Polly tried to hide the excitement from her voice. Could the answer to their woes be so simple?

"Yes. That's what I've been saying, isn't it? It's why Mother isn't here today. She's taking Laura to see her favorite milliner."

Will gave Eleanor what appeared to be a sympathetic look. "How long has it been?"

"Forever." Eleanor let out a long sigh. "Here I am, trying to plan a wedding, and Mother is busy entertaining these people."

Mary nodded and touched the woman's arm gently. "Having recently married myself, I can only imagine how trying that must be for you. Planning a wedding is so much work. Why would your mother let them stay so long if it's interfering with your plans?"

"Well that's just it," Eleanor said. "I assume since we're here in the pastor's office, you won't breathe a word to anyone. But honestly, I'm so upset by the whole thing, I have to get it out."

They all murmured their agreement that of course they wouldn't share what Eleanor told them.

"Did you hear about that horrible murder that happened in Denver? An actress was brutally killed right there, in the Orrington Grand. Can you imagine? A murder. Right there. Just down the hall from where Mother and I were sleeping. Why, it could have been us."

Polly bit her lip to keep from reacting. This could be even better information than they'd hoped for.

"The papers say it was the woman's husband, acting in a jealous rage, but what if it wasn't? There's a madman on the loose, and we were nearly victims."

Instinctively, Polly reached for Mitch's arm, giving him a sympathetic squeeze. He'd most likely heard worse, but it had to be hard to hear someone sensationalizing what had happened. And at least Eleanor was willing to give the husband the benefit of the doubt.

"After the deputies questioned us, Mother was intent on getting us home to our own beds, where we didn't risk being murdered in our sleep. But when we went to check out, James Booth was there, and he was absolutely insistent on having us for lunch. It was very kind of him to want to be sure the deputies weren't too hard on us, but he just kept asking questions, making us miss the train."

Eleanor let out another long sigh. "By then, Laura had joined us, and she was so upset that a murder had happened in her hotel, and then reporters were there, asking questions, and it was horrible. Mother felt so bad for poor Laura that she invited them to come stay with us until the talk died down."

With an imploring look toward all of them, Eleanor continued, "James asked us not to let anyone know they were here because he didn't want the reporters to find them. Who would have thought that the accused murderer would have family in Leadville and he'd come to the very town where the Booths were staying? Fortunately, Leadville is large enough these days that we're not likely to cross paths, particularly since we don't spend time in that part of town. Father assures us that we're perfectly safe. Supposedly, the man's gone into hiding or some such, but I can't imagine why the Booths would remain, except that Mother keeps insisting Laura stay."

Polly glanced at Mitch, whose blank look didn't reveal any reaction to Eleanor's words. But she noticed Will taking them in with great interest. No one said anything but let the talkative young lady continue her tale.

"I know Mother means well in befriending Laura, but why should she take such an interest in this other woman when she has her own daughter's wedding to plan? I probably shouldn't have told you all of this, but honestly, I am at my wit's end. How much longer are those people going to stay with us? I fear my wedding is going to be a disaster."

Eleanor burst into tears, and her fiancé, who'd stood silently by, pulled her into his arms, comforting her. "There, now, darling, it's going to be all right."

The gentleman looked over at Uncle Frank. "That's why we asked to meet with you, sir. Naturally, we'd like to discuss the wedding, but we're also hoping you could suggest ways of entertaining the Booths so Eleanor's mother can focus her attention back on her daughter."

"Oh, Eleanor." Mary put her hand on the other girl's back. "You know that those of us in our Bible study group would be happy to help with your wedding. Why, I think even Emma Jane Jackson would be pleased to give her assistance."

Eleanor turned around, her face reddened with tears. "You think so? Mother said we shouldn't be so presumptuous as to even invite the Jacksons to our wedding, but if you think Emma Jane would be willing…"

The Jacksons were one of the wealthiest and most powerful families in Leadville. And now that Emma

Jane was married to Jasper Jackson, her involvement in a project almost assured its success. Even though they seldom took advantage of their friend's elevated social status, sometimes being able to remind others of their friendship aided their cause.

Eleanor didn't know it, and Polly was sure none of them would mention it until they saw the case through, but she'd just provided Will and Mitch the breakthrough they needed.

"Emma Jane would be delighted, I'm sure," Mary said, smiling first at Eleanor, then turning her gaze on Polly. "Don't you agree, Polly?"

Polly had no idea if Emma Jane would be delighted, and given that everyone thought Polly would be delighted to do any number of things that Polly was not delighted to do, she was reluctant to volunteer Emma Jane for anything.

However, between Mary, Will and Mitch insistently staring at her, and the hopeful stares of Eleanor and her fiancé, Polly couldn't bring herself to disagree. So, she settled for a compromise.

"We can certainly ask her. She's always happy to lend a hand when she can."

The conversation quickly turned toward wedding plans, and Polly was hard-pressed to find an excuse to leave. She'd never planned on a wedding for herself, so she'd never given consideration to things like flowers, music and decor. But every time she sighed at having to think on such things, both Mary and Will shot her sharp glances.

Polly couldn't bear to look at Mitch. After all, even if all they exchanged were sympathetic glances, it would only add fuel to the fire that they were pining after each other. Which they most certainly were not.

But the few times Polly allowed her mind to wander, she couldn't help but wonder if she'd been wrong in so vehemently opposing marriage.

Chapter Fifteen

Mitch couldn't believe the gold mine they'd discovered in meeting Eleanor. He would have liked to have explained his side of the story to the young lady, but Will cautioned him not to say anything. The chatty young woman might accidentally reveal too much when she returned home, and it would ruin their chances of getting an unrehearsed reaction from James. Once they finished helping her sort out what she needed for her wedding, they gratefully accepted an invitation to stop in for tea the next day.

"I'll pay Nick Steele a visit later," Will told him as they walked back toward the parsonage. "He's ridden out with us a few times when we needed an extra man. I'll see what insight he can give us before we have tea. I'd like to have the element of surprise, but I also don't want to blindside Nick. He's a good man, and I know he'll do what he can to help."

"I should go—"

"No. We don't know if Booth is there or not, and he might recognize you. Given that he ran even with the blame being placed on you, there's no telling what he'll do if he knows you're looking into him. Right now, he thinks he might have gotten away with it, and public attention is on you, not him. Let's keep the element of surprise for as long as we can."

Though the other man's words made sense, it didn't feel right in his gut. It made him feel weak and helpless letting someone else fight his battles for him.

"It will be all right," Polly said, looping her arm through his. "I know it must be frustrating not to do anything, but your time will come. Let's do this right, so your children aren't visiting you in jail instead of taking you on picnics."

Her hand felt warm resting in his arm, a source of comfort he hadn't been expecting. The generosity in Polly's spirit was about giving to all, helping all. She meant nothing by the gesture, Mitch knew, but he could feel Will's questioning glare on him.

Mitch gently disentangled Polly's arm from his. "If you're trying to keep people from remarking on our relationship, then you're doing a terrible job of showing it."

As her face flushed, Mitch's stomach fell. "I'm sorry," he said quietly. "I didn't mean to hurt you. I know you were just trying to be kind, but others seem to think there's more to it than that."

Polly nodded slowly. "Of course. I wasn't thinking. I don't understand why everyone thinks I have to walk the path they've chosen for me."

The pain in her voice wasn't about him, and like she'd just tried to do for him, Mitch wanted to comfort her in some way. But even though they'd disentangled and taken a step away from one another, he could still feel Will's watchful eyes on him.

"I don't think they mean it maliciously," Mitch said, still keeping his voice low. "They care about you, and it's clear they want you to find the same happiness they have."

"I'm not sure that's possible for me." Her voice was almost a whisper, and he barely caught it.

Mitch wanted to argue with her and tell her all the reasons why any man would be fortunate to have her, list all the many reasons why she could have love in her life.

But as he started to think about her kindness, her compassion, her wit, he had to question his own attachment to her.

As much as he tried reminding himself of the heartache he'd faced at Hattie's hands, he knew they were excuses that didn't measure up. He would have never described Hattie as having Polly's qualities.

Polly wanted to leave, yes, but it wasn't the same wanderlust he'd seen in his late wife. Truth be told, he hadn't looked any deeper into Polly's motivations than resisting her family's meddling.

Was he wrong in dismissing the possibility of romance with Polly?

Mitch opened the door to let the ladies in, and as Will approached, he said, "Hold up a minute. We have a few things to go over."

"Sure." He closed the door and faced the other man. "What's the plan?"

"The plan is you need to be straight with me about your intentions toward Polly. Her brothers are up at the mine, or else I'm sure they'd be having this conversation with you."

The other man's stare bore into him like a drill into solid rock. Will might be a younger man, but he had a good few inches on Mitch and broad shoulders that dared any man to challenge him. There was no pretense of politeness or friendliness in Will's posture, and though Mitch didn't like having it aimed at him, at least he knew how the other man appeared when questioning people for a case.

Except Mitch wasn't guilty of anything. He squared his shoulders and returned Will's look. "She's my nanny. At times, I'd like to think we're friends, but too many people keep reading into it more than what it is, so we're trying to keep our distance."

That was the real shame. It had been a long time since Mitch could count anyone as a friend, but because of other people's assumptions and aspirations, he couldn't rely on his friendship with Polly.

"That so?" Will's gaze didn't flinch. "I've seen the way you look at her."

Apparently, everyone thought that he thought Polly was chocolate cake.

"She's a beautiful woman," Mitch said slowly. "But I do my best not to dwell too much on that."

"Exactly. You try too hard not to look."

Mitch closed his eyes for a moment. There was no winning in this situation.

"What would you have me do, gouge my eyes out?"

A hint of a grin appeared at the corners of Will's lips, but otherwise, he seemed just as hard as he'd been throughout the conversation.

"If that's what it takes to keep our Polly safe." His expression softened slightly. "She might seem like she's hard as nails when it comes to dealing with men and romance, but her heart's as delicate as they come."

"You don't need to tell me that." He could have told Will a thing or two about Polly's delicate heart. Hadn't he seen it in action as she cared for his children? As she tried to bridge the gap between him and his children?

He'd even seen it in the moments when he'd tried to put a respectable distance between them and ended up hurting her feelings.

"Obviously I do."

What was he supposed to say? In defending his knowledge of Polly's heart, it would only prove exactly the point Will was making. And yet, Will failed to understand the complexity of the situation.

Will continued staring at him like he expected an answer, and Mitch couldn't see the point in continuing the conversation. He couldn't give the other man the answers he wanted, and to keep talking about it would only serve to frustrate them both.

"I understand your point," Mitch finally said. "But you don't have anything to worry about on my account."

The look Will shot him could have slain Goliath himself. "I can't tell if you're lying to me or to yourself. Either way, you'd better figure it out soon. I won't let an innocent man go to jail, but I promise, you hurt Polly, and jail will seem like a far more pleasant place."

Then he tipped his hat and went inside.

Everyone had been right in saying Will Lawson was the best man to put on a case. Mitch had no doubt that Will would find a way to get the right man behind bars. Now to convince Will that Polly's heart was in no danger. Had he been open with the man, he would have told him that the heart most in danger was his own.

Mitch went inside to find the others all chatting merrily in the kitchen. Will stood with his arm protectively around Mary, laughing at something Frank said. He couldn't fault the other man for wanting to protect Polly, and as Polly entered the room, carrying Isabella, Will gave her a warm smile.

"I see someone missed you," Mary said, touching

Isabella's arm gently. "Emma Jane said the children all behaved for her. And, judging from how she spoiled this little one, I think she's hoping for a little girl of her own."

"I wouldn't mind a little girl," Will said, patting Mary's still flat stomach.

"Oh, I don't know about that." Mary grimaced. "I can't imagine the torment you'll put her suitors through. I know your talk with Mitch outside was not just a friendly chat."

Polly turned to Mitch. "It wasn't about the case, then?"

Mitch shook his head, not wanting to say much more and risk inciting Will's wrath.

"Honestly!" Polly gave Will a look far deadlier than any Will had given him.

"I am a grown woman, perfectly capable of looking after myself. I know you all think you know better than me, but this is my life and I'll thank you to stay out of it."

Then she turned to Frank. "You asked me earlier about being overworked and why I wanted so badly to make a life of my own. This is why. Mitch has done nothing wrong, but everyone is warning him and then trying to push us together. Even if he were interested in me, I can't imagine why he would want to get involved with someone with such a meddling family."

Tears ran down her cheeks, and it took every ounce of strength not to run and comfort her. Though he ached to see her hurting, his actions would only cause more strife among them.

"They only want what's best for you," Mitch said quietly, trying to break the rock-solid tension in the room. "It wasn't so long ago that I didn't appreciate your meddling in my life, but now that we're closer to answers than I ever got on my own, I understand that you were able to see things I couldn't."

She turned her fiery gaze on him. "So you're saying that they're right in how they're acting over us?"

"No." Mitch met her gaze, then turned his attention on Will. "The truth is, even though Andrew was good in taking us in to escape the attention we received after Hattie's death, I'm not as close to my family as I'd like to be. When I met Hattie, they warned me. Told me that I was ruining my life. And when everything fell apart, I never went to them for help, advice or comfort. I had too much pride to listen to one more 'I told you so,' and the gap between us widened."

His throat tightened as he realized just how much he'd missed the closeness he once shared with Andrew. The backs of his eyes stung, and he took a deep breath to calm the emotions he hadn't realized he'd been stuffing down for so long.

"Andrew used to be my best friend, my closest confidant, and being here with you all has made me realize how much I've missed my brother. But every time I think of talking to him about what's really happening, I hear his voice in the back of my head, telling me not to come crying to him when my life falls apart."

A tear trickled out of the corner of his eye, and Mitch did his best to ignore it. These people had no idea how much of his insides they'd torn open, allowing the green festering ooze to spill out. It wasn't fair to dump this all on them, not when the situation was really about Polly, and him doing his best to defend her while keeping his heart intact.

With all that he'd broken open these past weeks, he couldn't afford to let her run away and take it with her.

"Don't do that to Polly. She is the strongest, bravest woman I know, but if you push her too hard, her pride will never let her come back. We've both told you where we stand on our relationship, and that's where you need to leave it."

He glanced at Polly again and gave her a nod. "Polly, you are a good, honorable woman, and were circumstances different for the both of us, there might be a chance of something between us. But you've made your wishes clear, and I respect you too much to ask otherwise."

Eyes filled with tears, Polly whispered, "Thank you."

Once again, Mitch returned his attention to Will, giving him the steely gaze that he'd subjected Mitch to just minutes earlier.

"Maybe Polly and I are lying to ourselves. And maybe we're just being honest about the fact that attraction isn't enough for a lasting relationship. I know all about being led astray by a pretty face, and I've lived enough life to know what I will and won't settle for in a marriage. I'm sorry if you don't like that response, but I will not answer to you again on this subject."

Without waiting for a reply from any of them, Mitch turned and walked out of the house. He wasn't fit company for anyone right now, and now that he'd gotten to the core of where he was hurting, he had a lot of thinking— and praying—to do.

Polly watched Mitch leave, and somewhere in the haze of her tears, she felt Mary's gentle hand on her arm. And then Uncle Frank's on her other arm, gently taking Isabella from her. Somewhere behind Mary was Will. Polly couldn't speak, and though she knew she was crying, she wasn't sure she could even feel anymore.

Her pain wasn't just about how smothered she'd been feeling by her family, but about Mitch's warning. And how he had lost so much over Hattie. Though she was certain he didn't blame her for losing his close relationship with his brother, Polly could see where that, too, was another casualty of Hattie's life.

Somewhere in the recesses of the fog surrounding her emotions, she heard footsteps, and then she could smell the faint lilac smell of her mother, until she was enveloped in her mother's arms.

Ma... Polly felt like a baby sobbing against her mother's chest. Feeling the warmth and comfort that she hadn't had for so long, aching because she'd held everything in and hadn't needed to.

"I'm sorry, baby," Ma said. "I didn't know. So much I didn't know, and you kept it all to yourself because you didn't want to hurt anyone."

The soft brush of lips on top of her head made Polly feel more protected than she ever had. Not by the strength or might of the lawman in the room but by the mother who cherished her.

Ma shifted her weight, and Polly felt the air against her face as Ma turned. Polly wiped away her tears and watched as Ma addressed everyone.

"I know we all want the best for our Polly. But we've got to give her room to live her life, to make her mistakes. I thought that if I sheltered her from all the bad surrounding us that it would be better for her. Instead, she took on interpretations that were false, and it's led her to believe things that I never wanted in her head."

She gave Polly a look of such love it made Polly's heart melt like a pile of snow on a hot summer's day. "I am so sorry, and I know I can't take anything back, but I want to be here for you now."

"It's all right," Polly said, hugging her mother tight. "I'm sorry, too. I know I've been hardheaded, and I should have been more open with you."

When Ma pulled away, Mary stepped in to hug Polly. "And I'm sorry, too. I don't think any of us have paid much attention to what you wanted, and instead were focused on what we thought was right for you."

Mary turned and smiled at Will. "I am so happy, married to Will, and now with our baby on the way, I can't imagine anyone not having this kind of content-ment."

Bringing her gaze back to Polly, Mary gave her a tender look of love. "But just because I love my life doesn't mean it's the life for you. I hope you know that no matter where life takes you, I'll always be here to support you."

"I'm sorry, too," Will said. "I was hard on Mitch, thinking he'd finally declare himself, and the two of you would be on the road to happiness, like we are. I was wrong. You need to figure these things out on your own, not because we pushed you into something you weren't ready for. I'll apologize to Mitch next time I see him."

The heaviness that had been weighing Polly down seemed to disappear. She looked around, realizing that Uncle Frank had also disappeared. "Where is Uncle Frank?"

"He and Maddie went to take over watching the chil-dren for Emma Jane. She had to get Moses home for his nap," Ma said.

The children! Polly's hand flew to her mouth. "Oh, no! I forgot all about them! What kind of nanny am I?"

Ma smiled. "The kind who has a loving family to support her when she needs them. When I was going through all the things I did with your pa, there were plenty of times I forgot about the children, and I was always grateful to find that you had things well in hand. I suppose it's high time we paid you back."

Picking up an apron and tying it around herself, Ma continued. "It's a fine line between meddling and doing what's needed to help someone we love. I daresay we often cross it more than we think we do, and more than some folks like. But as long as you know it's rooted in love, sometimes you just need to let it go."

Then Ma handed her a bucket of potatoes. "Mostly, though, I think we all have to be grateful that we have someone to care about us, since there's lots of folks who do without. Now you get to work on peeling these here potatoes so Maddie's not behind in fixing supper. There's a time for talking, but then there's time to get work done or else we'll have lots of complaining over not having a decent supper."

Polly couldn't help but grin as she dutifully took the bucket of potatoes and carried them to the table. As she peeled potatoes, she noticed that Ma had put both Mary and Will to work, even though they had their own house down the street. Watching the easy banter between everyone, Polly couldn't imagine why she'd wanted anything more.

True, she hated peeling potatoes above all else, but Maddie's kitchen was full of the kind of warmth that didn't come from a fire.

Her heart ached as she realized Mitch's children had never had that until now. And wouldn't when Polly left. Though she'd told them that she'd stay as long as she was needed, Polly couldn't imagine that such a time would ever come.

After all, who better to love Mitch's children than

Polly? If all those other nannies hadn't been able to see into their hearts and care for them, could someone else?

Which then begged the question, was she wrong in refusing to see Mitch as a romantic possibility?

Polly sighed. No, romance with Mitch was about more than just what was best for the children. Mitch might have admitted being attracted to Polly earlier, but he was also equally firm on the notion that attraction didn't make for a lasting marriage.

As she finished the last potato, the back door opened, and the children came running in.

"Polly!" The chorus of happy voices filled Polly's heart and made it more full than she could have possibly imagined.

She set the potato down, wiped her hands on her apron, then stood and gathered the children in her arms. How all five managed to fit into that embrace, she didn't know, but as far as Polly was concerned, it was the perfect fit.

Once their hug was complete, the children all started chattering about their day, how they enjoyed Sunday school and how much fun they'd had with Emma Jane and her baby, Moses.

She could almost not hear for all the din, but she caught enough snatches of words to know that here, in Leadville, the Taylor children were blossoming. She uttered a silent prayer, thanking God for giving her this treasure she hadn't even known she'd wanted.

Maddie entered, pulling off her hat and muttering about all the commotion in her kitchen.

Polly grinned. Everything was right in the Lassiter house. "Come on, children, let's go into the parlor, and you can each take a turn telling me about your day."

They didn't need another invitation, as all five raced

out of the kitchen. Polly started to follow them, but Uncle Frank gently took her by the arm.

"I'm sorry I missed out on the entire conversation in the kitchen, but I knew you'd be concerned about the children and I wanted to keep that worry at bay. I want you to know that I heard you, and I understand. Sometimes we do meddle too much. I'm sorry. I hope you know that we only do so because you are so very dear to us, and we only want the best for you."

Polly nodded, tears once again filling her eyes.

"I also hope you know that Mitch is a fine man. He's been hurt deeply, but I believe that when he finally allows himself to love and be loved, it's going to be a deep love that can't be shaken. A woman would be most fortunate to have a man like that."

She could only shake her head as she left the room to join the children. But this time, rather than being annoyed at the not-so-subtle attempt at pushing her in Mitch's direction, warmth filled Polly's heart knowing that the people around her truly cared. Not just for her, but for Mitch.

As she reached the parlor, the front door opened, and Mitch came in.

"There you are. I was wondering where you'd gone," she said, offering him a smile. "The children were just about to tell me about their day. You should join us."

His eyes met hers, and she saw something in them she didn't understand. A connection, yes, but something deeper. But as they entered the parlor and the same five children who'd so eagerly embraced her wrapped their arms around their father, the connection was broken. With a promise that they had much to discuss later.

Chapter Sixteen

Mitch had been too busy since returning home the previous afternoon to speak with Polly alone. He didn't know what to say to her, except that he felt as though there were too many unsaid things between them.

"It's a fine day, isn't it?" Polly said, stepping in line with him as they walked to the Steele house to collect on their tea invitation.

Their party, consisting of Mitch, Polly, Will and Mary, seemed fine for afternoon tea, but Mitch worried that it wasn't right to have the women along to confront James Booth.

"You don't have to do this," Mitch said, looking over at Polly. "The kind of man Booth is…"

"We have a deputy with us, and Will says that Nick Steele has helped them on many an occasion. Besides—" her eyes met his "—I don't want you to have to do this alone."

Alone. Mitch swallowed the word, but it stuck in his throat. He'd been alone for a long time, and while part of him reveled in having Polly by his side, the other part of him was just waiting for her to decide to leave.

"I have Will," he said. "He apologized to me this

morning, just so you know. Said he was wrong to interfere and he was sorry."

Then Mitch grinned. "But he did say it wasn't permission to break your heart."

He'd have liked to have told the other man that Polly's heart wasn't in as much danger as his, but their friendship was still too tenuous. All of his relationships were too tenuous, but after last night, he'd vowed to make them better. Starting with Andrew. Mitch would have liked to have talked to his brother before they visited Booth, but there wasn't enough time. So later, when the dust settled, Mitch would stop by and work on undoing that wrong.

Pink tinged Polly's cheeks, but she turned her head away before Mitch could examine it further. Did Polly have feelings for him?

Attraction, yes. They'd both admitted their mutual attraction in some ways, but for him, it wasn't enough. Where he might have said something flirtatious in response to Polly's blush, Mitch remained silent. Apparently, Polly didn't want to talk about Will's pronouncement either, so they continued their walk to the Steele house without further conversation.

The Steele house was a smallish abode, larger than the typical Leadville home, but nothing nearly so grand as the mansions in Denver. Andrew had explained it to him when he'd arrived that the expense of getting materials to Leadville necessitated the smaller homes. Mitch had been astonished at the much higher cost of goods in Andrew's store, but when he saw the shipping costs, he'd understood.

As a maid led them into the parlor, Mitch saw the evidence of the Steele family's social standing. From the thick luxurious carpets, to the silk wall hangings and the gold leaf ornamenting every accessory, the room demanded respect for the amount of money that had gone into its decor.

Mitch eyed a chair that was designed more for appearance than comfort. He appreciated that while the Lassiter house was one of the larger homes in town, which would have ordinarily screamed "wealth," the comfortable furniture and modest arrangement made it seem far more like a home than this showplace.

A tall thin man with a long beard entered the room. "Will Lawson! Such a pleasure to have you in my home."

Will shook the man's hand. "Nick. Nice to be here. I'd like you to meet my friend I was telling you about, Mitch Taylor. And you remember, of course, my wife, Mary, and our dear friend Polly."

"So glad to meet you," Nick Steele said, shaking Mitch's hand. "I am terribly sorry to hear about your troubles."

The man looked to be only a few years older than Mitch, and his welcoming appearance made Mitch think Nick was the sort of man he could be friends with. His expression was genuine, warm and open.

"Thank you. I appreciate you allowing us the opportunity."

Before Nick could answer, three ladies entered the room.

"Ah, here they are. I'm sure you all remember Eleanor, and my dear wife, Patricia, and this is Laura Booth, our houseguest." He smiled amiably, then turned his gaze on Laura Booth. "But where is your husband? I thought he'd be joining us."

She blushed, then looked at the ground. "He hasn't yet returned from last night's festivities."

A dark expression flashed across Nick's face, but then he gave the woman a gentle look. "There now, it's not your fault. I'm sure there's a reasonable explanation for his absence."

Mrs. Booth murmured noncommittally, then exchanged glances with Patricia Steele. Clearly, the women were in each other's confidence, and from their expressions, neither was surprised by Booth's actions.

Mrs. Steele gestured toward the uncomfortable-looking chairs and an equally uninviting set of sofas. "Please, sit. We have tea and refreshments. I am so grateful to you all for helping with Eleanor's wedding planning. I had no idea just how neglected she's been feeling."

She gave her daughter a loving smile, and Mitch wondered if there'd been something in the air that had caused so many heartfelt conversations yesterday.

Eleanor smiled back. "It's all right, Mother. I should have said something sooner."

Then Eleanor looked over at Mary and Polly. "I saw Emma Jane Jackson at the dressmaker's this morning. She was so gracious, just as you said she would be. I can't believe she offered to host a luncheon at the Jackson Mansion in honor of our wedding. However, she did tell me I was wrong not to discuss my feelings with Mother and insisted I go right home to talk to her. So I did."

Mrs. Booth gave her daughter an indulgent smile, then turned her attention back to Polly and Mary. "I cannot thank you enough for the kindness you did for Eleanor. And to also have a word with Mrs. Jasper Jackson on her behalf…it is almost too much."

"Mother," Eleanor chided. "She told me that we are to call her Emma Jane."

Mitch watched the interplay with interest, not so much that he cared anything about the matters of the heart, but because he saw again the strength of Polly's character. She and Mary had gone round to see Emma Jane after supper to tell her about Eleanor's plight. He'd been so used to seeing women of standing wielding their power like weapons, forcing others to bend to their will and shunning anyone who didn't fit the expectations of society. Which was why his children had fared so poorly in Denver.

Here, Polly, Mary and their friends used their social standing to bring others up, to help them and do good. His children had been embraced by the other children, in large part due to Polly's influence. As the women continued to banter back and forth in a pleasant conversation about weddings, he couldn't help but continue to marvel at how engaging Polly was, even in conversation about what had to be her least favorite subject—weddings.

The front door opened, and from his vantage point, Mitch could see two men enter. Nick stood.

"Baxter? Is that you?"

"Oh, Baxter, darling, you've returned!" Eleanor jumped up and by the time the two men had reached the doorway, she had gone to meet him with all the enthusiasm of a young bride in love.

"I'm sorry it took so long." He kissed her cheek, then gently pushed the other man into the room. "Probably too drunk to be of much use, but you can try."

Then he seemed to notice the other women in the room. "Begging your pardons, ma'ams. Didn't mean to subject you to such indelicacies."

"It's all right, Baxter." Nick waved a hand at one of

the sofas. "Why don't you help Mr. Booth take a seat, and then we can have ourselves a nice chat?"

"I'm sorry," Laura Booth whispered. "I didn't mean for him to be any trouble."

"None doing," Nick said, shaking his head. "You didn't force him to go out. You didn't force him to drink. Seems to me that a man has to own up to his behavior and not hide behind his sweet wife."

Then he looked over at Booth. "How drunk are you?"

"I'm not drunk," Booth muttered, staggering into the couch before sitting. "Can't believe you took me away from my winning streak for a tea party."

"Actually," Will said, "it's not a tea party."

Booth looked over at his wife. "You'd better not be trying to divorce me again. You know what happened last time."

The poor woman blanched, and Mrs. Steele patted her hand.

"No." Nick glared at him. "But if she should want to divorce you, my wife and I are happy to give her our full support. Especially after we discuss what Will is here to talk to you about."

"I don't owe you money, do I?" Booth's speech was slurred, proving his claims to be sober a lie.

"No," Will said. "But you do owe us some answers."

Booth tried staggering to his feet. "I swear I thought that mining stock was valid."

Baxter held out an arm, keeping him from standing.

"That's not what this is about, but I'll be asking the sheriff to look into any mining stock you might have sold."

Will grinned. "Now, is there any other dirty laundry you'd like to air before we ask you about Hattie Winston?"

Booth turned a shade of sickly green. "The husband did it. It was all over the papers."

The desperation in the other man's voice almost made Mitch feel sorry for him. There was no doubt in his mind now that James Booth had killed Hattie.

"Why didn't anyone see the husband at your hotel?" Will asked.

"We had dinner with them there the night he killed her." Then Booth glared at his wife. "Didn't we, my dear?"

His menacing tone made Mitch want to cringe. Had they had dinner together, he and Mrs. Booth would have recognized one another, but even when they'd been introduced, she didn't seem to even know the name.

Mrs. Steele turned to Mrs. Booth, a quizzical look on her face. "How is that possible? We had dinner with you that night, and as I recall, you were with us most of the evening."

She then turned her attention to Booth. "Of course, you left early, but I am certain that Laura was with us the rest of the night. You might have had a second dinner with the poor woman who was killed and her husband, but Laura wasn't there. We had an interesting conversation on making your own lace rather than buying it as I recall."

Mrs. Steele looked over at Laura. "And don't think I don't remember that you said you'd help me with Eleanor's lace. I've never seen a girl who wanted so much lace in all my life."

Will made a noise. "So, Booth, tell me again how you and your wife had dinner with Hattie and her husband."

"Well." Booth looked around the room. "I suppose we might have mixed up our days, but I'm certain we've entertained Hattie and her husband. Hattie confessed to me that she was terrified of him."

Mitch's stomach clenched, and he felt Polly's hand on his arm. She hadn't needed to stop him from saying anything, but it felt good to know that he didn't need to say anything for her to see how ridiculous Booth's claims were.

"Do you recall what Hattie's husband looked like?" Will's question was casual and seemed almost crazy, considering Mitch was sitting right there. But then, had Booth actually dined with them, he would have recognized Mitch right away.

"I can't quite rightly remember," Booth said slowly, shifting in his seat, then adjusting his already loosened tie. "It's been a while, and I do meet a lot of people. Quite an unremarkable man I suppose, except, of course, that he killed his wife."

Polly made a funny noise. When Mitch glanced at her, he could see the mirth in her eyes. Booth's obvious lies would never hold up in court.

"And could you tell me why your cuff links were in Hattie's room, covered in her blood?" Will leaned in toward Booth.

Booth's eyes widened. "I paid good money for that deputy to—" Then he realized what he was saying. "That is, they were quite expensive, and I had a deputy looking into their theft. Whoever stole them must have killed that poor woman."

Mitch took a deep breath. No wonder they'd done such a shoddy job investigating Hattie's murder. Clearly, Booth had paid someone to hide evidence of Booth's presence and place the blame on Mitch.

"And the expensive gifts you gave Hattie? The fur coat? Was that just in friendship, then?" Will's voice was calm, but as Mitch glanced around the room, he saw tears running down Laura Booth's face.

"That little—" Booth's face turned red. "She wasn't supposed to— That is, she…"

Booth stopped speaking. Looked around the room again. "Which one of you's the law?"

"I am," Will said. "At least here in Leadville. But I'm sure once we have a chat with my good friends in Denver, they'll be mighty interested in your story."

Booth grinned. "I doubt it. I have too many friends in Denver. Deputies who have the ear of the sheriff. No one will believe you."

"Yes they will," Baxter said. He looked up at Will. "I'd stand, but I think we'll keep Booth close. In all the chaos over Eleanor's disappointment in our wedding plans, and then everything today, we were never properly introduced. Baxter Campbell, US Marshal. They'll believe us."

This time a giggle slipped out of Polly as Eleanor beamed. "He saved one of Papa's silver shipments after it was robbed. Brought down a whole gang of bandits. He's a real hero, just like in the dime novels." Eleanor gave a long sigh as she looked at her fiancé.

"It was a group effort," Baxter said, giving his intended a loving smile. "I've been on leave, spending time with Eleanor and preparing for our wedding. But I'm afraid that once we're married and I'm back to work, she's not going to think my job so romantic."

Will grinned. "Pleased to have you on board. I'm sure Mary will be more than happy to help Eleanor adjust to being a lawman's wife. While we're making introductions, I might as well make one of my own."

He gestured toward Mitch. "This here's Mitch Taylor. Hattie Winston's husband."

Mitch couldn't help but smile as he watched Booth turn white. "When did you say we had dinner again?"

"I...well, I suppose..." For a moment, Booth looked as though he was going to explode. But then calm spread across his face as he smiled.

"You know, for someone so nosy, you have a lot of secrets, Taylor," Booth said.

"What do you mean?" Mitch could feel the gazes turn on him. He had nothing to hide, so why was Booth acting like he did?

"Hattie shared some personal information with me. About your children. It would be a shame if the press got wind of it. I wonder what would happen if the truth about those children got out. Seems to me that a man who wanted to protect his children from that ought not say anything, you know what I mean?"

Mitch's face heated as he felt the blood rising in his head. "You wouldn't—"

"Of course he would," Will said calmly, putting a hand on Mitch's shoulder. "He killed a woman. Ruining your life, your children's lives, that's nothing compared to what he's already done."

Forcing himself to swallow the sourness rising up in his throat, Mitch took a deep breath. Reacting to Booth only made things worse. It only gave power to a man who didn't deserve it.

"I suppose by the time they put you on trial for Hattie's murder, no one will believe you anyway," Mitch said calmly. "After all, you've just proven yourself to be a liar right here in this room. How many more will be willing to come forward once you're behind bars?"

Fear darted in and out of Booth's eyes, and Mitch realized that once they started looking for evidence of his involvement in the murder, they were going to find it.

"So why'd you kill her? Did Hattie tell you about the baby and how she thought you'd finally divorce your wife and marry her now that you had an heir on the way?" Mitch spoke directly at the shadows in Booth's eyes.

"You shut your dirty mouth!" Booth tried to lunge at him, but Baxter held him back.

"Hattie was so happy," Mitch continued. "That was our last conversation. Yes, we fought, but the thing I remember most about that night was how convinced she was that the two of you were going to finally live the life you'd always promised her. The life she'd always dreamed of having. But you lied to her, didn't you?"

"I said shut up!" Booth's words were an angry crescendo of hate and guilt all wrapped up into a neat little package that would hopefully convict him.

"You think you're so smart," Booth said. "You can't prove any of this. I have men who will testify against you, who will say that you did it. No one's going to speak against me. Laura is going to say exactly what I tell her to say, and she knows it."

Then he smiled, a sickening expression of victory that made him seem all the more vile. "So you'd best leave while you still can. Take those children and hop on the next train to Mexico, or as far away as it will take you. Because mark my words, you will rot in prison—if they don't hang you."

Those words would have made Mitch shake in his boots just a few short weeks ago. But now, he saw them for what they were—empty threats.

"The only one who's going to see the inside of a jail cell is you, Booth." Will stared down at the man with more confidence than Mitch had ever had in dealing with men like Booth.

"I don't think so." Booth's voice shook slightly, almost imperceptibly, but enough for Mitch to know that even Booth was beginning to doubt his own words.

"I'm sure the sheriff will think otherwise," Will said with a grin. "I can't wait to tell him the good news. He'll be putting the right man in jail, and he'll probably still be reelected. That's all he really cares about anyway."

Booth grimaced. It probably finally occurred to him that no friend in the department was going to stay on Booth's side when all the sheriff cared about was having someone pay for the grisly crime.

"We'll be long gone before he can get anyone up here to bring me in." Then Booth gave Will a self-satisfied look. "And you've no jurisdiction to hold me."

Mitch's heart sank. Had this all been for nothing? If Booth got away now, what would they do? No, he told himself firmly. They'd found a way this far, there had to be a way to keep going. But he sent a silent prayer heavenward asking God to please help them find that way. It didn't hurt to be too sure.

Nodding his head slowly, Will looked over at Baxter. "Marshall Campbell, is it your professional opinion as an officer of the law that this man's conduct could be considered drunk and disorderly when you brought him here today?"

A slow smile spread across his face. "Why yes, Deputy Lawson, I do believe so. There are plenty of people who would be more than willing to testify that Mr. Booth was drunk and disorderly in the saloon I found him in, and then on the street on the way here. And, of course, these good people here have all borne witness to Mr. Booth's drunken and disorderly conduct. Why, it would be a threat to the public at large if we let him loose on the town."

The longer Campbell talked, the more wild-eyed Booth became. "You wouldn't dare."

Will shrugged. "Seems to me the safety of this town is at risk, and I have no choice but to bring you in. Marshal Campbell, would you be so kind as to assist me in escorting this fellow to the jail?"

Booth strained against Baxter's grip, but the other man easily held him. Within a few minutes, Will and Baxter were walking out the door, a struggling Booth with them.

Though Mitch should have felt relief at having Baxter in custody, he knew that they could only hold him for so long on the accusation of being drunk and disorderly. Hopefully, it would be enough time for the Denver sheriff to arrive to arrest him for Hattie's murder.

As the door closed behind the men, Laura Booth burst into tears. For a few moments, everyone in the room stared at her in stunned silence.

"You haven't won," she said, her voice muffled by her tears. "He'll make you think you have, but trust me, he's already got a plan in motion. I've tried to leave him more times than I can count, and no matter how smart I was in doing it, he was already two steps ahead of me."

A sob shook her body. "Once, he beat me so bad that I crawled to the sheriff's office. And when I got there, do you know what they did?"

She looked up at them, puffy faced, tears streaming down her cheeks. "They brought me back home."

Every cell in Mitch's body ached at knowing the torment this poor woman must have suffered.

He watched as Polly got up from her seat, then knelt in front of the sobbing woman, taking her hands in hers.

"He may have won in the past, but never again. I've worked with Pastor Lassiter in helping dozens of women leave this kind of situation. You will never have to fear him again."

The power in the young woman's voice made Mitch wonder if there was anything Polly couldn't do. She had so much strength, especially in defending the weak and powerless, just as she'd done when she'd seen his children at the mercy of the nanny's unkindness in the Mercantile.

"I am so sorry," Mrs. Booth—no, Laura—said. Though she hadn't given Mitch leave to call her by her first name, he couldn't think of her as being married to that animal.

Laura looked over at the Steele family. "I should have never allowed James to accept your invitation. I knew he was running from something, but I thought perhaps it was just another gambling debt. It never occurred to me that he'd killed that woman."

Another loud sob wracked Laura's body. "I should have known. James has a terrible temper, and I know he'd kill me, given half a chance."

But then Laura looked up and gave a wry grin. "But he won't, because the money is all mine, and it's locked up in a trust that he can't break. If I die, he doesn't get any of it. Mother and Father feared he only married me for my money, and they were right."

Then Laura straightened and dabbed her eyes with the handkerchief Polly had given her. "I want to help you. I have no doubt that James killed poor Hattie Winston. But you have to understand, James knows a lot of people, and they are very dangerous. I've seen many who got in James's way disappear."

A heaviness, like lead, settled in the pit of Mitch's stomach. He'd known Booth had a wife, of course, but he hadn't imagined that going after him would put

Laura in danger. She seemed like a good woman, and she didn't deserve to be put in this position.

"You're still welcome here," Nick said. "We knew something wasn't right, but none of us could figure it out. I'm grateful that Will came along and told us what was happening so that we could bring your husband to justice."

A new set of tears streamed down Laura's face. "I appreciate everything you've done for me. But this is the first place James or his men will look. I can't put you in any danger."

"You'll come home with us," Polly said firmly. "As I mentioned, I've helped the pastor in these situations, and he's kept many a woman safe. If he perceives any danger to those living in the parsonage, he has other places you can stay. But we'll not discuss that now. The fewer who know about those things, the better. It's how we keep people safe."

His Polly was a tigress, that was for sure. How could a man not love someone like her? Wait. Mitch closed his eyes. His Polly? He started to deny it in his own mind, then he heard Will's voice accusing him of being a liar.

All right. Fine. He'd been lying to himself about not having feelings for Polly. The trouble was, even if he admitted the truth to himself, it wouldn't change the facts.

And the facts were, there was no way he could give his heart to her.

Chapter Seventeen

Polly knew from the way Laura shook that she was desperate for a way out of her marriage. But she was also desperately afraid he would hurt her again. She'd seen it all too many times before.

How many terrified women had she helped give a safe place to stay after they left abusive husbands, or after they fled a house of ill repute that didn't want them to leave?

"You don't know how evil he is," Laura said, her voice shaking. "Hattie wasn't the first person to fall for James's lies. You have no idea how many cast-off mistresses have shown up on my doorstep, begging me to set him free so they could be married."

Laura looked up at her. "Is it true that she was expecting?"

"That's what she told her husband," Polly said quietly, looking over at Mitch, who nodded.

"It wouldn't be the first time she came home with another man's child," Mitch answered. "I'm sorry for what they did to you."

Tears streamed down Laura's face, and Polly handed her a handkerchief.

"I've never had a child," Laura said. "James used to hit me and say it was my fault. I always hoped…" Then she sighed. "I guess it was my fault after all."

Not all abused women were receptive to being hugged, but Polly couldn't help but take her in her arms and hold her close.

"It isn't your fault. It's no one's fault." She wished she could give Laura more comfort.

"Indeed," Patricia Steele said. "You mustn't trouble yourself with such things. What's important is that you're safe from that man. Though I echo my invitation for you to stay, I agree that Pastor Lassiter is much better suited at finding you a safe place. But know you always have our friendship and support."

Laura gave her a watery smile. "I'm sorry I subjected you to this situation. I hope you'll forgive me for putting your family in danger."

"There is nothing to forgive, my dear." Patricia's expression was warm and loving.

"No, nothing," Nick agreed. "And if money is an issue, I insist that you allow us to help you."

Laura shook her head. "I'll be fine. That's why James had so many gambling debts. The trustees wouldn't release additional funds when he asked for them. He tried so many schemes for making money, but in the end, they all failed and he needed my fortune just to survive."

"Why didn't you tell them what happened?" Patricia's gaze was sympathetic. "Why didn't you tell us? Especially when I asked about the bruise on your arm?"

Polly could have given her a list of reasons. But it wasn't her story, and what mattered was helping Laura feel safe so she could heal.

"When I went to the authorities, they sent me back

to him. As far as the trustees…" Laura sighed. "I'm just a woman. No one listens. Why would you be any different?"

Her gaze returned to the ground. "When Mother was alive, she used to tell me that I simply wasn't trying hard enough. But I did everything he wanted. The only thing I couldn't do right was give him a son."

The anguish on her face when she looked back up nearly rent Polly's heart in two. "But I don't think he would have been satisfied even if I had."

Once again, Polly held her tight as she sobbed. "You're probably right," she said softly. "But that isn't your fault. There's nothing wrong with you, but with him. James Booth is an evil, evil, man, and it has no bearing on you."

Two watery brown eyes looked up, meeting hers. "But I married him. I fell for his charm. Do you think I would have married a man like him? No. He was kind, and generous, and…"

Her voice shook slightly. "I couldn't see it. How could I have been such a fool to not see what kind of man he was?"

"We all have lapses in judgment," Polly said. Her own poor judgments were many, too many to even count. Which was why, as she faced so much turmoil in her life about Mitch, she wasn't sure what to think or believe in terms of her own feelings.

She glanced in his direction and noted that he was speaking quietly with Nick, probably making arrangements. Patricia had joined them, and Mary was sitting with Eleanor, which she'd done as soon as James had been brought in. Polly had to admit, she and Mary made a team when it came to helping with the ministry. Each seemed to instinctively know what the other needed without anything having to be said.

Polly had worried how having this confrontation in Eleanor's presence would work out. A sensitive young woman who'd had no exposure to the rougher side of life, Eleanor was the sort who might go into hysterics. But she'd held up well, remaining silent but wide-eyed throughout the situation. A good thing if she were to marry a marshal. Mary would likely bond with her and help her with the transition to being a lawman's wife.

Which left Polly comforting a sobbing woman whose husband was now accused of murder.

"It's going to be all right," Polly said gently. "He won't be able to hurt you anymore."

Laura looked up at her. "How can you say that? You don't know what he's capable of. When he gets out…"

"He's not getting out." Polly used a firm tone as she stared into Laura's eyes. "With what you told us, plus with what further investigation is going to prove, he'll be in prison for a long time."

Laura nodded slowly, but fear lurked in her eyes.

"Are you ready?" Mitch gently put his hand on her shoulder. "I'd like to get Laura settled before word gets out."

"Yes." Polly turned her attention to Laura. "Will you come with us? I promise we'll keep you safe."

Experience had taught her to ask for permission, because the women who came unwillingly were always the ones who went back.

"How long can they keep him in jail?"

"A few days," Polly said, wishing she had a different answer. "But knowing Will, he'll find other charges on which to hold him. By then, folks will be up from Denver to take him. And I can't see them letting him out."

Laura looked over at Mitch. "You're out. And they think you did it."

"I had a good lawyer," Mitch said. "And I made bail. Had to use my house and my store, as well as those of my brother, as collateral. Everything I own is tied up in my legal case. If all the money is yours, I can't see Booth making bail."

"But his friends…"

Mitch shook his head. "Which ones? The ones he owes money to? How many people will actually stand by him when it all comes out? I didn't do it, and were it not for a brother who believed in me, I would still be in jail. Everyone else, including people I thought were good friends, abandoned me. No one wants to be connected to a murderer."

"But you have Polly, Mary and Will," Laura said.

"I met them after my life fell apart. And I will always be grateful for their support."

Then, eyes shining, he looked at Laura with such tenderness, it made Polly's heart nearly break in two. "And you have them, too. You will never meet more loyal and devoted friends. I promise you are safe with them."

He reached over and put his hand on top of Polly's, which still held Laura's hand in hers. She met his eyes as he said, "I mean that. You have no idea the precious gifts you've given my family. That you've given me, and I will treasure our time always."

His words sounded like a goodbye. Ridiculous, of course, but Polly's eyes stung and her chest hurt at his words.

"Thank you," she said, pulling away, then standing. She shifted her weight to put her back to them as she wiped her eyes. This wasn't about her, or her feelings.

They were saving a woman, Laura, from her abusive husband. Which was all in a day's work as part of their ministry.

Laura also stood, and after saying goodbye to their hosts, they returned to the Lassiter house. They all quickly retreated to Uncle Frank's study, where he was apprised of the situation. Because James was in jail, he decided that for now, the safest place for Laura was to remain at the Lassiter house. When the sheriff arrived from Denver, they'd want her close so she could tell him her side of the story. He didn't want them all going back and forth between safe houses and risk their operations being discovered.

Polly was moving her belongings into the attic with the children so Laura could have her own space, when Laura walked in.

"You don't have to do that," Laura said. "I would be perfectly fine in the attic."

"But the children are used to me. And this way, you have some privacy. Trust me when I say that they will give you no privacy whatsoever."

As if to prove her point, Clara and Isabella came bounding in. "Can we help?"

Clara's voice was suspiciously overearnest. Isabella merely lifted her arms up to be held. Polly picked up the little girl.

"I think we're fine. Uncle Frank said I should keep my dresses in the closet here, since there isn't a good place for them in the attic, and I just have this one small bag."

Polly held up the bag and smiled.

"Who's she?" Clara eyed Laura suspiciously.

"She's our friend, Laura, and she'll be staying with us for a while."

Though Caitlin and Nugget were familiar with the comings and goings of people in the house, this was the first the Taylor children had experienced.

"She's not a nanny, is she?"

"No." Polly smiled at the little girl. "I'm the nanny, remember?"

Clara's eyes narrowed. "You don't think you're going to be marrying our father, do you? Because we don't want you. If anyone's going to marry him, it's Polly."

Polly sighed. They still hadn't been able to convince the children they weren't getting married. Now they had to convince them that Laura wasn't a threat to the status quo.

"I told you, I am not marrying your father. We don't suit."

"Yes, you do!" Clara's scowl deepened. "We made a list of everything we want in a mother, and you're it. He looks at you like he wants to kiss you, and you want to kiss him. So you should marry him already."

From chocolate cake to kissing. Polly took a deep breath as she tried to find the right words to say to this little girl, who knew nothing about kissing.

"And who told you about kissing?" A teasing approach might be the best way to handle the situation.

"Everyone around here does it. Every time Mary walks into a room, Will kisses her and pats her tummy. Joseph and Annabelle do it, too. Yesterday, he even kissed her big stomach when he left. I saw Jasper kissing Emma Jane yesterday at church. At church!"

Polly tried not to giggle at the little girl's indignant expression.

"There's a whole lot of kissing going on around here, and you and Papa look at each other like you want to do it, too. So marry him already!"

Clara turned on her heel and stormed out. Isabella burrowed her face deeper into Polly's shoulder. Polly gently kicked the door closed and burst out laughing. Laura joined her, and the melodic laughter coming out of the other woman only served to make Polly happier. Laura would survive. And thrive.

As for Polly…well, that was another story. Some days she wondered if she'd be forced to marry Mitch just to get the children to stop.

"I'm sorry about that," Polly said when she finally stopped laughing. "No matter what we say to the contrary, the children are convinced that Mitch and I should marry."

Laura smiled. "You two do have a way of looking at each other."

Polly didn't bother to hide her groan. "Not you, too. I'm so tired of everyone and their matchmaking. Mitch and I have made it quite clear to one another that we don't suit."

Laura nodded slowly. "Why don't you suit?"

Polly stared at her. No one had asked that question before. "Well, because." She paused. Everyone else had simply assumed they knew the answer, and they all thought she and Mitch suited quite well.

"I suppose it's because we want different things out of life."

"Like what?" Laura's expression was gentle, understanding. She wasn't trying to push Polly into feeling something she didn't, or into a relationship she didn't want.

"Well, for one, I don't want to get married and have children. And Mitch has said that after what a disaster his marriage to Hattie was, he has no intention of ever remarrying. So for two people who don't want to get married—marrying each other, why, that's ludicrous."

Laura appeared to consider her words, then said, "Why don't you want to get married?"

Another question most people didn't ask of her. And now, having had a heart-to-heart with Ma, Polly wasn't fully sure of her answer. Especially with Isabella snuggled up to her, filling Polly's heart with more uncertainty as to the direction she'd so firmly plotted out for herself.

"Because I've seen too many marriages go wrong," Polly said. It seemed to be the simplest answer, given that of all the things she knew to be true, and the things she questioned, at least this remained constant.

"In what way?" Again, Laura's question was gentle, seeming more curious than judgmental.

"Do you know how women end up working in brothels?"

Laura shook her head.

"Many of them are either running from abusive husbands, or are widows with nowhere else to go or have no family to care for them. Some choose the life, but so many do it because they have no other options."

Polly took a deep breath. "Uncle Frank started his ministry in the mining camps, where we still do a lot of work. That's where we met him, Annabelle and his late wife, Catherine. Until we met them, we lived a hard life. I helped Ma the best I could. Some people think miners are beyond salvation, and I don't blame them. They're a hard lot. I know what a man's fists can do to a woman's face."

Trying to get the images out of her head, Polly closed her eyes and tried to bring to mind the feeling of hope she'd found in helping others. Then she turned back to Laura.

"I understood your pain and fear because I've seen it too many times to count. What happens if I marry a man and he turns into a monster?"

Polly could still remember hearing various couples fighting, back when they lived in the mining camps and all they had for shelter was a tent. Sometimes she still had nightmares about the things she'd heard.

Sympathy filled Laura's face. "I can understand that. What evidence has Mitch given you that he's going to turn into a monster when you two marry?"

Laura's words hit her square in the chest.

"What evidence did James give you of being a monster?"

Laura let out a long sigh. "None that I could see. But my family saw. My father told me not to marry him, and when I did, he did everything he could to protect my fortune from him. I don't know why I didn't see it when everyone else did. Has anyone warned you that Mitch may not be who he seems?"

Polly's heart sank as she realized that not only had no one warned her against Mitch, but they all seemed to be pushing her in his direction. Were they right after all?

"No," she said quietly.

"I barely know you," Laura said. "And I barely know Mitch. But I can't fathom how a man who would raise the children of his wife's indiscretions and give them the kind of love I've seen in this family would somehow turn into a cold-blooded murderer."

She let out a long sigh. "I knew the first minute you all started talking about James and the murder that he did it. Had I been willing to open my eyes, I probably would have seen it the moment her body was discovered. I'll own that I have been a poor judge of character. You may have, too. But I am putting my very life on the line on the belief that Mitch is a good man."

Polly hadn't thought about it that way. Trusting Mitch in this situation, at least for Laura, was a matter of life and death. If she was wrong in trusting Mitch, and Mitch was the murderer, or even if he was a bad man, Laura could wind up in more trouble than she'd bargained for. She was trying to escape an abuser, not run headlong into more trouble.

"His children clearly love you," Laura said, gesturing to the little girl asleep in Polly's arms. "And I have no doubt that if you would get past your fear, he would love you, too. You deserve happiness, Polly. A woman with as big of a heart, helping people like me, you shouldn't spend your life alone simply because you're afraid of being hurt."

Isabella stirred in Polly's arms. "I should probably put her down."

"Think about what I said." Laura gave her another gentle smile. "Just because James hurt me, it doesn't mean I don't still believe in love. I've spent barely an afternoon in this house, and everywhere I look, I see deep, lasting love. You may be so used to it that you don't see it, but I hope you open your eyes before it's too late."

Remembering Clara's words about all the kissing that happened in their midst brought a smile to Polly's face. There was an awful lot of kissing around her, and it wasn't the way most places were. But most places weren't firmly centered in God's love. Most marriages weren't supported by such an incredible group of people who vowed to love each other as family.

"Thank you," Polly said as she exited the room.

Laura was right—Polly had been blind. She'd let the ugliness and fear from her past cover her eyes and keep her from seeing the incredible examples of love right before her. Even the love of Uncle Frank and Catherine, when she was alive, had encouraged others in pursuing a deeper connection.

Polly was so deep in thought that she nearly ran into Mitch on the landing. He held out his arms to keep her from colliding with him.

"Whoa! Everything all right?"

"Sorry." Polly looked up and her eyes locked with his. A deep blue sky of compassion met hers. She used to feel the same peace lying on her back watching the clouds.

Even when he was the angriest, when he had the right to be the angriest, Mitch had never raised a hand to her. He'd never raised a hand to his children, though they'd all confessed to being beaten at times by nannies. Mitch had been horrified to learn that.

"What's the worst thing you've ever done?" she asked, searching his eyes.

"What?"

"Tell me." She stared at him. "It's important."

"I've never committed a crime," he said slowly. "If that's what you're asking. What's going on here?"

"I need to know. What's the worst thing you've ever done?"

He finally seemed to understand what she wanted, because she wasn't even sure herself. But for some reason, that question burned inside her.

"When I was a boy, I was supposed to be watching my brother. But I wanted to play with my friends, so I made him sit by a tree. He wandered off, and it took hours for us to find him. I've always felt guilty for not being a better brother."

Mitch let out a long breath. "I promised to make it up to him, and I've done a poor job. I still haven't figured out how to be a good brother to him, but now that I've realized my mistake, I'm doing my best to do it differently moving forward. Which is all we can do."

No, you couldn't change the past, or even how things happened. But you could, as Mitch said, do your best to do better.

"Thank you," Polly said. It was on the tip of her tongue to tell him how she felt about him, but something about it felt wrong.

"What about you? What's the worst thing you've ever done?"

"I'm prideful and stubborn. I guess we all know that, but I'm realizing just how much I allow it to blind me. Now I need to figure out how to keep it from making me make the worst decision of my life."

Mitch smiled at her. Gently. Kindly. And, if she were to be so bold, lovingly. "Take it from a man who has made more than his share of worst decisions. Even your worst decision can become your best decision, if you give it time. You don't have to live your life perfectly as long as you're willing to learn from it."

Then he chuckled softly. "I suppose that's where working on our pride has to happen."

Isabella lifted her head from Polly's shoulder. "Papa?" She turned and reached for him just as the thunder of footsteps sounded up the stairs.

"Papa's back!"

The children entered the room, chorusing their questions of where he'd been.

Over the din, Polly said, "Yes, where did you go? You disappeared earlier."

Mitch gave a small shrug. "I went over to the sheriff's office to give my version of the events. They'll want to talk to you to confirm what was said at the Steeles', but it sounds like they've already got folks from Denver coming up."

"Is that good?"

Clara, Rory and Thomas wrapped their arms around Mitch as he said, "I think so. Will sounded hopeful."

Polly watched as Mitch greeted his children, hugging each one of them, even pulling Louisa, who'd been standing off to the side, into an embrace.

She'd have said that she lost another piece of her heart to this man and his family, but as she continued down the stairs, she realized she'd given it to them a long time ago.

Now to figure out what to do about it.

Chapter Eighteen

Mitch walked home from the Leadville sheriff's office, a load off his back. The Denver sheriff had come up overnight and had insisted on meeting with Mitch first thing. Mitch's story, as well as what Will found out about James Booth, had put together missing pieces in the investigation. Though Booth was still loudly protesting his innocence, this time they were convinced they had the right man. All charges against Mitch would be dropped.

Passing his brother's store, he noticed the reporters had all left. Now that Booth had been arrested, they'd abandoned their interest in Mitch's family. Mitch entered the store. Andrew greeted him with a warm smile.

"I see we have good news."

"Yes." Mitch looked around to be sure the store wasn't busy. Fortunately, no customers appeared to be about. "I'm sorry I didn't tell you sooner."

"I understand." Andrew shifted uncomfortably.

"No, you don't." Mitch came closer to his brother. "I didn't do a very good job of telling you much of anything, and that wasn't fair. A very wise person told me something about pride yesterday, and how she let her pride stand in the way of her happiness. Or something like that."

Mitch looked at Andrew, realizing how little he knew his brother. He'd let too much distance come between them. "You see, I was hurt by what you said when I married Hattie. You told me not to marry her, and I didn't listen. When things went wrong, I had too much pride to confide in you. But being around Polly's family has made me realize just how much I miss our closeness."

His throat felt tight as he said, "I'm sorry."

Tears filled Andrew's eyes. "No, I'm sorry. I could tell you were having a bad time of things, and I should have offered my support sooner. I wish I could have done more than just offer my house and store as collateral for your bond." Then he grinned. "But I'm mighty glad to be getting it back."

Andrew came around the corner. "But all that's water under the bridge now. I understand Polly has your terrors in hand, so maybe we could do more together as a family."

"I'd like that," Mitch said, giving his brother a hug.

The door jangled, and a group of customers walked in.

"I should get back to the children."

Andrew nodded. "We'll talk soon."

Mitch left and arrived home to a quiet house. Funny how this place had already become home. Now that the reporters weren't dogging their every move, he supposed they could go home to Denver. But he didn't want to.

Taking advantage of the quiet, he went up to his room to grab his Bible. A note lay on the bed.

Mitch,

I was wrong in not giving you a chance. Me and my pride. The truth is, I'm in love with you, but

I'm scared. What if you don't love me back? I
don't want things to be awkward between us, so
if you share my feelings, meet me at the livery so
we can go on a picnic. If not, I'll understand, and
I promise never to mention it again.
Love, Polly

Mitch closed his eyes. He'd told them no more. How
was he supposed to get the children to understand that
being with Polly was impossible?

He went downstairs to find the children at the
kitchen table, hard at work on their studies.

"Children!" He knew his voice sounded harsh, but he
couldn't help himself. They didn't understand. Couldn't
understand.

"Yes, Papa?" Louisa's voice was all sweetness, her
eyes all innocence.

"Which one of you left the note on my bed?"

"What note?"

Four sets of eyes looked at him in what would have
been perfect innocence had he not known better.

"Fine." He looked over at Gertie, who appeared to
be supervising their studies. "Where's Polly?"

"She had some errands to run. I offered to help the
children this afternoon. I'm sure they didn't mean anything by their prank. You know how they are."

"Yes, I do." He glared at them. "You will each write
one hundred sentences. They will read, 'I will never
meddle with my father's love life again.' Do you understand?"

"But that's not fair!" Louisa jumped up. "We didn't
do anything."

He turned his attention to Clara. "Did you or did you
not tell me just this morning that I should kiss Polly?"

Tear-filled eyes looked up at him. She nodded.

"From now on, if I hear any of you mention anything romantic with Polly, marrying Polly, prayer requests at church about getting a new mother, you will all write one hundred sentences. And you will keep writing until you learn to stay out of my affairs."

Then he looked at Gertie. "None of them are to leave the table until they all finish their sentences."

"Mitch…" Gertie looked disappointed. "Don't you think…"

"What I think is that these children have too much time on their hands if they have the time to keep arranging love notes." He held up the note, then stomped over to the stove and tossed it into the fire.

"There will be no more of this nonsense. Polly is not your mother, and she never will be. Taking care of you is her job, just like my working in the store is mine. She does not want to get married, she does not want a family and you need to leave her alone."

Then, without waiting for a response, Mitch stormed out of the kitchen, slamming the back door behind him.

"They are just children," he could hear Polly's voice saying in the back of his head. He'd been unfair to them, and he knew it. Gertie knew it, and she probably thought terrible things about him for it.

But what else was he supposed to do? If one more person tried pushing him toward Polly, he was going to lose his mind. Yes, he cared for her. And yes, in answer to Clara's very nosy question this morning, he did want to kiss her. More than he'd ever wanted to kiss anyone else.

Polly, however, did not want those things. And even if he could convince her to try, what kind of man made a woman give up her dreams? Oh, he knew Polly wasn't

Hattie, but how could he do that again? Polly wouldn't have affairs or leave them, but how long would it take for her to resent her decision to stay?

Love was letting someone go and giving up your right to have that person by your side so that they could be happy.

Did he love Polly?

Most desperately.

Which was why she could never know. Never settle for the life she didn't want.

Polly waited at the livery until long past the time she'd told her mother she'd be back. Mitch wasn't coming.

At first, she'd tried telling herself that he'd been held up at the sheriff's office. But she'd seen Will, and he'd stopped to say hello. He told her that everything wrapped up nicely, and James Booth was already on his way to Denver, where he'd be officially charged with Hattie's murder.

Though they'd had the clue of the cuff links, apparently the sheriff's office had other evidence not linked to Mitch that they'd been hiding—evidence that proved James had done it—including James's prized statuette, which had been used to kill Hattie. Some of it had been pushed aside because it didn't fit with the theory of Mitch being the murderer. But others, like the cuff links, had been deliberately hidden by a deputy on Booth's payroll. The deputy would be facing charges of his own.

Great news for Mitch. Great news for Laura. But it didn't seem to matter when Mitch wasn't here to celebrate.

Polly turned to walk back to the parsonage, wishing she didn't have to face him. She'd said that she'd never speak of her feelings for him again, but it was still humiliating to have to see him. As much as she loved the children, how was she going to be in his presence knowing that she loved him and that he didn't love her back?

She'd been a fool to think that just because she'd experienced a change of heart, Mitch had as well. After all, hadn't he made it clear that he had no intention of remarrying? That his heart was no longer available to romance? He'd assured everyone, including Polly, that his feelings for her were nothing more than platonic.

He'd given no indication of his feelings being any different. Polly sighed. Deep in her heart, she must have already known that, which was why she'd left him a note, rather than having to see his face when he rejected her.

Somehow she'd thought it would be easier to not see the look in his eyes when he rejected her.

And now she wondered how she'd even be able to look at him at all.

Her stomach knotted, and she wanted to be sick. Why had she been so foolish as to go against her better judgment and fall in love with Mitch? Why had she expressed those feelings, knowing he didn't feel the same?

Once again, Polly had allowed her heart to blind her to common sense. Would she ever learn?

She looked up to see a familiar face.

"Polly!" Eleanor Steele greeted her warmly.

Despite the churning in her stomach, Polly gave her friend the best smile she could manage. It seemed almost cruel to run into someone glowing with the happiness of a woman in love—and loved in return. While she was genuinely pleased for Eleanor, Polly wasn't sure she could hold her broken heart together if she had to listen to the other girl talk about the joy Polly would never have.

Eleanor gestured to the woman next to her. "I'm so glad you're here. You can be the first to meet my dear friend, Rebecca Ashworth, who is here to help with the wedding. Rebecca just finished teacher training school in Denver, and after the wedding, she'll be looking for a job. She wanted to go to work right away, but I convinced her that she should stay with me for a while first. When else will she be able to enjoy her life? Once she starts teaching…"

Rebecca groaned. "It's not going to be that bad. It's a pleasure to meet you, Polly. Eleanor has told me so much about you."

"The pleasure is all mine." Polly smiled at the other woman. As much as she'd dreaded having to hear more about the happiness she'd never experience in her life, running into Eleanor just might be the answer to Polly's problems.

"I'd love to hear more about that teaching school. I've been hoping to attend myself."

"We were just on our way to tea at the Rafferty. Join us," Rebecca said with a smile.

Polly smiled back, but she didn't feel much like it. This is what she'd said she wanted all along, but as she followed her friends into the hotel, she felt more like her entire world had just ended.

Chapter Nineteen

Betrayal was not strong enough of a word to describe Mitch's feelings as he listened to Polly in Frank's study, outlining her plan to go to Denver.

"You promised the children you'd stay as long as you were needed," Mitch said, trying to keep his voice steady.

"They appear to be doing fine," Polly said, turning toward Laura. "Laura has agreed to help with them."

Laura nodded. "I've always wanted children. And, given that I won't have children of my own, I rather like the idea of being able to care for yours. I'm sure we'll get along."

Mitch snorted. "Until they set you on fire."

"What is wrong with you?" Polly glared at him. "They've grown. Changed. I'm sure they would never do such a thing."

Then she added with a small smile, "Again."

"Fine," Mitch said. "Have a nice life."

He started to turn to leave before his anger got the best of him. Before the pain of Polly tearing herself from him engulfed him in a fire that burned hotter than anything his children had ever set.

"Please, Mitch, don't leave angry. I want us to be…"

He waved a hand at her. "Don't. We've discussed this. I knew your involvement in our lives was temporary. I just didn't think you were going to leave so soon. I'm sure it's better this way anyway."

Yes. That's what he needed to tell himself. Had been telling himself. Better for her to leave now, when he was just beginning to fall in love with her, than later, when he'd given her his entire heart.

Mitch shook his head. Who was he trying to fool? Despite all of his efforts, he'd already done that.

"I need to check on the children." He didn't give her a backward glance as he turned to go.

When he opened the door, five faces stared back at him. Then they rushed past him.

"Don't go, Polly," they wailed.

"We'll be good, we promise," Rory said.

"Papa already punished us. We'll never try to get you two married again. Just don't leave us." Big, fat tears rolled down Clara's face.

"Please, Polly, we still need you."

Louisa's tearful admission had probably cost his daughter far more than anyone realized. How long had she argued that they didn't need a nanny?

But Polly hadn't just won his heart. She'd won the hearts of five children determined to never give theirs up either.

It's not fair, Lord, he prayed. *Why did You do this to us? To them?*

"I'm sorry, children," Polly said softly, her eyes puffy and red. Why she cried, he had no idea, since it was her decision to leave.

"But there's a class that starts next week, it's a special class, and it will allow me to..." Tears streamed down her face. "I may never get a chance like this again.

But it'll be like I promised. I'll write, and we can visit sometimes."

Her voice cracked as she said, "And the truth is, you don't need me anymore. You've all done so well, and I've hardly been doing anything the past few days. Louisa, you've proven to me that..."

Sobs kept Polly from saying whatever she'd meant to say, and only the devastation on his children's faces kept Mitch from feeling sorry for her.

"We won't write to you." Louisa glared at her. "You're a liar, and we never want to see you again."

His daughter turned and stormed out, taking the rest of the children with her. Mitch wanted to call her back and tell her that she was behaving inappropriately, but he didn't have the heart to. She was only telling the truth, and he, too, felt like he'd been lied to.

Polly began to sob like her heart was breaking. All it did was remind Mitch that his already had. And somehow, he'd have to go upstairs and find a way to put together five other broken hearts.

He should have known this was a bad idea. Should have known not to bring someone into their lives who had every intention of leaving. He'd just expected Polly to have more integrity and keep her promise to stay until they no longer needed her. The trouble was, Mitch couldn't imagine that such a time would come.

Which was why, he told himself, it was better for her to leave now. Had she waited any longer, and gotten everyone's hearts further entangled, he wasn't sure how he would pick up the pieces. Even now, it seemed to be a Herculean task.

Everyone in her family thought she was crazy. They didn't say it, but Polly could tell from the way they looked at her. More than a few times, she saw one of them start to open their mouth to try to talk her out of it, but then her mother would shoot them a glare to remind them of their promise not to meddle in Polly's life.

On one hand, Polly wished they would meddle and talk her out of this nonsense. But the looks on Mitch's and the children's faces told her that she'd already done too much damage. There was no way that they'd take her back, even if she spent every second since the horrible words came out of her mouth regretting her decision.

She trudged up the steps, also regretting her decision to give up her bedroom for Laura. She'd have to sleep in the attic, listening to the children's gentle breathing and hating herself for the hurt she'd caused in their lives. Polly wouldn't sleep a wink, but that was the price she'd pay for her actions.

Why did she think declaring herself to Mitch was a good idea? All she had was everyone else's word that he cared for her. He'd never said he had feelings for her, just that he was attracted to her, and that wasn't the same thing, now was it?

When she reached the top step, she felt something funny under her feet. But before she could determine what it was, she felt herself falling.

With a thud, Polly landed at the base of the stairs. Pain shot through her leg, surging through her body. Unable to help herself, Polly cried out.

The first person to open his door was Mitch. "Polly! What happened?" He looked down at her and he said carefully, "Don't move. Frank!"

Uncle Frank opened his bedroom door. "What's going on here?"

"Polly's been hurt. We need a doctor."

She thought she heard Ma's voice, but she couldn't be sure as the pain seemed to overwhelm everything else. Darkness tried claiming her, and while she thought she might need to fight it, everything hurt too much to try.

When Polly regained consciousness, she was in her mother's bed, quilts wrapped around her and her leg propped up.

"Don't move," Ma said quietly. "Your leg was badly broken, and while Dr. Owens was able to set the bone, he said you need to lie as still as possible to give it the best chance of healing."

"What happened?" Polly looked around the room. "Why am I in your room?"

"It seemed easier." Ma gave her a small smile. "As for what happened, the children rigged a contraption to the attic door, thinking they'd keep you out. Unfortunately, you didn't see it and tripped over it instead, causing you to fall down the stairs. You landed on your leg, breaking it in several places."

Polly's heart sank. "The children—"

"Are upstairs packing. Mitch is horrified at what happened. Now that he's been exonerated, he wants to get them back home to Denver. We told him it wasn't necessary, but he feels it's best to resume their normal lives."

"Can I see them?"

Ma looked away.

"They need to know I'm not angry." Polly sighed. "I'm sure they didn't mean to hurt me."

"Mitch would prefer that you didn't." Ma didn't sound happy about it, but she hadn't seemed happy during any of the conversation. But who would be at having their daughter laid up so?

"Could I talk to Mitch?"

Seeing him would hurt more than the throbbing in her leg. But she had to tell them that she was sorry. And that she wasn't upset with the children. She should have known that they'd act out. And she should have known that they'd take their frustrations out on her.

"He's waiting outside."

Ma got up and opened the door. "You can come in now. I'll be outside, but I need to leave the door open. I'm sure you understand."

Polly fought the urge to laugh. There was no risk of violating propriety here.

Mitch stepped in, his hair disheveled and dark circles under his eyes. "Polly, I'm so sorry."

"Don't be. I deserved it."

He nodded slowly, like he agreed with her but didn't think it was right to say so.

"They did it on purpose. They wanted to make sure you learned your lesson." He closed his eyes, and she watched the pain crease his face. "But they didn't intend for you to be so badly hurt."

"I forgive them. You should, too." Though it took more effort than she thought it should, she smiled. "I know I have no authority over them anymore, but I'm asking you to please not punish them. They don't deserve it. I do."

Tears rolled down her cheeks. "I hurt them, so they wanted to hurt me. I understand. My leg will heal."

"Maybe," Mitch said. "But I heard your mother and the doctor talking. I know your mother is trying to be positive, but your leg is broken in multiple places. The doctor isn't sure how it's going to heal."

"I hope you weren't trying to come in to cheer me up," Polly said, trying to laugh but finding that effort just as difficult as anything else.

"Why?" He looked at her, tears in his eyes.

"Why what?" They'd probably given her something for the pain, but surely that wasn't enough to make their conversation so fuzzy.

"Why did you do this to us?"

He wasn't talking about her injury. She'd rather he did, because the prospect of not walking again seemed so much better than ripping her heart open again.

"You know why."

"No, I don't." Mitch's voice shook. "I haven't slept at all because every time I close my eyes, I try to understand why you would leave us. Why, after knowing how important it is to me, you would break your promise to us."

The words that had been in her head since she realized he wasn't going to show up stood at the tip of her tongue but wouldn't come out. Instead, they rolled down her cheeks, globs of everything she'd been holding in but couldn't say.

"You owe me at least that."

She didn't really owe him anything, not when this was all his fault anyway. Now, the children, she owed them, and that was why she'd accept this injury as her due.

"I didn't know what I was promising," she finally said. "I didn't know how hard it would be to look at you every day, knowing how desperately I loved you, and knowing that you didn't return my feelings. For the children, I should have tried, I know that. But I couldn't."

The tears fell harder and faster, tears she thought she'd already cried, but apparently, they hadn't been enough. Would they ever be?

"You could have at least told me." His expression was unreadable, making the pain even worse.

"I did. I left you a note. You didn't even meet me."

Mitch started laughing. "You left me a note?"

"Yes." She couldn't believe he'd mock her like that after everything.

He shook his head. "I don't suppose your mother or the children mentioned that I punished them for leaving a love note for me. They denied it, of course, and that just made me angrier. I'm afraid I was a little harsh on them."

Polly closed her eyes. It hadn't occurred to her that Mitch would think it was a prank. The children had been so good about listening…

"Polly, look at me."

She obeyed his request and saw his eyes shining in a way she hadn't seen before. "I was angry because I was tired of being taunted with something I could never have. I am in love with you, and I didn't think you'd be willing to give up your dreams and share your life with me."

"But you never said anything."

He shrugged. "Neither did you. I suppose we both had too much pride to risk our hearts being broken."

"And when I took that risk, and you didn't respond, I was too ashamed to face you."

Mitch handed her a handkerchief. "And that's why you decided to leave?"

Polly nodded, wiping her face. "I was so embarrassed. I finally realized that all of my fears were foolish, and that life with you and the children wasn't going to be anything but wonderful. But when I admitted it to you, you rejected me."

"In the future, let's not rely on notes to communicate."

"All right." Polly took a deep breath. "So what happens now?"

Mitch grinned. "I'm told that there's an awful lot of kissing happening in this house, but we're not part of that. I think, if you're feeling up to it, we need to rectify that situation."

"Oh, I'm up for it."

Polly reached up and put her arms around him as Mitch bent down and kissed her. Just as their lips met in a most satisfying way, she heard a voice.

"It's about time!"

They turned their heads, and Clara was standing in the doorway. "Now that you've kissed, are you going to stay?"

Polly grinned. "I don't know. I hear you're leaving."

Clara groaned. The rest of the children joined her at the doorway.

"We're not going anywhere," Louisa said.

"We like it here." Rory glared at his father. "You might have been planning on leaving, but we had a plan to stay."

Then, with a grin, he looked over at Thomas. "You can wash those spots off your face. We don't need 'em."

Polly tried to laugh, but it hurt too much. "Are you sure I broke my leg?"

"You might have also broken a rib or two," Mitch said slowly. "But we were trying to break the news to you gently."

"Were you trying to kill me?" Polly looked at the grinning children.

Clara shrugged. "That wasn't part of the plan. But I'd say the rest of it worked perfectly."

All five children had the nerve to grin. Even Isabella,

who probably had nothing to do with the plan, wore an expression of mirth. Mitch just shook his head.

"And you're sure you think a life with these wild creatures is going to be wonderful?"

Warmth filled Polly's heart. Or was that another injury they hadn't told her about? No, she decided, it was everything finally being put back together. And if her heart could heal, so could the rest of her body.

"We're waiting," Louisa said, hands on her hips.

"For?" Mitch looked at his daughter. "We already kissed."

Clara groaned again. "Kissing is just the second step. The third step is you asking Polly to marry you, and her saying yes. So get on with it, because Maddie thinks we're out getting berries, and pretty soon, she's going to realize we're gone and then we're going to get in trouble."

"Again," Rory muttered.

"I think Maddie will let this one slide," Ma said from the doorway. "But Polly does need her rest, and the rest of us would like to know that things are finally settled between you two, so we can all stop our worrying."

Polly fought the urge to giggle as Mitch looked down on her. "Are we ever going to be able to live our own lives?"

"Probably not," he said, kissing her on the forehead. "But I wouldn't have it any other way."

"Neither would I."

"Would you get on with it?" The voices in the doorway all seemed to be in unison, and Polly turned to see that Uncle Frank, Maddie, Mary and Will were all also standing there.

"Should I wait for Annabelle and Joseph?" Polly said, looking around.

"You could, but they're going to be a while. In fact, that's why we're so eager for you two to hurry up. The baby's coming, and Gertie is supposed to be there to deliver it. Annabelle is never going to forgive you if your ma misses it because you're too busy dithering over a marriage proposal." Mary gave her a mock glare, but then Will elbowed her in the ribs.

"But do take your time," Mary said with a smile. "After all, a woman only gets proposed to once."

Mitch grinned. "This woman, anyway." He planted another kiss on her forehead. "And this woman deserves a little privacy for her special moment. So you're all going to close the door, walk back to the kitchen and when I open the door again, you'll be able to congratulate the future Mrs. Taylor."

"Wonderful," Maddie said. "With as stubborn as those two are, we might get such a pleasure after Mary's baby is born."

"I'm sure they'll be hungry before then," Uncle Frank reassured her.

Everyone laughed as they shut the door.

This time, when Mitch's eyes sparkled as he looked at her, Polly knew exactly what they meant.

"I meant what I said about accepting their meddling as part of being in a loving family." He grinned. "But that doesn't mean we're not entitled to our privacy from time to time."

He brought her hand to his lips. "Polly MacDonald, will you do me the great honor of becoming my wife and the mother of my children?"

"Yes!" She tried to bring her arms around him to embrace him, but the effort hurt more than it had last time.

Mitch seemed to understand as he bent to kiss her.

"We have the rest of our lives for that. For now, just let me handle it."

And so she did.

Epilogue

"Hurry! You're going to miss it! Polly's going to throw the bouquet!" Clara tugged at Mitch's pants as he accepted congratulations from Joseph.

"I don't think you want me to catch it," Mitch said, ruffling his daughter's hair.

"No, but we rigged it so Laura would." Clara grinned as she ran out to the garden.

Mitch just shook his head as he pointed to the baby girl in Joseph's arms. "I hope you know what you've gotten yourself into."

Joseph gave the baby a squeeze as he kissed her. "I wouldn't trade Catherine for anything in the world, and I'm pretty sure no one could convince you to give up Clara."

"True."

He heard shouts from the garden and knew the deed had been done. "Shall we go see what the damage is?"

"At least we don't smell smoke." Joseph grinned.

Mitch patted the other man on the back. "True, true."

He thought it best not to mention that his children had many other ways of creating mayhem. Fortunately, they'd mostly reformed their ways.

Unless they wanted something really, really badly.

Which was why Mitch kept finding baby everything everywhere.

He shook his head. Why the children were set on another sibling, he had no idea. He blamed Annabelle for that one, bringing over her baby every day and making Polly and the children gush over it.

As they entered the garden, Will greeted them with a grin. "That's another one for the Taylors."

"She caught the bouquet?" Mitch asked, knowing he didn't need to.

"Of course she did. I don't know how they do it, but they're good. I'm looking forward to what they try to accomplish next," Will said.

Mitch sighed. "They want a baby."

Will clapped him on the shoulder. "Mine isn't here yet, and I already don't think I'd have the strength."

"Strength for what?" Polly asked, giving her pa a squeeze as she let go of his arm to give Mitch a kiss as she joined them.

Mitch quickly kissed his wife back, mindful of everyone's eyes on them. Especially Polly's father's. Polly had been spending more time with him lately, repairing the bond that had been broken between them. And while Mitch knew Collin MacDonald approved of the match, it still felt awkward to kiss his daughter in front of him.

"The children want a baby," Mitch told Polly, shaking his head.

"But we've just gotten married."

As if they knew they were being talked about, the children came running up to them, followed by Andrew and Iris, who'd agreed to watch them so Mitch and Polly could have a proper honeymoon. At first, Mitch was surprised they'd offered, but then Iris admitted that her own little darling might have played her own role in not getting along with his children. Now that Mitch had decided to relocate to Leadville and leave management of the Denver store to his staff, the two Taylor families were spending more time together.

"Mama," the children all said in unison.

They'd decided that the children could choose what to call Polly after the wedding, but as soon as they announced their engagement, the children had started calling her Mama. Mitch had to say, the name fit her well.

Polly wrapped her arms around them, and if one didn't know better, they'd never guess that Polly hadn't given birth to them.

"What's this I hear about a baby?" she asked, looking directly at Clara.

"I was too little to enjoy Isabella when she was a baby, and I think I'm rather good with them. Annabelle's baby is lovely, but we have to give her back. But if you had a baby, we could keep her forever. And I do love babies." Clara let out a long sigh.

Joseph held up the baby in question. "Well, I don't love changing her, and she needs one. Why don't you take her inside and get some practice in for when your baby comes."

Clara took the baby and did as he asked, the other children following, chattering about what a wonderful baby Catherine was.

Mitch shot him a glare. "Really?"

"I'm not sure how your children will manage having a role in it, but I do know Clara. And when she's determined about something, well, you may as well save yourself a whole lot of trouble and give in right away."

Polly groaned. "We have got to work on getting that girl to accept the word *no* as a final answer rather than a challenge."

Andrew nodded. "Please do. She's starting to rub off on our daughter."

They laughed, and Mitch couldn't help but again be grateful for his renewed closeness with his brother. Polly, though, still wore a concerned expression on her face.

Taking her into his arms, Mitch asked, "So you're saying you don't want a baby?"

If he hadn't already been hopelessly in love with her, the look in her eyes would have sent him over the edge. "Oh, I want all the babies you're willing to give me. And maybe a few we find along the way."

She turned in the direction of Emma Jane, who was bouncing her son, Moses, on her lap.

"I do like how you think," Mitch said, bending down and kissing her. "But if it's all the same to you, I'd like to focus on one at a time."

Polly kissed him back, filling him with so much love, he hadn't known it was possible. How he'd ever survived without her, he didn't know, but he would always be grateful having her by his side.

* * * * *

If you enjoyed Polly's book, pick up the stories of Polly's friends, also set in Leadville, Colorado:

ROCKY MOUNTAIN DREAMS
THE LAWMAN'S REDEMPTION
SHOTGUN MARRIAGE

Available now from Love Inspired!

Find more great reads at www.LoveInspired.com

Dear Reader,

Originally, I intended to write Polly's story right after *Rocky Mountain Dreams*. But finding the right hero for her proved to be more elusive than I thought. When I finally found the man I thought was the perfect hero for Polly, my editor wasn't sure he'd be a good fit. And, as much as I hated to admit it, she was right. She and I had a great conversation about the kind of man Polly needed, and I finally realized why none of them worked. Polly's perfect match had to be someone who, at least in Polly's estimation, was the absolute worst marriage prospect on the planet. Otherwise, she was never going to let her guard down enough to fall in love. I remember blurting to my editor, "He's got FIVE kids!" The gleam in her eyes told me that I had finally found Polly's hero.

Polly needed a man who would challenge her and make her question a lot of her preconceived ideas, but also someone would could love and appreciate her indomitable spirit—and not break it. What Polly needed was something we all need—someone who will challenge us, push us and make us stronger without breaking all the marvelous qualities that make us who we are.

Whether it's a friend, relative or significant other, I pray you find that kind of relationship in your own life.

I love hearing from my readers! You can visit me online at the following places:

Website: *http://www.danicafavorite.com/*
Twitter: *https://twitter.com/danicafavorite/*
Instagram: *https://instagram.com/danicafavorite/*

Facebook: *https://www.facebook.com/ DanicaFavoriteAuthor*

Sending abundant blessings and love to you and yours,

Danica Favorite

COMING NEXT MONTH FROM
Love Inspired® Historical

Available October 4, 2016

MONTANA COWBOY DADDY
Big Sky Country • by Linda Ford

With a little girl to raise, widowed single father Dawson Marshall could sure use some help—he just didn't expect it to come from city girl Isabelle Redfield. The secret heiress who volunteers to watch Dawson's daughter wants to be valued for more than her money, but will hiding the truth ruin her chance of earning Dawson's love?

THE SHERIFF'S CHRISTMAS TWINS
Smoky Mountain Matches • by Karen Kirst

After confirmed bachelor Sheriff Shane Timmons and his childhood friend Allison Ashworth discover orphaned twin babies, Shane offers to help Allison care for them—temporarily. But as Shane falls for Allison and the twins, can he become the permanent husband and father they need?

A FAMILY FOR THE HOLIDAYS
Prairie Courtships • by Sherri Shackelford

Hoping to earn money to buy a boardinghouse, Lily Winter accompanies two orphaned siblings to Nebraska. But when she discovers their grandfather is missing and the kids are in danger, she hires Jake Elder, a local gun-for-hire, for protection—and marries him for convenience.

THE RIGHTFUL HEIR
by Angel Moore

Mary Lou Ellison believes she inherited the local newspaper from her guardian...until Jared Ivy arrives with a will that says his grandfather left it to *him*. The sheriff's solution? They must work together until a judge comes to town and rules in favor of the rightful heir.

———————

REQUEST YOUR FREE BOOKS!

2 FREE INSPIRATIONAL NOVELS
PLUS 2 *FREE* MYSTERY GIFTS

Love Inspired® HISTORICAL

Sheriff Shane Timmons just wants to be left alone, but this Christmas he'll find that family is what he's always been looking for.

Read on for an excerpt from
THE SHERIFF'S CHRISTMAS TWINS,
the next heartwarming book in the
SMOKY MOUNTAIN MATCHES *series.*

"We have a situation at the mercantile, Sheriff."

Shane Timmons reached for his gun belt.

The banker held up his hand. "You won't be needing that. This matter requires finesse, not force."

"What's happened?"

"I suggest you come see for yourself."

Shane's curiosity grew as he followed Claude outside into the crisp December day and continued on to the mercantile. Half a dozen trunks were piled beside the entrance. Unease pulled his shoulder blades together. His visitors weren't due for three more days. He did a quick scan of the street, relieved there was no sign of the stagecoach.

Claude held the door and waited for him to enter first. The pungent stench of paint punched him in the chest. His gaze landed on a knot of men and women in the far corner.

"Why didn't you watch where you were going? Where are your parents?"

"I—I'm terribly sorry, ma'am" came the subdued reply. "My ma's at the café."

"This is what happens when children are allowed to roam through the town unsupervised."

Shane rounded the aisle and wove his way through the customers, stopping short at the sight of statuesque, matronly Gertrude Messinger, a longtime Gatlinburg resident and wife of one of the gristmill owners, doused in green liquid. While her upper half remained untouched, her full skirts and boots were streaked and splotched with paint. Beside her, ashen and bug-eyed, stood thirteen-year-old Eliza Smith.

"Quinn Darling." Gertrude's voice boomed with outrage. "I expect you to assign the cost of a new dress to the Smiths' account."

At that, Eliza's freckles stood out in stark contrast to her skin.

"One moment, if you will, Mr. Darling," a third person chimed in. "The fault is mine, not Eliza's."

The voice put him in mind of snow angels and piano recitals and cookies swiped from silver platters. But it couldn't belong to Allison Ashworth. She and her brother, George, wouldn't arrive until Friday. Seventy-two more hours until his past collided with his present.

He wasn't ready.

Don't miss
***THE SHERIFF'S CHRISTMAS TWINS** by Karen Kirst,*
available wherever
Love Inspired® Historical books and ebooks are sold.

www.LoveInspired.com

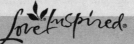
She leaned back in the seat and covered her face with her
hands. "I am angry. I'm mad because I don't know what to
do for Colby. And the person I always went to for advice
is gone. Grant is gone. I think Colby and I were both in
a delusional state, thinking they would come home. But
they're not. I'm not getting my brother, my best friend,
back. Colby isn't getting his parents back. And it isn't
fair. It isn't fair that I had to—"

Her eyes closed, and she shook her head.

"Macy?"

She pinched the bridge of her nose. "No. I'm not going
to say that. I lost a job and gave up an apartment. Colby
lost his parents. What I lost doesn't amount to anything. I
lost things I don't miss."

"I think you're wrong. I think you miss your life.
There's nothing wrong with that. Accept it, or it'll eat
you up."

Tanner pulled up to her house.

"I miss my life." She said it on a sigh. "I wouldn't be anywhere else. But I have to admit, there are days I wonder if Colby would be better off with someone else, with anyone but me. But I'm his family. We have each other."

"Yes, and in the end, that matters."

"But…" She bit down on her lip and glanced away from him, not finishing.

"But what?"

"What if I'm not a mom? What if I can't do this?" She looked young sitting next to him, her green eyes troubled.

"I'm guessing that even a mom who planned on having a child would still question if she could do it."

She reached for the door. "Thank you for letting me talk about Colby."

"Anytime." He said it, and then he realized the door that had opened.

She laughed. "Don't worry. I won't be calling at midnight to talk about my feelings."

"If you did, I'd answer."

She stood on tiptoe and touched his cheek to bring it down to her level. When she kissed him, he felt floored by the unexpected gesture. Macy had soft hair, soft gestures and a soft heart. She was easy to like. He guessed if a man wasn't careful, he'd find himself falling a little in love with her.

Don't miss
THE RANCHER'S TEXAS MATCH by Brenda Minton,
available October 2016 wherever
Love Inspired® books and ebooks are sold.

www.LoveInspired.com

LIEXP0916